DEATH OF A PRINCESS

As Detective Superintendent Mark Pemberton investigates the death of a woman nicknamed The Princess, he finds himself asking the question – accident or murder?

The last of the Milverdale family, The Princess has been found shot in the grounds of her Estate. Was the bullet that killed her a stray from a poacher's gun, or did someone deliberately set out to shoot her? Pemberton suspects murder as he uncovers rumours suggesting there are many who would wish The Princess harm.

Nonetheless, Pemberton becomes convinced that the key to her death is a deep family secret. Could there be an heir? And how far would he go to gain his inheritance?

DEATH OF
A PRINCESS

by

Nicholas Rhea

Magna Large Print Books
Long Preston, North Yorkshire,
BD23 4ND, England.

British Library Cataloguing in Publication Data.

Rhea, Nicholas
    Death of a princess.

    A catalogue record of this book is
    available from the British Library

    ISBN   0-7505-1578-3

First published in Great Britain by
Constable & Company Ltd., 1999

Magna Large Print is an imprint of Library Magna Books Ltd.

Printed and bound in Great Britain by
T.J. (International) Ltd., Cornwall, PL28 8RW

1

The shallow moorland stream rippled over sunlit pebbles behind the freshly leafed alders. In front of the alders, a brilliant patch of wild bluebells dominated the low-lying field with a spread of incandescent colour. It was an oasis in the moors, a picturesque and idyllic scene. It was marred only by the woman's body lying dead among the flowers. She had been shot in the head, according to the local constable.

Detective Superintendent Mark Pemberton, tall, fair-haired and immaculately dressed, halted some distance from the corpse. Motionless in concentration, his dark suit, polished black shoes and black briefcase were, like the body, incongruous in these surroundings. More apt were the piles of cow dung, hundreds of them. Their age varied from fresh to very dry, he noted, but there were no cows in sight.

To his right was a bank of deciduous trees, a wood of ancient oaks interspersed with ash, elms and beeches which grew in profusion on Mill Bank to form a backcloth to the meadow. Dressed in the new green of spring, the trees of Mill Bank Wood rose above a carpet of thick bracken and granite rocks. Above and behind those trees were the houses, shops and people of a moorland village. Out of sight from here, it was called Campsthwaite End and was the higher part of the village. The lower part lay at the foot of the dale. That was called Campsthwaite – the residents of the higher portion liked to make that distinction.

To his left, Pemberton saw the waters of Cam Beck, clear today but sometimes amber-tinted due to their passage from distant peat moors. The beck flowed over rounded stones and pebbles and was a haven for wildlife, particularly trout. Pemberton could hear the water rippling softly in the deathly silence of that mild and sunny afternoon. It was the music of nature enhanced by the notes of a willow warbler, a recent arrival in this green and springtime land.

There were no signposts or paving stones here, but the field bore evidence of several footpaths, little more than tracks defined by the occasional passage of human feet or the movement of cattle. One ran along the banks of the beck, another passed through isolated clumps of bluebells in an erratic route among the grass and meadow flowers. One path might even have been made by the dead woman. If she came regularly, she could have created that path. It wound

6

haphazardly across the field, sometimes veering from its route beside the stream to weave through the grass and bluebells. But Pemberton was interested in the section which disappeared into the trees ahead. That path went towards the old mill.

Formerly Milverdale Mill and now called Mill House, it lay sleeping among the dark bank of trees which filled the shallow dale ahead, stretching from the rising slopes to his right and reaching the edge of the beck to his left. The dense canopy of trees concealed and shaded most of the atmospheric old house. It must be lost in deep shadow for the whole of each day. It was hardly a desirable country residence, Pemberton thought; it was far too gloomy and remote.

No other house was visible from this quiet place. There were stepping stones behind him to his left; they crossed the beck not far from the farm gate. Even the farm, directly behind him and through whose yard he had driven to reach the bluebell field, was out of sight about a quarter of a mile away. Neither the farmhouse nor its outbuildings were visible from where the victim had fallen but the cow pats had probably been deposited by its livestock. This field appeared to be part of their grazing ground. The farmer might be able to help with Pemberton's enquiries.

The other indication of human presence

was the single track railway line which served the dale. It passed the bluebell field at the far side of the beck where its elevated route lay on an embankment rich with primroses. The track ran almost parallel with the beck and was about quarter of a mile or so from where he stood. It approached this point through a three-arch stone viaduct which was out of view from here, hidden behind the rising landscape. He'd have to establish the times of local services – a passenger or crew member might be a vital witness.

Standing in silence among the bluebells, Pemberton realised he would be visible from a wide area even if he could not be seen from the farm or the village. Surrounded by the undulating, picturesque landscape, the bluebell field was like a central stage with the auditorium rising all around at differing levels and in different forms. With the scene imprinted on his mind, he turned and saw Detective Constable Lorraine Cashmore walking slowly towards him, tall, graceful and beautiful.

'Ah, Lorraine, you've made it!' She halted about twenty yards away, pale-faced in the afternoon sunshine, and rewarded him with a fleeting smile. 'So what did the doctor say?'

'I'll tell you later, sir,' she said as the smile

vanished, the brief nod of her head acknowledging the presence of the uniformed constable only feet away.

'All right.' He studied her carefully, wondering what news she brought, then turned his attention from domestic matters to professional duties. 'Now, this is what we must do. The entire scene – this field of bluebells, the wood, all of it, right up Mill Bank to the village boundary, the banks of the stream on both sides and the woodland at the far side of Mill House – all of it must be preserved for scientific examination. Mill House too, inside and out, and the track leading to it, the one down through the wood from the village. This is a bizarre death. She's been shot dead in such a lonely place but with so many places to aim from. We've got to take great care with this one.'

Pemberton then addressed the uniformed constable who had been waiting patiently nearby. He had done such a good preliminary job in coping with the first moments of this reported crime.

'She's been shot, you said so in your call, PC Wardle? A head wound?'

'Left temple, sir,' said PC Wardle, the village constable for Campsthwaite. 'It looks like a bullet wound. I could be wrong, of course. It might be some other type of injury...'

'Any sign of a weapon?'

'No, sir, unless it's under the body.'

'So the chances are that she hasn't committed suicide. You didn't turn her over?'

'No, sir. She was cold, I touched her face and knew she was dead, I thought it best to leave her.'

'Good man. We need this scene kept in pristine condition for our scientific wizards. So who is she? Any idea?'

'Alicia Milverdale, sir. From Milverdale Hall. The big house at the far side of the railway, near the bottom of the village. You can't see it from here.'

'Family seat, eh?'

'A landowning family, sir, she's the last one. Was the last one, I should say. She never married.'

'Is she from an historic family? A rich one?'

'I'm not sure whether she could be described as rich, sir, although she did live in a rather grand house. She never flashed her money around, but claimed she had a very impressive pedigree.'

'So do we have a murder or was this a very unfortunate stray shot? This is shooting country, I believe?'

'Yes, sir, rabbits, pheasants and partridges in season, grouse on the moors in season, vermin of all kinds. The local farmers and their lads shoot regularly, mainly with shotguns of course. Some do have .22 rifles and air guns though.'

'It's not a shotgun wound, in your opinion?'

'No, sir, a twelve-bore wouldn't make that kind of wound, even at close range. I've seen farmers who've committed suicide with shotguns, it's not a bit like that. It looks like a revolver shot or even a rifle wound to me.'

'We'll see what the pathologist says. We need to trace the weapon and establish the trajectory of the shot. In a place like this, it could have come from anywhere! A .22 rifle is lethal up to a mile. Just think, some rabbit-shooter might have killed her without realising. Or has somebody shot her deliberately? Right, Lorraine, we need a doctor to certify her death. Who's the local GP, PC Wardle?'

Wardle responded by flicking open his notebook and reading an entry in the back cover. 'Dr Allison, sir, on 273688.'

'OK, Lorraine. Get Control Room to send him as soon as possible, then arrange for a forensic pathologist to visit the body at the scene. Force photographers and video teams to record everything. Scenes of Crime officers and Task Force to search the whole scene. If it is a bullet wound, we have to find the ejected shell – talk about looking for a needle in a haystack!'

'I'll get started, sir.' Pemberton recognised a lack of commitment in her voice.

'Are you all right?' His reaction registered

his concern.

'Yes, sir, fine,' she said with an effort.

He frowned as he studied her, but continued, 'Tell the teams to come through the farmyard. I want all other routes examined before they're trampled on. Then we'll set up an incident room. It's a bit remote, there's not many places to set up a busy office at a moment's notice!'

'Remote but lovely, sir!' breathed Lorraine with a fleeting smile. 'What a beautiful place, a paradise you'd want to keep to yourself for moments of peace.'

'Not the sort of place one expects murder. So, PC Wardle. How did you come to find her? You'd better hear this, Lorraine.'

The constable said, 'She has a live-in companion, sir, a woman. A maid or housekeeper. A Miss Farrow. She found her. Alicia, that's the deceased, always goes for – went for – a morning walk before breakfast. She always came here. It was her favourite place. She owns all this land, the field, the wood, the farm behind us–'

'Did she come alone?' interrupted Pemberton.

'Yes, sir, so I understand.'

'No dog? Horse?'

'No, sir. Completely alone. She set off at seven and got back at eight.'

'Then what was her routine?'

'After her morning walk, Alicia always had

12

a shower then had breakfast while she read the papers and dealt with her mail.'

'Until this morning, eh?'

'Yes, sir. This morning, when she didn't return as usual, Miss Farrow wasn't too worried because Alicia would sometimes pop into Mill House for a while – it's hers, nobody else uses it – and Miss Farrow had her own jobs to do, but when Alicia hadn't returned by noon and there was no word from her, Miss Farrow came to look for her. She found her lying where you see her now.'

'She approached the body?'

'Yes, she went to see if her mistress had tripped and fallen or maybe collapsed for some reason, then touched her. She realised Alicia was dead, she saw the blood on her head and ran to Mill House to ring me from there.'

'And you came immediately?'

'Yes, sir. I happened to be at home, lunchtime you see. Miss Farrow had left when I arrived. Alicia was lying just as you see her, so I radioed my sergeant from the car. Like you, I parked in the farmyard, it's the quickest way to get here. The sergeant said I should call you direct from the scene. He told me to preserve it and remain with the body to stop anyone trampling all over the place.'

'Good man. Did you see anyone as you arrived?'

'No, sir, no one. Not many people come down here, it's private property. There are no public footpaths through this land.'

'Right. Now, this was a regular outing for Alicia?'

'Yes, part of her daily routine. Most of the villagers knew she came here, it's all part of Milverdale Estate.'

'So we've a lot of suspects hereabouts! They could have shot her without anyone realising until some time afterwards.'

'Yes. If Constance Farrow hadn't come looking, she'd have been there for ages.'

'And no one would see her or her killer arriving or leaving. Right, can you remain with us, PC Wardle? Stop unauthorised people entering the scene, then when my officers get here they'll seal the area and arrange night-time supervision.'

'Very good, sir.'

'When things settle down, I'll need your local knowledge – the names of likely suspects, for example, someone with a grievance against Alicia, a motive of some kind. And I need to know who's got access to guns, people like poachers and so on.'

'Right, sir.'

Pemberton turned to Lorraine. 'While you're talking to Headquarters, Lorraine, ask them to send Dr Preston, will you? In addition to the pathologist, I need a forensic expert to examine the body *in situ* and he's the best. Go and start your calls while I'm examining the body. And where can we set up our incident room, PC Wardle?'

'There is a village institute, sir, next door to the vicarage. It's large enough.'

'Good. And food for the troops? Is there a pub that can produce bar snacks for a lot of hungry coppers? Lunchtime and evening?'

'Yes, the Miners Arms. It's only a minute's walk from the institute.'

'Fine. We might pick up bits of gossip there. Now to look at our victim more closely.'

As Lorraine departed, Pemberton watched with an ache in his body, an ache of desire fuelled by a new uncertainty as he admired her graceful movements. His colleague, his woman, his best friend, his partner in life...

With an effort, he concentrated on the corpse. He could see the route she had taken through the bluebells. It was marked by crushed plants, consequently he approached from a different direction. There might be footprints in the soft earth beneath the grass and flowers – her footprints perhaps, or those of her killer. They would have to be preserved.

A virgin route brought him towards her head where he halted and looked down at the body without touching her. He saw a woman in her middle or late forties with a

15

head of dark brown, slightly auburn hair turning grey. It was rather unkempt. The wound in her left temple was covered with congealed blood and partially hidden by her hair. She wore no spectacles, no ear-rings, no necklace and no make-up or lipstick. Her eyes were closed. Her mouth was partially open and he thought she sported her own teeth, all in good condition. Her face was round and full, he noted. Of average build, not too stocky or too slim, she appeared to be taller than most women and was lying on her back with her right arm outstretched among the flowers, palm uppermost. Her left arm lay across her breast. Her left wrist bore a watch, he noted. A silver one on a leather strap. It was showing the present time. There were no rings on her fingers, and her hands were delicate with well-manicured nails. They bore no evidence of heavy or manual work, no roughness from activities such as keeping horses, tending the garden or general outdoor work.

She wore a short-sleeved T-shirt, dark green in colour with no motif or design upon it, and faded blue denim jeans with frayed edges around the bottoms. Her clothing did not appear to have been disturbed. That fact tended to rule out any sexual motive for the attack. Her feet bore a pair of white Nike trainers, and he could see she wore pale green socks. She was dressed for the weather, a mild and dry morning in May, and her body did not appear to have any wounds or injuries, other than the one on her head.

Stretching forward, he touched her eyelids to confirm that the constable's diagnosis was correct. There was rigor mortis in the eyelids, one of the first places on a dead body to be subjected to that condition. An additional light touch on her forehead told him her body temperature had dropped considerably – not surprising in the open air but it did indicate she had been dead a few hours. It might not be possible for the pathologist to provide a precise time of death but it was likely she had died during her early morning walk, sometime between 7 a.m. and 8 a.m.

Her handbag was nowhere in sight, nor were any other personal belongings scattered around her. This suggested robbery, that her killer had fled with her bag and its contents. He hadn't taken her watch, though. But would she have brought her handbag on such a regular morning trek? And if she was going to Mill House, surely she would have carried the key? The housekeeper had run to Mill House to raise the alarm, so had she used the same key? If not, how had she gained entry?

It was tempting to turn over the body and search her clothing but for the time being he must leave her precisely where she had fallen. Her position did suggest she had been spun around, perhaps partially, perhaps fully, by the impact of the bullet, to fall dead in a whirl of arms and momentary agony. And she did appear to have been shot from a distance – there were no discernible powder marks or burns on her flesh to suggest a close-range execution. A rifle shot rather than a pistol fired at closer range? He could see no relevant marks among the bluebells other than those made by Alicia and the absent cows.

How tall was she? That would be determined during the post-mortem. She looked to be around five feet seven or eight inches perhaps, a significant point if the elevation of the fatal shot was to be determined. Pemberton, standing slightly more than six feet tall, looked around in an attempt to identify possible firing sites. A position in the surrounding woodland was one obvious choice, an elevated position near the railway was another, the banks of the beck too, or the field at the other side of the beck, or even somewhere in this open field of bluebells. And Mill House? In spite of its seclusion, could it offer a suitable sniping position? Or might the killer have lain prone among the profusion of flowers in the meadow? In such an unpopulated place, the victim, defenceless and alone in this natural

18

arena, would have been as vulnerable as a hunted rabbit. But, reasoned Pemberton, if the killer *had* lain in wait for her, he must have known her daily routine.

Having completed his initial examination, Pemberton carefully retraced his route. Lorraine had returned after making her calls, and was waiting some distance away with PC Wardle at her side.

'We've a very tricky one here,' he told them. 'Shot in the middle of nowhere, probably from a distance. Precious little evidence at the scene or on the victim. No obvious motive like a sexual attack although we can't rule out robbery. Her handbag isn't here but he's left her watch. So is it an accidental killing or a local villain with a score to settle? Did you manage to raise the necessary support services, Lorraine?'

'I did, sir,' and she called him 'sir' because they were in the presence of another officer. 'I've directed them to rendezvous here after parking at the farm.'

'It'll be cows from that farm who've left their deposits all over this field, I'll bet?' Pemberton grinned at the constable.

'Yes, sir, they graze here. It's a rented farm, rented from Alicia's estate in fact, Cam Beck Farm.'

'So where are the cows now?' asked Pemberton.

'I had them moved out, sir, to stop them

congregating around the body and trampling all over the scene. You know what cows are, they're curious about anything or anyone in their field and would stand in a circle around her, just looking. I thought we'd better have them shifted.'

'More good thinking! So our assassin would have to avoid a herd of cows when he shot her?'

'Unless they were in the byre being milked at the crucial time, sir,' Wardle suggested.

'Right. So we need words with the farmer. What's his name?'

'Midgley, sir. Geoff Midgley, a decent man.'

'Not a likely suspect, you think?'

'I would doubt it, sir, she got on well with all her tenants.'

'We'll see what he has to say about his whereabouts this morning. Am I right in guessing he knows about the crime?'

'When I arrived, I told him Alicia had been attacked, sir, then later, when I asked him to move his cows, I thought he should know she was dead. I told him to expect a lot of vehicles and police officers. He agreed to us parking on his premises.'

'Good,' Pemberton said. 'And what time did you ask him to move his cows?'

'Not long after I arrived, sir. He used a dog to move them.'

'So the cows would have been returned to

this field after the morning's milking? They'd be here until you had them removed?'

'Yes, sir.'

'Then they might have trampled on valuable evidence! At least we know what might have caused some of the footprints around here. Now, if my reckoning is correct, the fact that you alerted the farmer to something out of the ordinary means the whole village will know by now. Village gossip travels faster than the Internet! Can you help me to learn more about this place? The old mill house for starters? Is it occupied?'

'No, sir. Alicia used it as a kind of retreat. She spent hours there.'

'Alone?'

'Not all the time. The local schoolchildren used to come.'

'Children?'

'She liked children, sir, she helped at the school with art and drama classes. Some of the pupils came to Mill House with her.'

'Did they? And have you searched Mill House today?'

'No, sir, I thought it best if I left it alone. If a killer had been hiding there, he'd have gone long before I turned up.'

'So he would, but we'll need to trace all those children who used it if only to eliminate them from the enquiry. The killer's prints might be in the house too, so we need to trace anyone who might have gained entry for reasons best known to themselves, legal or otherwise. Now, PC Wardle, while we're waiting for the cavalry to arrive, what can you tell me about the late Alicia Milverdale?'

2

John Wardle, Campsthwaite's village constable for the past five years, was a large homely man in his late thirties whose uniform looked slightly unkempt and whose dark brown hair was always in need of a trim. In fact, compared with Pemberton he looked positively untidy. But the man inside the well-worn dark blue serge oozed friendliness, confidence and efficiency; he was a man who knew his patch, a very experienced village policeman.

He told Pemberton that Alicia Milverdale was something of a character, an oddity perhaps, almost a stranger living among these down-to-earth Yorkshire moor folk. She did not 'fit in'; she was different and yet she tried so hard to involve herself with village matters. She liked to organise the annual Christmas pantomime with children from the primary school. She enjoyed running art classes for them too, or occasionally arranging a sports day. In spite of her efforts, said Wardle, the local people did not warm to her. She was rarely, if ever, asked to help at village events; she had to make the initial approach but was often told, 'No, thank you, Miss Milverdale, it's good of you but we've enough helpers.'

She had a cultivated accent and a fine home full of antique furniture, and she used an ancient and rather spectacular Rolls Royce whenever she needed transport to town, to engagements or to Rainesbury railway station for trips to London. She tried to appear genuinely interested in local matters and people, but even though Alicia's ancestors had lived in Milverdale Hall for several generations and owned a number of village properties, she was always regarded as an outsider.

'Would you say she had enemies?' Pemberton asked.

'No, it wasn't like that,' Wardle explained. 'I don't think she had any enemies here. The locals just got on with their lives as if she didn't exist. She had no real part in the social life of Campsthwaite. You'd never see her at a WI meeting, for example, having a snack in the pub or going to the post office or shop. Miss Farrow did her shopping. That sort of thing set her apart, Mr Pemberton, but it was deeper than that. I don't think the WI ever asked her to be president, like they did with her mum. I reckon that was a snub of some sort, but I never did know why. The villagers don't tell me everything, they're deep, they like to keep secrets from the police.'

'You're set apart too – the job does that,' smiled Pemberton. 'But with her background and breeding, I can see why some villagers would want to keep her at a distance. At the same time, I think it's odd she was snubbed, as you suggested. What had she done to antagonise them? The whole community, I mean, not just the odd individual.'

'I don't know, sir. There's something in the air, it's always been there. I can sense it, an undercurrent of sorts. I'm sure the villagers are keeping something from me. I reckon I'm a good village bobby, but there's a fair bit I don't know about this village, or the people in it. They do keep things very much to themselves.'

'That's inevitable in a small community. You've tried to fathom it, I imagine?' smiled Pemberton.

'Oh, I have, sir. But it's got me baffled. I must say I liked her even if the people kept her at a distance. She wasn't snooty. She was very good and generous to her tenants, she cared for them if they needed help, she was kind and warm-hearted. Her rents were the lowest around the moors. She paid good wages. There were a lot of good things about her but no one got very close to her, sir. There was always a respectful distance between her and her tenants, and the other villagers. I don't think she's ever upset any

25

of them, I've never known open animosity towards her. I've never known anyone say she was hated and I can't think of a tenant or villager who would want to harm her. And she did care a lot about children.'

'Then you'd expect her efforts would have done something to bridge any gap between her and what the papers call ordinary people.'

'Yes, but that didn't happen here.' Wardle shook his head. 'If she wanted to organise something which involved the children, such as the annual pantomime, she had to make a tremendous effort to get people interested. Recently, she approached the new schoolteacher – she travels in every day, a Mrs Donaldson, Margaret.'

'A fellow outsider?' smiled Pemberton.

'In a way, yes, sir. She was someone Alicia could approach knowing she wasn't a tenant or a relation of a tenant! Mrs Donaldson helped Alicia with the last pantomime. She persuaded the children to take part and go to rehearsals. Alicia did need some help, there was too much for one person. She organised art classes through the school too.'

'Held in the school, were they? Her art classes? And pantomime rehearsals?'

'She liked to use Mill House on Saturday mornings, that's until very recently. Then there was a fuss so they used the school all the time.'

'Fuss? What kind of fuss?'

'Some parents objected to their children going to Mill House, sir. I don't know why. The new teacher seemed to like the idea and they started going again.'

'Down through the wood? That way, not the way we came?'

'Right, sir. Anyway, that was stopped as well, only recently. I never did find out why – unless parents didn't like bairns walking through that dark wood all alone.'

'They have to walk through the wood to get here from the village?'

'Yes, it's the only way, other than the long trek round by the farmyard. The track approaches the far side of Mill House. You can't get a car down it, it's all right for mountain bikes. A four-wheel drive cross-country vehicle might just make it.'

'It could be an access route for our killer. I'll get Scenes of Crime to examine it. Now, it's important we establish precisely which youngsters came to Mill House. Were the pantomimes well supported? By villagers who didn't warm to Alicia?'

'Yes, there was always a good attendance. There's no doubt Alicia did a good job. She was very good with scenery, painting most of it herself, or getting the youngsters to do it under her guidance. And costumes. She could make lavish costumes and I wondered if she had contacts in the theatre world,

27

being able to acquire unwanted costumes. But in any case, parents will always attend a show in which their kids take part, won't they?'

'True. So was Alicia a theatrical type?'

'She did like dressing up but I don't know much about her early life or her time at university. Although she was from a wealthy and cultured background, she wasn't horsey. You never saw her riding or going out with the hunt or following country pursuits like breeding dogs or going to agricultural shows. That means she didn't fit in with the county set either.'

'An outsider in more ways than one, eh?' agreed Pemberton, thinking that Alicia's isolation by differing strata of village society might explain her desire to generate companionship from children. 'Have you a child, PC Wardle? It would be nice to talk to one who's actually been to Mill House.'

'I have a little son, sir, Harry, but he's only three. He's not started school and he's never been to Mill House.'

'Right. So it seems she was more of a theatre type than a county or horsey type. What about gossip? Snippets of local information? Scandal even. What about her trips to London? Or people who've been to visit her or stay at the big house? Famous names she's been in touch with?' Pemberton pressed the constable for more details.

'Very little, sir. She may have been involved in London theatreland, hence the trips to London, but really I've no idea, sir. She never spoke of being involved with actors or knowing any of the big names in the theatre world. And there never seem to be any visitors to the Hall.'

'Fine. This is most helpful. Now, PC Wardle, her family background. She's not titled, I note.'

'No, sir, and neither were her parents.'

'Perhaps there was a title somewhere in the family?'

'Possibly, sir, in the distant past, or with another branch. I just don't know. I've never had reason to investigate her family background.'

'Fair enough. We'll look into that. Now, you say she never married? What about brothers and sisters? Parents?'

'She was an only child, sir, that's how she came to inherit the estate. Her mother died about nine years ago – she's buried in the family vault in the parish church alongside her father, Roderick Milverdale. He died five years ago, he was eighty and lived at Milverdale Hall until his death.'

'With Alicia?'

'Yes. I think she was away at boarding school as a child, then went to university, Bristol I believe, but apart from that I understand she's always lived there, with her parents. She never had a formal job, sir, her time was spent looking after them, and learning how to manage the estate with a view to taking over from her father eventually.'

'We'll have to trace her nearest relative. There must be someone somewhere who's related, however remotely.'

'I don't think so, sir, not according to local information. She's the very last of the Milverdales on both sides of the family.'

'Even so, it's amazing how long-lost relatives can come out of the woodwork when there's an estate up for grabs!' laughed Pemberton.

'That might happen once the news gets out, sir.'

'Yes, it might. So if there are no known relatives, what will happen to the estate? There must be speculation about it, particularly as so many people depend on it for their homes and work.'

'I understand a trust was established to temporarily administer the estate if Alicia died without an heir. Old Mr Milverdale, Alicia's father, wanted the tenants to have an opportunity to buy their homes or farms before the estate was disposed of, and the staff to find new work. I believe the trust is allowed to run Milverdale Estate for three years before selling it.'

'That's not long to sort out something as

complicated as the end of a dynasty, but it's a pleasing idea,' smiled Pemberton.

'The Milverdales did have the needs of their tenants and staff in mind, sir, they were very good like that. Once those three years of grace are over without an heir turning up, with some tenants having purchased their homes, then whatever is left of the estate will be sold, with the proceeds going to charities. I've not seen this in writing but it is general talk in the village.'

'I can check but it makes a good starting point for our investigations. Do you know who are the estate's solicitors?'

'Snowdon and Hurst in Rainesbury, sir. I had dealings with them once, over some straying cattle and broken fences.'

'I know them, I've had dealings with them too. I'll have to tell them about Alicia's death anyway. So were the tenants aware of these provisions?'

'Yes, Mr Milverdale wanted it known. A few would like to buy their homes or farms but not many can afford to although some have been making long-term plans. They knew Alicia would never produce an heir. She wasn't the marrying sort.'

'And she died somewhat sooner than expected,' murmured Pemberton.

'Right, sir, and someone might benefit from that.'

'I find that rather ominous. Quite

suddenly, we have a clutch of key suspects.'

'She ran a very efficient office, sir, I've been there a number of times. You'll find everything you want to know about the estate.'

'I'm sure I will. Now, PC Wardle, is there anything else you can tell me about Alicia? Any juicy gossip? Love life? Dodgy finances? Character quirks...'

'Just one odd thing, sir. She was nick-named the Princess by the villagers, if that's of interest.'

'The Princess? Why was that?'

'She often said her family had royal origins, that she should be a princess by rights. She mentioned that to the children and they spread the tale around the village. That's how I heard it. The children called her the Princess too, they thought she was very famous and important.'

'Is there any truth in those claims?'

'I don't really know, sir. She did come from a good background, but some thought she lived in a fantasy world, making up stories and re-enacting them on stage with children. She wrote her own pantomime scripts, by the way, always with a princess in them.'

'But even if she did live a fantasy life, that story could be true. There are families who are genuinely descended from the love-making antics of past sovereigns and their mistresses. There are lots of claimants to the throne, or to the royal lineage out there, all thwarted for the sake of a marriage certificate!'

'It shows the importance of a piece of official paper, sir! But she's never caused gossip through her love life, there's never been a man so far as I know, or a woman for that matter.'

'But it seems she liked the company of children. Sexless, was she?'

'I wouldn't know about that, sir! I'd have thought some gold-digging male with an eye for a country estate might have tried his hand. But I don't think she was regarded by any of the local men as a romantic challenge...'

'Most people exert some appeal to someone, PC Wardle. Perhaps she had never found her true love ... like some princesses!'

'Or perhaps she was very choosy, looking for a handsome dream-like prince in shining armour, sir!'

'But he never came, did he? So what about her financial dealings?'

'I think she was honest, sir. I never came across anything to suggest otherwise and she never flashed her wealth around, except for her old Rolls. It must be forty years old, a real vintage model, so she wouldn't have to pay for that, it was her father's. In lots of ways, she led a very modest life.'

'So we have an unusual victim.' Pemberton pursed his lips. 'A real character study for us to unravel, but who'd kill such a kind and eccentric lady – and why?'

'A real puzzle for you, sir.'

'I relish the challenge! Do keep your eyes and ears open, PC Wardle. You are my admission ticket to the local community!'

'Very good, sir.'

'Right, now here comes the local doctor. That means the troops will soon be here and we can get this show on the road. In the meantime, can you keep guard on our boundaries until one of our officers relieves you?'

'Yes, sir.'

'And Lorraine?'

'Sir?' She had been standing patiently beside Pemberton and Wardle during this interchange, listening to every word and, unusually, not making a contribution.

'Take my car. Drive out to Milverdale Hall, will you? Explain to Miss Farrow what we will be doing, chat to her, be friendly. We shouldn't leave her alone in that big house at a time like this. Get her talking about her mistress. I need to know everything I can about Alicia, her family, friends, contacts. Get her talking about herself too. We need to know all about her.'

'Yes, sir.'

'And could you ring the estate solicitors

from there? Give them my compliments, tell them I'm engaged at the scene for an indefinite period, but inform them of Alicia's death. Say we're waiting for confirmation about the cause of death and for the formal identification, but I'll be in touch in due course. As soon as I've finished here, I'll join you at Milverdale Hall for a chat with Miss Farrow.'

'Yes, right, sir,' she said softly.

As Pemberton watched her striding away, he realised they'd not yet spoken about the visit to her own doctor. He must make time for that.

By mid-afternoon, a dozen detectives assisted by half a dozen civilian clerical staff had begun to establish the incident room in Campsthwaite's village institute. They were supervised by Detective Inspector Paul Larkin, highly experienced so far as the running of incident rooms was concerned. Computers including HOLMES (the Home Office Large Major Enquiry System), a photocopier, office furniture, telephones, fax machines, an email modem, radio sets, piles of stationery and paper, blackboards, coffee-making facilities and all the paraphernalia of a busy office were being installed as, deep in the woodland below the village, the scientific examination of the scene got under way. The body of

Alicia Milverdale had not yet been removed.

Some four or five hours of daylight remained and Pemberton was obliged to be present during these initial stages. By five o'clock a small tent had been erected over Alicia's remains and the entire scene was contained within yards of yellow tape bearing the words 'Police – Keep Out'. Dr Allison, Alicia's GP, had examined her body and pronounced life extinct. It was a formality but a legal necessity. Dr Paul Lewis, the forensic pathologist, conducted a visual examination of her head, including her eyes and mouth and the wound in the temple. He followed with a swift but expert appraisal of her entire body, including her fingernails in case she had fought and scratched an assailant, an action which would produce deposits under the nails. He loosened her clothes to seek wounds, bruises or other marks but he did so with all the safeguards of his calling, bearing in mind the necessity not to destroy even the tiniest particle of evidence. Something as small as a hair or speck of dust could be important.

'I need to turn her over,' he said to Pemberton eventually. 'I need to examine her back just to make sure she's not been shot there, or stabbed.'

'Jack?' Pemberton addressed the forensic scientist, Dr Preston, the man who would attempt to determine the source of the fatal shot. 'Can we turn her over?'

'Yes, I've got what I need. Usual care, please. She'll fall back into position when you've finished.'

Lewis hauled Alicia, now stiff with rigor mortis, on to her right side, swiftly examined her back including her skull and neck, found no further injuries, and gently lowered the body to its former position. During those moments, Pemberton noted there was no weapon or door key hidden beneath the body and asked the hovering photographer to record those facts.

Lewis, leaving the confines of the small tent, halted in a place now earmarked as safe, and said, 'Mark, my instincts say this is murder, although I can't rule out a stray shot. That head wound has all the appearances of being caused by a bullet fired from a distance. There's no exit wound which means the bullet is still in her head, so you can recover it. I'll take her to the lab very soon and will do the PM this evening. I'll call with my findings, with the written report to follow.'

'Thanks. Any idea of the time of death?'

'It's always a rough estimate as you know, Mark, but I'd say this morning, probably between seven and eight as you believe. It might be an hour or two either way though. I can't be precise. Now, Jack,' and Lewis turned to Dr Preston, 'you've watched all this. Anything to contribute?'

'Not yet, but I'd like to attend the post-mortem,' he responded. 'I need to examine the angle of entry and path of the bullet if I'm to calculate its point of origin. If she was deliberately shot from a distance, then I'd say a skilled marksman was responsible.'

'That's ominous,' muttered Pemberton.

'Could be,' said Preston. 'From the position of her body, I'd say she was hit while moving, even in mid-step, which is another reason to suspect a very skilled marksman. I find that possibility most in-triguing!'

'An assassination, you mean?' asked Pemberton.

'Either that, or a bloody unfortunate accident. Judging by the size of the wound – and I know it's all speculation at this stage – I'd say it was something with a larger calibre than a .22 rifle. Not a rabbit-shooter's weapon, something much more lethal. Again, that points to murder rather than an accident.'

'And very few have legal possession of such a gun!' observed Pemberton.

'Exactly, Mark. Paid assassins have access to powerful rifles, legally or otherwise, and there are some very exotic firearms in cir-culation. Illegally held, most of them.'

Pemberton pursed his lips. 'Or it could be

a military weapon, there must be a few ex-military men who could get their hands on a gun that size. I'd better wait until the ballistics people give their verdict.'

'The circumstances would suggest some kind of expert involvement, but as you say, let's wait until I've seen that bullet and the ballistics people have examined it. If she was shot from a distance, the killer probably won't have touched her body or been in direct contact with her; there'll be no transfer of substances, no evidence on her body apart from the bullet. The killer's footprints will not be near the body either. There's lots of cattle hoof marks around but I have isolated some of her trainer prints; there are other prints too. Yours, PC Wardle's, DC Cashmore's and those of the person who found her.'

'We were all at the scene at some stage,' confirmed Pemberton. 'Any other prints could be from her killer.'

'Unless we've had snoopers we don't know about. I'll need to examine the shoes of those I've just mentioned.'

'No problem. Now, if you're suggesting a skilled marksman is involved, are we talking of a hired killer? Or a tenant with military skills? Or even a crack shot with access to a wartime heirloom? Someone who won't wait any longer to buy his place? We need to know more about our enigmatic Miss Alicia

Milverdale. Detective Constable Cashmore is already talking to her housekeeper,' said Pemberton.

'Fine.' said Dr Preston. 'And I need to get the victim and her clothing into the lab, then tomorrow, in daylight, I'll examine the scene.'

'While you're doing the PM,' Pemberton addressed Dr Lewis, 'can you secure a DNA sample for me? From Alicia?'

'No problem, Mark, that sort of thing's routine nowadays.'

'Thanks.'

At seven o'clock, the three senior investigators – Pemberton, Dr Preston and Dr Lewis – agreed that the body could be transferred to the pathology laboratory at Rainesbury General Hospital. Her clothing and control samples of soil from the field in which she was found would also be examined. This would determine whether she had died where she was found or whether the body had been transported to the bluebell field after death.

Still aware of his need to speak to Lorraine and to Alicia's housekeeper, Pemberton left the bluebell field but decided he should first address those officers who would be gathering in the incident room. It was time for them to be made aware of the basic facts.

He arrived to find some forty detectives

had assembled from all parts of the county. Wasting no time, Pemberton placed his briefcase on the table, called them to order and provided brief details of the death. Then he continued, 'I'm treating this like murder, even if it might be an accident. Bear that in mind even if I refer to it as a murder. I think she was killed where she was found; I've no reason to think she was transported to the bluebell field after her death – getting her body there would be almost impossible if just one person was involved. Our top priority is to find the murder weapon. It's certainly a rifle of some kind and it can't be far away. We need to find someone with a motive – a tenant wanting rid of Alicia to clear the way to purchase his house or farm, perhaps with some speculative gain in mind. Have we a tenant or villager who's undertaken military service? There could be a military element here, bearing in mind the type of gun used and the skill of the fatal shot. Or is it something else? Jealousy somewhere? Had she been blackmailing someone who couldn't pay? Has someone been black-mailing her? I've no grounds for thinking that, but we have to examine every possibility. Or was it suicide with someone removing the weapon before we got there? That's a good way of making a suicide look like an accident or murder! Or is there a secret heir who couldn't wait for her to die naturally? Or is the entire affair just a tragic accident? Tap into local gossip and ask questions until you are sick of asking questions but don't ignore any possibility, however unlikely it might seem.'

He paused to allow his words to be digested.

'I need house-to-house enquiries in the village and surrounding farms. I need to know the deceased's family background and ancestry, how she spent her time, who she spent it with, what problems she faced in running her estate, who came to her main home – Milverdale Hall – and who came to her nest in the woods, Mill House, an old mill. She took children into the old mill, from the local school, and that doesn't seem to have pleased their parents. We need to talk to the teacher for starters, as soon as possible; we can talk to the children later. Remember, very young children do not make reliable witnesses, though, and memories can be fallible. I need to know who goes walkies in this village – anywhere in the village, that is – between seven and eight every morning and perhaps in the hours either side of those times. Find out who the early movers are – delivery vans, postman or woman, milk rounds people, dustbin men, home helps and nurses, people setting off for work at distant places by car, bus or train. Or returning from night shift. There is a railway line through this village, and a railway station. Find out what time the early trains run and who was on board. They might have seen something. People out shooting rabbits or poaching. I need the names of everyone who owns any kind of rifle or pistol, particularly one which is out of the ordinary, and we need to closely examine *all* likely murder weapons. We don't know the calibre of the murder weapon yet, but meanwhile preserve any suspect weapons for ballistic and scientific examination. The entire scene will remain protected overnight, then tomorrow at daybreak we will recommence our search for evidence. In particular, I want the ejected shell of the bullet. Remember, everyone leaves something at the scene of a crime even if it's only a hair, a footprint or a fibre from their clothing. It's our job to find it. Familiarise yourselves with Alicia's life-style, her contacts and her relationship with the villagers, or any particular villager, young or old. Tomorrow we begin in earnest. There might be time for a few house-to-house enquiries tonight, but be here tomorrow morning at nine o'clock sharp. And now, before I knock off, I'm going to Milverdale Hall for a chat with Miss Farrow.'

And a talk with Lorraine, he told himself.

3

Pemberton's journey revealed that Milverdale Hall occupied an elevated site on the edge of open moorland about a mile from the bluebell field. Cam Beck, the railway line and a lofty ridge of picturesque countryside separated the Hall grounds from the bluebell field – one could not be seen from the other. Surrounded by lush meadows, extensive grounds and beautiful gardens which sloped the dale, the Hall was a substantial two-storey stone house built in 1825. Its frontage had a *porte-cochère* with a pair of fine Tuscan columns and several bay windows.

The railway line and Campsthwaite station were both visible from the Hall grounds while to the south-west was the site of a former ironworks. This was separated from Milverdale grounds by both the railway line and Cam Beck. Most of the ugly buildings and all three blast furnaces had been dismantled more than half a century ago and the land had been reclaimed for agricultural purposes. It was currently under cultivation by one of Milverdale's tenant farmers. A disused track ran through the former ironworks from Bottom Road, crossing the beck via a wooden bridge, then following its unsurfaced way towards the viaduct before terminating in the grounds of the Hall. In the golden days of iron-ore mining there was a lot of traffic on this route, but that had ceased long ago. The track was now overgrown but used occasionally by Alicia, the estate workers, the tenant farmer and anyone enjoying a long walk while visiting the big house. There was no public thoroughfare although stray ramblers did find their way on to it from time to time.

The main route to the Hall, the one in daily use by delivery men, estate workers, visitors and vehicles which needed access to the Hall, was fully surfaced and Pemberton followed its twisting route. In spite of having been on duty for almost twelve hours without a break, he continued to look immaculate – he had, however, had a quick shave with his battery-powered razor and had rubbed his tired face and grubby hands with a moist tissue, part of the travelling kit in his briefcase.

Day was turning to dusk as he was driven by one of his detectives through the splendid blossom-adorned landscape. The road climbed towards the Hall with spectacular views below and all around him; as he was a passenger he could take a leisurely look at the scenery. All this belonged to Milverdale Estate; the family Milverdale was, he felt, lord of all it surveyed even if there was no title. Now, with a bullet in a woman's head, that dynasty had ended.

As his car came to a standstill on the gravelled forecourt, he saw Lorraine's vehicle neatly parked to the left of the front door. There were lights deep in the big house. After thanking his driver, Mark Pemberton dismissed him and walked under the *porte-cochère* to ring the doorbell. Eventually, through the glass panels, he could discern a tall, slender and rather shadowy figure heading towards him. The dim internal light did not reveal any of the person's features but the silhouetted long skirt and flowing walk told him it was a female. She halted, peered at him through the glass, and before opening the door, called, 'Who is it?'

Her rather shrill voice sounded muffled due to the thickness of the door and its fine glass, but he shouted back, 'Detective Superintendent Pemberton, CID.'

In confirmation he waved his warrant card before her face as she peered through the glass.

'Oh,' she said, switching on the external light and then turning the key in the huge brass lock. She held the door open.

'Superintendent, do come in. I was expecting you. Miss Cashmore has been here a while.'

'Thank you,' and he stepped into a panelled hall smelling of polish and adorned with portraits in oils. 'You must be Miss Farrow?'

'Yes, Constance Farrow. Do come into the drawing-room. I can offer you a sherry, or perhaps coffee?'

'A coffee would be most welcome,' he smiled, remembering it was a long time since he had eaten anything. 'Milk, no sugar, if you don't mind.'

'I won't be long, the kettle has just boiled,' she said, edging away from him. 'That's the door on the left. Do go in and join your colleague.'

Constance Farrow was a tall, slender and rather gangly woman probably in her early fifties. With a rounded but rather sallow face, she had thick iron grey hair with hints of brown, no make-up or jewellery, and was dressed in an old grey cardigan with a handkerchief in one pocket. It matched her alert eyes behind large, horn-rimmed spectacles. The cardigan covered a pale blue blouse with an open neck and she sported a long denim skirt and dark blue sandshoes; she seemed to be wearing them as slippers and they made her legs look abnormally slender. He noticed that her hands were thin

47

too, on the end of very slim arms. A plain thin woman, he felt, humourless but probably very efficient. A spinster beyond doubt, and one who seemed very much in command, both of her emotions and of the situation. As she strode away, he watched her for just a second, then turned into the drawing-room. Lorraine rose to meet him.

'Hi,' he smiled.

'Lovely views,' she said, each of them knowing not to discuss the purpose of their meeting. You never knew who was listening. He decided against any reference to Lorraine's visit to the doctor too. She understood his restraint, and so they talked about inconsequential things, like the scenery outside and the décor of the beautiful room. During their chatter, Pemberton did not sit down; instead, he wandered around to admire the view across the valley as darkness intensified. A slight mist filled the hollows among the hills, and beyond the old ironworks the lights of the village began to appear, one by one, like candles glowing among the lush dark scenery.

The long, high walls bore several portraits, anonymous but once important figures both male and female in historic costumes, some with children in velvet at their knees and some with horses or dogs. There were rural scenes too, in oils, originals he was sure; one depicted a massive red stag standing on a heathered peak and another showed salmon leaping over a dam. Rural scenes, not theatrical scenes, he noted. Heirlooms or purchases? Pemberton professed no expertise in antiques. Then Miss Farrow was returning to his side bearing a silver tray of coffee and some biscuits.

Smiling briefly, she placed the tray on a low table before the settee, bade him be seated and poured a coffee. Then she handed him the plate of biscuits – famished though he was, he remembered his manners, took just one and accepted the coffee cup from her.

'Miss Cashmore, another coffee perhaps?' Miss Farrow asked.

'No thanks, I've had sufficient. You've looked after me very well ... it's been a long day for you.'

Constance Farrow sat in an armchair, helped herself to a coffee and biscuit and looked at him, not smiling but showing some nervousness as she perched on the edge of her chair to await his comments. Pemberton noticed a slight tic at the corners of her mouth.

'I'm sorry to call so late,' Pemberton apologised. 'I did intend arriving earlier, but there were things to do.'

'I understand.' She produced a quick flicker of a smile. 'It is good of you to come, superintendent. Miss Cashmore has been most kind and very understanding.'

'I'm pleased you could accommodate her. Now I need to talk to you, just for a while at this stage. Can you spare me the time now?'

'Time? I've all the time in the world, superintendent. It is such a shocking thing ... I just cannot believe what has happened ... What *has* happened to her, where is she now? Miss Cashmore said she was still lying in that field, after all this time...'

'We've taken her to the hospital at Rainesbury.' He did not add that the body would be taken for examination in the operating theatre of the mortuary complex.

'So when can I have her back? There's the funeral to arrange, you see, and such a lot to do ... it's all so harrowing and sudden...' and, quite unexpectedly, she burst into tears. Although Lorraine reached across to touch her sympathetically, Pemberton waited for her to compose herself, watching her closely.

'I'm sorry,' she quickly apologised for her lapse. 'It has been a trying day.'

'We understand,' he said kindly. 'Now, to answer your question, before any funeral arrangements can be made, someone must formally identify Alicia. That can be done tomorrow. When the post-mortem is over, the coroner will decide whether or not the body can be released for burial. I'm sure

Alicia's solicitors will want to be involved in the funeral arrangements. You contacted them, did you, Lorraine?'

'Yes, sir. I spoke to a Mr Browning of Snowdon and Hurst. He deals with the estate's legal affairs as well as the Milverdale family matters, and he is also Alicia's personal solicitor. He was most helpful and asked that we keep him notified of any developments. At my suggestion, he was happy that Miss Farrow should make the formal identification.'

'Alicia would want me to do that,' added Miss Farrow.

'Fine. I'll ring tomorrow to suggest a suitable time. One of my staff will drive you there and look after you.'

'Thank you, I'll cope, I'm sure.'

'What about informing her friends and acquaintances? You might want a notice in the local paper or *The Times?*' he suggested.

'I will discuss all that with Mr Browning, superintendent. There is no family, you realise, absolutely no one. I know she'd want me to inform the villagers and her tenants and staff. It will be something to occupy me. I can say she was murdered, can I? I do want to be careful about such things.'

'I'd prefer it if you said she died tragically. We are conducting a murder-type enquiry, but it might not be murder, Miss Farrow. It could be a terrible accident. We are not sure at this stage but you can say we are investigating the matter.'

'Yes, all right. I will be very discreet. She will be missed dreadfully, you know. She did such a lot for the village, such a lot. She wanted to help the people here, wanted to serve them in some way. I do hope they respected her for that ... she was so very kind.'

'I must talk to you at length another time because we do need to know everything about her, Miss Farrow. I shall rely on you for that kind of help.'

'I'll co-operate in any way I can. I've told Miss Cashmore a good deal, it was so nice having her here, someone to talk to, to be with me at this dreadful time.'

'We do our best,' Pemberton told her. 'But I'd like to ask you some questions now, even though you've had a very trying day.'

'I'm quite happy to carry on, super-intendent. I do want to get this dreadful matter over. And you will tell me exactly what happened, won't you, once you are able?' she asked quickly, thinking he was about to conclude their conversation. 'I did see that dreadful head wound. Who would do such a thing to Alicia?'

She was trying hard to control her emotions.

'We shall be conducting very detailed scientific and forensic tests, Miss Farrow.

One theory is that Alicia was shot by a long-range rifle – that might indicate murder, but, as I said, we can't rule out an horrific accident.'

'Accident? But she didn't have a gun, did she?'

'I'm not suggesting it was an accident by her own hand, Miss Farrow. It might have been someone loosing off a shot without checking where it went. People have been shot in the countryside without the gunman ever realising.'

'It's all so dreadful, superintendent, so damnably awful and wearying. Can I ask if the press are aware of it? She hated publicity, you know.'

'They will know we have a major enquiry in progress, but at this stage they won't know the identity of the victim, or the exact circumstances of her death. These will be given in a news release from my office, and I have not yet issued one. We can't release her name until she has been formally identified.'

'Will they start dragging up her past? Some of those tabloid papers are dreadful, aren't they? Digging into families, turning up dirt, ruining relationships...'

That remark made Pemberton wonder if Alicia or her family had something to hide – many prominent families did have dark secrets – but he said, 'I'm afraid I can't say how they will respond, although the death of the last in a long, historic line will be regarded as newsworthy. Alicia was a prominent person, Miss Farrow, she will be of interest to the media.'

'I shall not co-operate with them, superintendent. I shall not speak to the press, I shall do my best to maintain her privacy!' snapped Miss Farrow.

'I understand.'

'So, for your formal requirements, I must wait a little longer?'

'Until tomorrow, all being well. Of course, you're welcome to call or ring me at any time if there's something to discuss. More immediately, Miss Farrow, I have the distasteful job of asking you some preliminary but important questions – it's because you found Alicia, you see. We need to clarify some vital matters at this very early stage. So, Miss Farrow, tell me how you came to find Alicia this morning.'

She took a long drink from her coffee and breathed deeply as she licked her lips. The tic reappeared, he noted, and he wondered if she had put something into the coffee, whisky perhaps. Under the circumstances, he would not criticise her for such a thing. He waited.

'I've told Miss Cashmore everything about that,' she said.

'And now I'd like you to tell me, in your

own words,' he responded softly but firmly.

'She always goes for a morning walk, superintendent, starting off at seven as regular as clockwork. She goes along the lane which leads behind the Hall to the old ironworks, but she doesn't go all the way to the ironworks. She crosses the railway viaduct, and then climbs over the fence by using a stile on the right. That's just over the viaduct. There's a path from there, it runs down the slope and across the field which is on this side of the stream, almost parallel with the railway line, and then the path crosses towards the stream. Further along, there are stepping stones and an old ford – horses and carts would cross there, years ago, but cars never use it now. I suppose a tractor could get across. Anyway, she did that walk every morning. Once she was across the river, she turned sharp left and walked beside the beck, through the bluebell field and then to Mill House. She did that walk every day, superintendent, well virtually every day, and always at the same time. She might give it a miss if she was full of cold or setting off early to go somewhere. But it was part of her daily routine. She liked to check Mill House, to see if it was secure. It is very remote, you understand, and we do get unauthorised ramblers on our land. When I started work here, she took me to show me the beauty of the area, and we went into the old house. She loved Mill House, you know, she'd played there ever since she was a little girl. It was one of the first places she showed me. It was very special to her. Her own hideaway, although she said I could go any time I wished, even without her.'

'We'll examine it in due course,' he said. 'And what time did she return from her walk?'

'Eight o'clock. She was very punctual. It took just an hour. On occasions, though, she would spend the whole or perhaps just part of the day in the old mill, Saturdays especially, but generally she was home by eight. She had a shower, got changed and had breakfast which I prepared while she was out. She checked her mail over breakfast, read the papers then went into her office at nine o'clock to deal with estate matters.'

'Alone?'

'Yes, she ran the estate single-handed. She was quite a woman, superintendent, most capable, extremely practical and very knowledgeable.'

'And this morning? Did she set off at her usual time?'

'Yes, seven as usual.'

'Did she give any indication she might be delayed?'

'No, not at all.'

'So how did she leave the Hall?'

'By the back door. She always left that way for her morning walk. She goes across the courtyard and into the lane.'

'Alone?'

'She was alone when she left the Hall, yes. Once she'd turned left, though, she was beyond my sight, obscured by the buildings.'

'And her handbag? Did she carry her handbag on that walk?'

'Handbag? No, she never took that, superintendent. Not on her morning walks.'

'And she was not carrying anything else? A rifle, for example? Walking-stick?'

'No, nothing ... You don't think she was going to shoot herself?'

'No, but if she did meet an attacker, he might have stolen her handbag, or the rifle she was carrying and used it against her ... or there might have been a struggle. I have to consider these possibilities.'

'Oh, I see. No, she had nothing with her, superintendent. I can swear to that. She never carried anything on those walks.'

'Good. And what did you do after she had left the Hall?'

'My job is to prepare breakfast ready for her return, then I make her bed and begin work in the house. Once she'd gone, I prepared my breakfast. I have mine first and do hers later, closer to the time she returns so it will be fresh. I expected her back at eight. She didn't come, although she hadn't said she'd be delayed. Generally, she was good like that, always letting me know about any change of plan, however small, but this morning she didn't announce she'd be late. I wasn't worried, she could have popped in to see Mr Midgley at the farm or got talking to someone – that kind of thing did happen sometimes. I waited an hour without any word and I did get a little concerned, so I rang Mill House – there is a phone there. I wondered if she had decided to stay a while. I rang just after nine, and again at ten, but then I had to go out to the shop in the village. I needed things for lunch.'

'How did you get there?'

'I drove, Mr Pemberton. I have use of the estate vehicles; I'm even allowed to drive her Rolls! Quite an honour. But I went in the Landrover. It took about an hour, there and back.'

'I see. And then?'

'She hadn't returned by the time I got back. I rang Mill House again without success, so just before lunchtime, I decided to go and look for her.'

'You'd not alerted anyone else during this time?'

'No, I thought there was no need to panic. I thought she must have met someone she knew.'

'But your concern increased?'

'Yes, even though she'd sometimes told me not to treat her like a child! As time went by with no word from her, I did get worried.'

'And what time did you decide to do something about it? Before lunch, you said?'

'Yes, I can't be sure of the exact time, twelve maybe. Something like that.'

'So what did you do?'

'I made one more phone call to Mill House, then went to look for her.'

'Alone?'

'Yes, alone. The men would be at lunch, you see, and I don't like to disturb them during their free time. I wasn't all that worried anyway, even then I never dreamt she'd come to any real harm...'

'And which route did you take?'

'The one she would have taken, over the railway viaduct, down the fields and across the stepping stones. As I went along, I did wonder if she might have collapsed or hurt herself, and I looked in all the likely places. Then I found her. Among the bluebells. It was awful, superintendent, truly, truly awful...'

He spoke gently to her now. 'So what did you do? I must know exactly what you did at that point.'

'I ran towards her, shouting her name I think, and touched her ... She was cold, so cold, Mr Pemberton, and then I saw the blood on her head. That awful bullet wound.'

'You knew she was dead?'

'It was obvious, superintendent. There was no one to help so I ran to the old mill and rang for PC Wardle. I think he told me to wait until he arrived, but I couldn't, I ran home, all the way, crying and not believing what I'd found...'

'Now, how did you approach her? By that, I mean did you approach her from her feet or her head or from the side?'

'Must you ask all this? It is really upsetting, having to go over it all again like this...'

'I'm sorry, but it is most important.'

'Her feet, superintendent. I approached from her feet. I saw her legs and feet towards me as I went through those bluebells...'

'There was nothing you could have done at that stage,' he said softly. 'Nothing at all. Did you touch anything? Remove anything?'

She frowned at his question.

'No, for God's sake!'

'I must ask – if she'd committed suicide, the gun would be near the body. Some people have been tempted to remove the gun in such circumstances. We have to know every detail, I know it's harrowing...'

'Oh, I see, sorry. I should realise you must

60

ask these things. No, I just touched her hand, the one that was outstretched, and then her forehead ... but I didn't move anything. There was nothing to remove, she had nothing with her.'

'And you let yourself into Mill House to call for help. How did you get in?'

'The key, it's always kept in an outside toilet, at the back of the house.'

'And it was there, in its usual position?'

'Yes, the place was locked up.'

'So you don't know whether or not Alicia had been into Mill House this morning?'

'No, I couldn't say.'

'All right. Now, Miss Farrow, I must ask which shoes you were wearing at that time.'

'Shoes?'

'There are footprints near the body – mine, PC Wardle's for certain, DC Cashmore's, and I would expect yours will be there. That is why I had to ask about your direction of approach.'

'Oh, I see,' and her face produced the tic once again. 'Yes, of course they will be there. They must be, mustn't they?'

'Yes. So I need to examine the shoes of everyone who approached the body – and if there are any prints which do not match mine, yours, Lorraine's and PC Wardle's, then they could belong to her killer. It means I need your shoes for elimination purposes.'

'You are very thorough, superintendent.'

'We have to be,' he smiled.

'I'll just go and get them for you.' She went out and returned with a pair of light black shoes caked with mud, grass and cow dirt. She placed them at his side.

'Were there cows in the bluebell field when you arrived?' was his next question.

'Yes, they were crowded near the end of the field, close to the farm gate, not far from the stepping stones. They did not trouble me, and weren't anywhere near Alicia.'

Pemberton smiled. 'They've left footprints too,' he said. 'I hope they've not destroyed any evidence. Now, in the time between Alicia leaving the house and you finding her, did you see any visitors around Milverdale Hall? Unexpected visitors? There was no one around the bluebell field, but how about the Hall and the places you can see from there?'

'I had no callers.' She shook her head. 'Apart from the usual, that is. Postman, milkman, paper boy, they'd all been.'

'Do they come early?' he asked.

'Around half past seven as a rule,' she said. 'I have known the paper boy give the papers to the milkman'

'So none of them would see her departure?'

'No, nor her return. They'd been and gone by eight o'clock.'

'What about hikers, people walking dogs, strangers to the village? People out shooting or just rambling? You've a wonderful view from Milverdale Hall. If there was anyone wandering on your land, even with permission, I'd like to know. They might have noticed something or seen someone acting oddly.'

She shook her head. 'When I'm working on a morning, I don't notice anyone in the grounds at the front. You could ask our estate workers, they arrive before eight.'

'All right, I'll get their names later. I'm very anxious to establish whether Alicia encountered anyone on her walk. A hiker on the old ironworks path or someone in the fields near the stream? Someone she knew? Someone sleeping rough in one of the outbuildings, or in the woods? There are many possibilities.'

'I saw no one, superintendent. As for the track over the viaduct, it's very rare anyone used it, except for Alicia and me. Once she turned left out of the Hall, she was out of my sight. I've no idea whether she completed her walk alone or not.'

'Thank. you, Miss Farrow. Had she any enemies, do you think?'

'Not a soul, superintendent. Miss Cash-more asked me to think about that and I've been trying to think of someone who might have had a grudge, someone who might hate her so much they'd want to harm her, but there is no one. Absolutely no one. They all loved her, everyone loved her.'

'I understand her tenants were all very happy with her as their landlord? And the estate workers liked her as their boss?'

'I've never known a grumble from any of them since I came, superintendent, and that is quite an achievement, mark my words. We've had tenants in here with all kinds of problems and she was always helpful. She always responded to their requests efficiently and quickly. She was the ideal property owner, superintendent, such an example to others. She will be missed greatly,' and she sniffed back more tears.

'And she liked the company of children, I understand?'

There was a momentary pause which Pemberton did not miss, then she responded rather haughtily, 'As any sensitive woman would, superintendent. I hope you are not suggesting her activities with children were anything but wholesome.'

'I must consider a wide range of possibilities,' he said, changing his direction of questioning. 'Now tell me about your role at Milverdale Hall, Miss Farrow.'

'I'm the housekeeper, superintendent. That is my official position. I answered an advert in *The Lady,* it was Alicia wanting a live-in housekeeper. I'd just left Lady

Featley's employment – she needed twenty-four-hour care and so she went into a home. She didn't need me any more so the post with Alicia came at exactly the right moment. That was two years ago.'

'Clearly you are happy here?'

'Yes, utterly ... or I was until today,' and the tears burst into a torrent. Lorraine touched her on the arm once more as Pemberton waited for a few moments before continuing.

'So what are your duties? Was there a secretarial role or was it just a domestic housekeeping post?'

'Housekeeping, superintendent,' she sniffed, 'although she did sometimes send me to look at crops or examine tenants' houses if we got requests for upgrading or repairs. I enjoyed that. I had wide responsibilities – basically, though, it was looking after her and the house, but I never did any office work! I'm no good with files and typewriters and things like that, or with those computers they use nowadays.'

'I need to examine her papers,' he said. 'Her birth certificate for one thing, then the estate records, names of her tenants and staff, that sort of thing.'

'Everything will be in her office, superintendent, she kept all her personal papers there. Do you want to see them now?'

'No, not tonight. Is the office locked?'

'It does lock, there is a key,' and the tone in her voice suggested she knew he did not trust her not to touch anything.

'I'd be happier if they were secure until I need access.'

'I'll get the key,' she said, once again leaving the room.

She returned with a large brass mortice key bearing a label marked 'Office' and passed it to him.

'Thanks ... I will ring you before I come to examine the papers. Probably tomorrow.'

'I shall be here, superintendent, I have nowhere else to go. I'll just let things go on as they are until I hear from our solicitors. I have no idea of the kind of work that is needed to keep the estate functioning, except for some very minor snippets Alicia told me during our conversations. She did have a girl in from time to time, a temporary secretary from the village. She could keep things ticking over on a temporary basis.'

'And who was that? Any idea?'

'Her name is Georgina Wallace, she lives in the High Street. She's married with a baby.'

'Thanks, I'll bear her in mind. Now, Miss Farrow, you are all alone here – does that worry you? I can ask our men to patrol the grounds tonight, if you wish.'

'No, I will be fine ... honestly...'

'Should you be thinking of temporary

accommodation somewhere? An hotel, perhaps?'

'No, superintendent. Please, I will be all right. I am not afraid. This is my home, there is nowhere I wish to go. Like Alicia, I have no family. My parents are dead.'

'You were friends, you and Alicia?'

'Yes, we were. Good friends. Very good friends in fact. It took time to understand her, she was quite a character, very strong and determined in many ways, but yes, we grew to like each other. I'd sit with her on an evening, for example, or go for a drive in that old car of hers or visit one of her tenants, share her table at dinner on occasions, that sort of thing. Friends, we were good friends. We trusted each other. But it was nothing more than that, if that's what you are thinking. We had separate rooms, separate bathrooms even. I have my own flat here.'

'I need to establish facts.' Pemberton produced another of his gentle smiles for her. It was almost a smile of sympathy. 'You were strictly mistress and employee then?'

'Oh, yes, that never changed! I knew my place ... I respected her, and never tried to take advantage of her friendship.'

'Well, my incident room is being established in the village institute and it will be staffed twenty-four hours a day. Don't hesitate to contact us on 728446 at any time if you need help. Night or day.'

'Thank you.' She made a note of the number.

'When I see you tomorrow, I'll be interested in any visitors Alicia might have had, professional or otherwise, especially strangers. I need to know everything about her recent life and work, Miss Farrow. Can you give some thought to that before to-morrow?'

'Yes, of course, superintendent. I'll do everything I can. I won't sleep a wink tonight, so your queries will have my undivided attention.'

After securing the estate office and retaining the key, Pemberton and Lorraine took their leave with him carrying Constance Farrow's shoes. He'd make a more formal examination of the Hall in daylight and tonight Detective Inspector Larkin would arrange for discreet all-night supervision of the house and grounds. Whether she liked it or not, or knew it or not, Constance Farrow would have a night-time guard of police officers.

And Pemberton wanted to talk to Lorraine.

4

'At last!' He kissed her on the cheek. 'Time to talk to you.'

'You've been busy.' Lorraine produced an understanding smile.

Easing the car away from Milverdale Hall, Pemberton glanced at her. 'So what's all this about seeing a doctor?'

'I went this morning, after you'd gone to work.' She almost whispered the words. He sensed the seriousness in her action.

'Why?' was his next question. 'What's wrong, Lorraine?' He felt he was dragging the news out of her.

'I found a lump,' she told him, followed by another long pause. 'In my breast, the left one.'

'Oh my God! When? When did you find it?'

'A couple of days ago.'

'You never said! You should have told me, Lorraine.' There was a flash of anger in his voice. 'You know we've no secrets–'

'I wasn't sure, Mark. I wanted to be sure, that's why I went to the doctor.'

'And what did he say?'

'I've got to see a specialist.'

'When?'

'He's making an appointment, soon. To have me properly examined.'

'You're telling me this is cancer?'

He sounded blunt and angry, but she recognised his concern. She paused for a long time before saying, 'I've got to consider that, haven't I? Under the circumstances, it's quite possible.'

'Yes, yes, it is ... your mother, you mean?'

'She did have a mastectomy, Mark.'

'I don't know what to say, Lorraine. God, I really don't know what to say... It might be just a lump, mightn't it? A harmless lump, nothing to worry about.'

'That's possible.'

'Is that what the doctor said?'

'He wouldn't commit himself, one way or the other. He said a specialist was necessary. If it's malignant, it'll mean an operation. To cut it out. Or worse.'

By this time, he had eased to a halt on the side of the drive, put on the brakes and switched off the lights and engine. He took her in his arms, a difficult manoeuvre within the confines of the front seat, and held her for a few minutes without speaking.

'Did he say when?' Pemberton broke the silence and released her. 'The specialist's examination, I mean.'

'No, but it will be as soon as possible.'

'You should press for a test the minute

there's a vacancy or a cancellation.'

'He said he would do that, Mark, but he wasn't going to rush me off to hospital at a moment's notice.'

'I'll ring him in the morning, some people need a bomb to get them moving.'

'Leave it, Mark, I can deal with it. I know what I'm doing.'

'But if it is cancer...' and his voice trailed away.

'If it is cancer, it can be treated,' she told him firmly. 'I've set the wheels in motion, Mark.'

'But you, of all people...'

She kissed him and discovered tears on his cheeks. 'Let's look on the bright side,' she said. 'It might not be cancer; if it is, it can be removed, and if things are very advanced, I can have a breast removed... I'm a long way from dying, Mark.'

He remained silent in his misery, restarted the engine, switched on the lights and pulled away. Moving slowly in the darkness, he emerged from the drive of Milverdale Hall and drove towards Campsthwaite village hall. He was struggling to compose himself, wiping his eyes with his handkerchief. In the light cast from their vehicle, Lorraine could see that his face betrayed the shock he had experienced, then he took several deep breaths, exhaling noisily after each one, and so she asked, 'Are you all right?'

71

'As right as I ever shall be. I'll cope, I don't have your worries. You're the one who has to really cope...'

'I'll do it with your help,' she told him, touching his hand.

'Let's hope I can provide the strength you need and deserve,' he said with a grim determination to take his mind off her devastating news. 'Perhaps we shouldn't dwell on it until we know more. Let's get back to the enquiry, shall we? What do you think of Miss Farrow?'

'She's like a schoolmistress I knew when I was little.' Lorraine managed a smile. 'Very proper and formal, no sense of humour, very much dedicated to doing the right thing at all times – or to be seen to. She's more like a butler than a housekeeper. I'm sure she's capable of running that place single-handed. The whole estate, I mean.'

'I agree, but is she a murderer?' It was a brutal question but it took her thoughts away from her own worries.

'A murderer?' She frowned. 'You don't suspect her, do you, Mark?'

'She found the body,' he responded. 'The person who finds the body is automatically suspect number one. They're in the frame until they are eliminated. And she's not been eliminated yet, shoeprints or no shoe-prints.'

'But her shoeprints will be at the scene,

won't they? She found the body.'

'Exactly. One set will either confirm her story or suggest she killed and "found" Alicia at the same time. Two sets on separate occasions will show she's lying – it means she made one visit to kill her or make sure she was dead, the second to "find" her.'

She considered his words, then asked, 'Do you honestly think she might be lying? She had no reason to kill her mistress, surely?' Already, Lorraine had pushed her private worries to the back of her mind and her professionalism was taking over, re-generated by Pemberton's accusation of Constance.

'We don't know anything about a motive, do we?' he countered. 'She might have had a reason we haven't uncovered. There might have been friction between them, bitter jealousy of some kind or some other deep impulse we've yet to expose. We know nothing about Constance Farrow, do we?'

'I did extract a good deal of her personal and family background during our chat,' Lorraine assured him. 'And I managed to get a run-down on the various posts she's had. I must say that everything looks absolutely normal to me – and so did she. I have no reason to suspect her.'

'She is the one person who had ample opportunity to kill Alicia. You'll have to check her story, Lorraine, every tiny fact.'

73

'She's just the housekeeper, Mark, a spinster lady working for a pittance, I would suggest, with never a hope of inheriting that estate. With Alicia's death, she'll be out of a home and out of a job. She's not a tenant wanting to buy her own home, so that's not a reason for killing Alicia. She could be a beneficiary under Alicia's will – that's something we'll have to check – but if she was going to kill her mistress, why not do it at home? Why stalk her to the bluebell field and shoot her there?'

'To make it appear as if someone else was responsible,' he returned. 'Or to make it look like an accident.'

'You are serious about this, aren't you?'

'I am. The more we know about Constance and Alicia, the easier it will be to conduct our enquiries, Lorraine.'

'Constance doesn't know as much as she thought she did,' smiled Lorraine. 'She lacks hard facts, family dates, but I gather Alicia was born in 1953. Here, at the Hall. That makes her forty-five. Her father died in 1993, three years before Constance came to Milverdale Hall as housekeeper. He was eighty, and his wife had died earlier, in 1989, aged seventy-five. Alicia had no brothers or sisters.'

'Constance would never have known the elder Milverdales, would she?'

'No, both died before she arrived.'

'I'd like to know more about the Milverdale family,' Pemberton said. 'I'll pop into the parish church tomorrow – there are bound to be memorials.'

'Good idea. And now?' she asked pointedly.

He paused and said, 'I think we ought to go home, after what you've been through.'

'Rubbish!' she retorted. 'I'm quite fit, Mark, it was just a routine visit to the doctor. I'm just the same as I was yesterday and the day before–'

'Finding a lump in your breast is not routine!' he snapped.

'No, but it doesn't turn me into an invalid!'

He sighed. 'I'm not sure I can face those detectives now.'

'Won't everyone have gone home?'

'Some of the teams were going for a bar snack,' he said.

'Then let's do that and give the incident room a miss! I can't say I fancy cooking when we get home.' Lorraine was showing her customary fortitude now.

'You know me, I'm not one for joining my teams socially during an investigation. After all, I am their boss! Besides, they keep quizzing me about the case. I need a break from that.'

'We don't have to sit with the others if you don't want to. We could find our own table in a quiet corner...'

'All right,' he capitulated. 'To the Miners Arms then. I must admit I'm famished. I missed my lunch. Then it's home for a good long restful sleep as we prepare for tomorrow.'

'Yes, but don't tell anyone about my news.' She had to adjust to her new situation. Sleep might not be easy tonight.

As they entered the pub, the first person they encountered was Detective Inspector Larkin.

'Oh, hello, sir, Lorraine. I didn't expect to see you two here.'

'The pangs of hunger have driven us here, Paul, I've had nothing to eat since breakfast and the thought of preparing a meal was just too much! I can't bear the wait!'

He reached for a menu, ordered a steak pie and chips for himself, lemon sole and salad for Lorraine after asking her choice, then ordered drinks from the landlord. Having undertaken those essential chores, he savoured the first sip of the deep rich flavour of the pint of best Yorkshire bitter while Lorraine settled for a dry white wine.

'That is very good!' he sighed after the first mouthful. 'Now, Paul, I'm not one for combining work with leisure, but have there been any developments in my absence?' Talking about work would avoid the risk of referring to Lorraine's news.

76

'There was a call from the pathologist, sir, to confirm that death was due to a bullet in the head. Otherwise Alicia was in good health if a little overweight. He found no other wounds or bruises once her clothes were removed. A clean shot, in other words, thought to have been fired from a distance. He's kept the bullet, it's not a .22, so he says, but he isn't sure of the calibre. He's having that established.'

'Not a .22, eh? Not a rabbit-shooter's bullet?'

'Dr Preston said he could arrange a ballistics examination. There's no sign of a sexual assault or any other form of physical attack. No bruises, no assailant's skin under her fingernails, nothing to indicate a struggle of any kind. Alicia's clothes were searched too. There was nothing useful there, a handkerchief in her jeans pocket, a comb in the rear pocket and nothing else. She travelled light.'

'She would, on a morning walk. Now, Paul, if she was shot from a distance it would suggest a villain with marksman-like skills. We need to examine all our firearms records for people authorised to hold pistols and rifles other than .22s. Try all the shooting clubs, do a check on their weapon stocks. And we might have to check the whereabouts of individual members. Check our crime reports for thefts of firearms.

Now for our side of things. We've just come from Alicia's housekeeper at Milverdale Hall, a lanky, sombre lady called Constance Farrow. Miss Farrow. She's confirmed that Alicia set off alone at seven o'clock for her walk. She wasn't carrying anything, not a rifle nor even her handbag. So her own gun wasn't used to kill her and she wasn't robbed. We've no sex motive for her death, and no robbery motive. I'm returning to the Hall tomorrow to go through the estate's files and we'll have to check the staff's movements during the material times. I hope to dig out some family history too, and delve into Alicia's background. Lorraine will do checks on Constance Farrow. Can you put their names through Criminal Records? Alicia and Farrow. Do all the standard checks for a murder suspect. Let's see if Farrow is who she says she is, or whether there's any mystery to *her* background.'

'No problem. And you think Alicia's background is relevant?'

'A murder victim's background is always relevant. Besides, the village bobby says she wasn't accepted by the villagers, he thinks they're keeping secrets from him too. Could they know something about Alicia's involvement with children? And the housekeeper seems bothered about the press unearthing some deep family secret. Maybe Miss Farrow is over-protective, but if there is

78

something, we need to know.'

'Some nasty skeleton in the family cupboard, eh?'

'Who knows? Dark family secrets can lead to some volatile and strange behaviour. Now, to change the subject, is everyone back from their enquiries?'

'All except DC Stokoe, sir. She went to interview the village schoolteacher, Mrs Donaldson. She's fairly new here and lives at Fortington, that's about six miles away. You suggested a speedy interview and I thought it would be best done out of school hours. I sent Stokoe, she should be back soon.'

'Good. I'm pleased you've made such a positive start. So how about you, Paul? Are you staying for a snack?'

'I'm just having one very quick pint, sir, my wife will have a meal ready.'

'You can join us if you want.'

'No, I'd better not be late.'

Carrying his drinks, Pemberton followed Larkin into the centre of the spacious bar where a crowd of noisy detectives were gathered around a table. He asked if they minded if he, Larkin and Lorraine joined them; he was warmly received and sat down with his drink.

'It's a change seeing you slumming with the troops, sir!' laughed one of the detectives, DC Norton.

'When you're as hungry as I am, you'll eat anywhere!' he chuckled in return.

'It's good to see you relax, sir. Anyway, we've hardly got started on the investigation, so there's not much likelihood of us talking shop.'

Not wanting to talk about work but wishing to avoid the temptation to talk about Lorraine's news, Pemberton did tell them about his first impressions of Constance Farrow but refrained from any suggestion that she might be guilty. He took care not to let the pub's regulars or the landlord overhear his words and found he was relaxing with his officers.

'We got nowhere,' Norton was saying with a shrug of his shoulders. 'We've only done a few houses but I get the feeling nobody wants to talk to us.'

'You mean they can't help?' Pemberton asked.

'No, sir, it's not that. I can't put my finger on it but I get the impression they won't help. They don't want us asking questions about Alicia, they won't talk about her. I got that impression from the start. I've come across this attitude before – a protective silence, I call it – but I've not experienced it during a murder enquiry.'

'This might support what PC Wardle told me. Is that what you've all found?' Pemberton's steak pie, a whopping edifice with hot gravy and piled high with chips and peas, was plonked in front of him by a teenage waitress and he smiled his thanks. Condiments were on the table, she told him, then gave him a knife and fork wrapped in a green paper serviette.

Lorraine's more delicate piece of white fish followed, prettily garnished with a salad.

'Yes, sir.' Detective Sergeant Williams joined the conversation. 'I got the same impression from houses at the top of the village.'

'We're in the very early stages of the investigation,' Pemberton countered. 'Some of the villagers will be shocked, perhaps they can't take it in yet. Let's see how things work out tomorrow. We can always revisit the stubborn ones! News of the murder should have reached everyone by then and they might find it easier to talk.'

'Let's hope so, sir. We won't get anywhere without their co-operation.'

As more food arrived, the pub was filling with local people and so the hungry detectives abandoned their discussions about the case and settled down to enjoy their hefty Yorkshire meals. Detective Constable Julie Stokoe entered about forty-five minutes later, noticed Pemberton among the throng and came to report to him. She outlined her chat with the primary school teacher, confirming that Alicia had offered to help with various school projects. She added that Alicia was always very keen to involve herself with the children, especially with the annual pantomime and art lessons. There was a standing invitation for any pupil to visit Mill House but Mrs Donaldson had told Stokoe that the parents did not favour them going there; they preferred those extra-mural activities to be arranged within the school with at least one teacher or parent in attendance. Mrs Donaldson had no idea why they felt like that. No one had explained. Pemberton asked Julie Stokoe to report her interview at tomorrow's conference of detectives. As a gesture of his appreciation, he bought her a drink and then she went off to join her friends.

While Pemberton was finishing his meal and debating whether it was prudent to leave, a man entered the bar, went over to the landlord and asked a question whereupon the landlord pointed to Pemberton. The man, a thick-set character with a bald patch and dark hair, and wearing a rather untidy dark suit, came across to the table. He'd be in his late forties, estimated Pemberton.

'Detective Superintendent Pemberton?' He looked down at the assembled detectives.

'That's me,' Mark answered.

'Haigh, Trevor Haigh, freelance reporter from Leeds, Mr Pemberton.'

'So what can I do for you, Mr Haigh?' He did not recognise the man; he was not a local freelance. Leeds was nearly sixty miles away.

'This murder—'

'We haven't confirmed there is a murder,' Pemberton stopped him. 'We are investigating a suspicious death which might be murder, but it could be an unfortunate accident. We can rule out suicide, though. If you want a quote, I can say that tests are being conducted and we are keeping open minds.'

'Alicia Milverdale is the dead woman, my sources tell me.' The reporter was already scribbling in his notebook.

'I can confirm that a woman has been found dead, but her name will not be released until she has been formally identified.'

'Come on, superintendent, we all know who it is!'

'You can say that the deceased is a middle-aged unmarried woman from Campsthwaite. That narrows it down. But there's no way I can confirm it is Alicia Milverdale until I get a formal identification.'

'All right. So what do you know about her?' was the next question.

'Know about who?' grinned Pemberton with just a hint of mischief.

'The subject of your investigation,' the reporter replied.

'Our enquiries are at a very early stage,' was Pemberton's practised reply. 'Our forensic experts are examining the scene but there's nothing else I can say at this point, except that the deceased died from gunshot wounds. There will be a news conference tomorrow morning at ten thirty.'

'I understand she is the last of a long and distinguished family line, Mr Pemberton...'

'Who? I haven't told you the name of the deceased.'

'I'm wondering if some long-lost cousin has come out of the woodwork in an attempt to claim the estate, you know the sort of angle I need.'

'All I can do,' stressed Pemberton, 'is to release the facts when they have been confirmed. If you want more right now, you can add that some forty detectives are engaged on the enquiry, that task force officers and Scenes of Crime experts have been called to the scene, and I am in charge. Pemberton is the name. Detective Superintendent. Now, I must leave, I have urgent things to do.'

'See you at the news conference then,' and as Haigh hurried out, Pemberton went over to the man he presumed to be the landlord.

'Pemberton,' he introduced himself. 'Detective Superintendent. I'm in charge of this enquiry.'

'Nelson, Andy Nelson. I'm the landlord. I heard what you said, we won't talk to him.'

'There's no harm in talking to the press, Mr Nelson, provided they print the truth. In fact, they can be very helpful,' smiled Pemberton. 'But we need to talk, Mr Nelson. You and I. Not tonight though.'

Nelson, built rather like an all-in wrestler with a crew-cut hair-style and a chest like one of his beer barrels, produced a cynical smile. 'You needn't waste your time, Mr Pemberton. There's nothing I can tell you, nothing at all.'

'You might have seen something out of the ordinary this morning, heard something in local gossip or noticed a stranger around the village...'

Nelson shook his head.

'I can't tell you or your men anything, Mr Pemberton. I know nothing, absolutely nothing,' and he turned to adjust the bottles on a shelf below the counter. 'But you and your men are welcome to use my facilities.'

'But we would still like to talk to you, to-morrow sometime.'

'When it involves Alicia Milverdale, superintendent, we know nothing and can tell you nothing, either now or tomorrow.'

'Nonetheless, I'll see you tomorrow in a

more formal atmosphere.' Pemberton had no intention of arguing or pressuring this man in his own premises while members of the public were present but he was determined to interview him.

'I'll be around most of the day,' Nelson said. 'Call any time. But I know nothing, absolutely nothing. I don't want to waste your time.'

Pemberton and Lorraine then left; Lorraine, after only one small glass of dry white wine, drove their car and they headed for the house they shared at Rainesbury, half an hour's drive away. Quite deliberately, Pemberton refrained from further reference to Lorraine's medical problem, doing his best to divert her mind from her examination. In doing this, however, he was rather more silent than usual.

'What are you thinking about?' she asked as they moved through the stunning Yorkshire countryside.

'You,' he said.

'And what else?' She knew him well enough to realise that his mind would not rest entirely upon her problem.

'I was wondering about this unwillingness to talk to us.'

'Some villages do adopt a closed-mouth policy,' she commented. 'They close ranks against outsiders, but I didn't think Campsthwaite was like that. It's a commuter village for Rainesbury and elsewhere, there are incomers living here.'

'Maybe they'll talk when they're not in the public eye or maybe the villagers are wary about talking too freely because they depend on the estate for work. I wonder if that landlord was putting on a show for the benefit of his customers?'

'That's likely. I didn't think this was one of those tiny-minded backwaters where you expect people to shun outsiders.'

'My sentiments exactly,' he nodded. 'So why do I get a feeling we're going to find some opposition?'

'Perhaps we're not,' was her light response. 'Perhaps it's your imagination working overtime. Perhaps everybody will love us and be most helpful.'

'I hope so. But if the locals *are* united in refusing to talk to us, Lorraine, who are they protecting – and why? And if some other villager died, would we receive the same kind of non-co-operation? Are they worried about their jobs or has this attitude to do with Alicia personally? Nelson more or less suggested that, didn't he?'

'I don't think we are in a position to answer any of those questions just yet.' She was trying to ease his concern. 'We're in the very early stages and you're basing those worries on two rather small incidents, Mark. Let's see what tomorrow brings, shall we?'

'I hope it brings bags of crime-busting information!' he laughed and settled down in his seat as the engine purred and the car swept through the lanes between the hedgerows and their brilliant displays of fresh new hawthorn blossom.

'Whose turn is it to make the cocoa?' he muttered, his eyes closing involuntarily as the smooth drive lulled him into a premature sleep.

'Yours,' she said. 'Definitely yours.'

His eyes were closed as he was thinking about her future, their future. Life without Lorraine was impossible to contemplate.

A tear slid down his cheek and he did not brush it away.

Using his private car, Pemberton left home ahead of Lorraine next morning. She was fast asleep; she'd had a fairly restful night but he did not want to disturb her as he made a very early start. First, he called at the newsagents for copies of all the national and local daily papers to see what Trevor Haigh and his colleagues had made of the story. Sitting in his car to read them he saw that Alicia's death was not headlines in any of the nationals but it did make the front page of the *Yorkshire Post* as the second-lead story. The account contained nothing to which he could take exception and there was no exposé of the Milverdale family background.

Content with this treatment, Pemberton began his drive across the moors to Campsthwaite. His intention was to arrive ahead of the teams to quietly study the statements and computer records already assembled and processed in the incident room. He told the night duty constable, bleary-eyed and tired, that he could go home and thanked him for his lonely duties. Pemberton then made himself a coffee and carried it into the ante-room which served as his office. Closing the door and plonking his coffee on a blotter, he sat at the desk, put the newspaper in his out-tray for Larkin to deal with, then turned to his in-tray, deep with copies of statements bearing highlights to mark sections which required his attention. As he worked, civilian staff and detectives began to arrive; he heard their chatter, listened to the chink of mugs and spoons in coffee jars, and then the phones began to ring.

As he tried to gain some kind of overall picture of the village and its association with Alicia, he ignored the passage of time and, happily, no one came to disturb him. His door remained firmly closed. But the statements told him nothing. They were all negative – people knew nothing and had seen nothing. This supported his feeling that the people of Campsthwaite had no wish to help the police with their enquiries.

Although this reaction could never be described as blatant obstruction – it was much too subtle for that – it did present a serious challenge; however, it was not one that would defeat Pemberton and his teams. One way or another, he would establish the truth behind this savage death.

It was approaching nine o'clock when he opened the door and walked into the body of the hall, now buzzing with noise and chatter. Paul Larkin was first to greet him.

'Good morning, sir,' he said. 'I had no idea you were here.'

'The early bird catches the worm, eh? We've a worm to catch, Paul, and I intend to be early enough to do so. Everybody here?'

'All except Lorraine Cashmore, sir.'

5

Lorraine did arrive just as Pemberton was about to begin his address to the detectives, and, with an apologetic smile, slid into a spare seat at the back of the hall. Relieved to see her, he opened the conference, and when it was over, Larkin said, 'Constance Farrow did not leave the Hall overnight, sir. Nor did she make any phone calls.'

'Good man. And Mill House?'

'No visitors. The Scenes of Crime teams are continuing at the bluebell field and in the woods. They won't enter the house until you say so.'

'I want to look around Mill House before our lads tackle it, it will help me to understand Alicia. Our bolshie landlord can wait and I want to have a look in the parish church. Then there's Alicia's formal identification to arrange.'

'I can deal with Alicia's identification, sir,' Lorraine's voice piped up.

'Thanks, that would be ideal.' He smiled.

'Sorry I was a bit late, sir, I got stuck behind a tractor.' She looked alert and cheerful this morning. 'It makes sense for a woman to accompany Constance while she's making the identification. Besides, it'll help me to get to know her better. But you'll want to talk to Constance as well, won't you?'

'Yes, in due course. I'll come to the Hall later, I'll bring some detectives to give the whole place a thorough search. Who knows, we might even find the rifle!'

'Do you want me to stay with her?' she asked him.

'If you could. I should arrive around the time you return from the mortuary.'

'I'll expect you when you arrive, sir.' She was formal because they were at work, and she was showing no sign of her worries. 'I'll make the arrangements now.'

He watched her leave, his heart aching but professional enough not to reveal his private concerns before subordinates.

'Paul.' He turned his attention to Larkin. 'Before I go, have we checked for any links between this case and the Muriel Brown murder?'

'I did a quick computer check, sir, for sightings of red cars, names which might be known arsonists or rapists living hereabouts, but nothing's turned up. I'll maintain comparisons through this investigation.'

'Just a thought,' smiled Pemberton. 'We've got to keep Muriel Brown in mind – I know it was sixteen years ago or thereabouts, but her murder was never solved.'

'If a link does ever turn up, the computers will identify it.'

'You and I will be superfluous soon, Paul, computers will be the new detectives. Right, I'm going to look at the Milverdale memorials, then I'll go to Mill House. I've got my mobile if you need me.'

The tiny church of St Helen stood within a yew-filled churchyard surrounded by dry stone walls. It was an ancient building whose tower dated to Norman times. Parts of the south doorway were erected in 1200 but the chancel was from the fourteenth century with nineteenth-century modifications. Smelling musty, it was illuminated with stained glass windows and boasted a splendid beamed ceiling on eight stone pillars.

Around the walls were several memorials, one commemorating an anonymous bearded man who had died around 1300, but those of the Milverdales were easy to locate. None was ancient, the family coming to the village during the nineteenth century when they built the Hall. Eventually, he found a white marble memorial shaped like a scroll; built into the south wall, it was dedicated to Alicia's parents. It recorded the death of Mrs Emmeline Milverdale of Milverdale Hall, aged seventy-five, on 8th September 1989, and her beloved husband, Roderick Milverdale, aged eighty, who died on 4th February 1993. So Alicia, born in 1953, had been the child of older parents – her father must have been forty at the time. A last minute rush to produce an heir, perhaps? A short phrase, 'Together in Eternity', had been carved at the base of that memorial, but the Milverdale memorials were few in comparison with those honouring more ancient families.

One was dedicated to Roderick Milverdale's parents, Roderick and Margaret, who had died in 1938 and 1940 respectively, and he found a more recent one to the memory of Audrey Milverdale. She had died suddenly on 7th September 1947 at the early age of thirty-two –'cherished daughter of Roderick and Margaret and sister of Roderick'. The memorial included the phrase: 'It's good to be honest and true.' She would be Alicia's maiden aunt, Pemberton realised, and it seemed Roderick was a family name.

There was little else of immediate interest, so he dropped a pound coin into the wall safe in response to a request for donations, then left for Mill House. He eased his car into a space among the array of vehicles already in the farmyard and donned a pair of wellington boots which looked slightly incongruous with his smart dark suit. As he made his way towards the bluebell field, he saw teams of detectives working to carefully made plans; he used a route clearly marked by yellow tape and hailed Inspector Fowler, the officer in charge of the Task Force.

'Morning, Brian. Any progress?'

'Nothing dramatic, sir. We've found more litter dropped by tourists, ramblers and children. Although the land is private, people do use it. I doubt if we can link any of the items to Alicia's death.'

'No bullets or bullet casings?'

'Not yet, sir, no.'

'Their absence supports the theory that she was shot from a distance, that her killer never set foot among these bluebells.'

'That's a fairly general view, sir.'

'Good, well, keep up the good work. Now, I want to look at Mill House before SOCO get their paws all over it. Where's DS Fenton?'

'He's with Dr Preston, sir, they're examining the stepping stones.'

'Stepping stones? Dr Preston's here already, is he?'

'He came early. He wonders if the gunman fired from the stones. If he did, the discharged shell might be in the water.'

'It's fairly shallow fortunately. I'll have words with him, he might like to join me in Mill House.'

Dr Jack Preston was a short and rather sturdy man in his early fifties, scarcely more than five feet six inches tall. He had a thick mop of neatly trimmed grey hair and a round pink face sporting an almost permanent smile, and he wore heavy horn-rimmed spectacles. He was wearing a light grey suit of very good quality, a white shirt and dark blue tie. Detective Sergeant Fenton, tall, balding and looking like a forty-year-old bank manager, was with him.

'Ah, Mark.' Preston spotted Pemberton. 'Good to see you.'

'Morning, Jack. You're out early?'

'I wanted to get here before anything cropped up to detain me,' he smiled. 'I was in the lab at six doing my paperwork and managed to get out before the phone started. I wanted to have a look at this scene... Fascinating case, Mark. Murder, is it? Or accident? I wouldn't like to be dogmatic, although I'm veering towards murder.'

'My sentiments too,' acknowledged Pemberton.

'If it is murder, the killer is a crack shot. A fatal head wound from, oh, one hundred yards? Two hundred? More? Bloody amazing accuracy.'

'Where did he fire from?' Pemberton asked.

'He might have been somewhere among the lower fringes of the wood where it borders the field, or on the river banks. Or even in Mill House or the bluebell field itself.'

'We can't rule any of those out, Mark. I

think he was fairly close.'

'Hidden, you think?'

'Who knows? If Alicia knew her killer, it wouldn't be necessary to hide, would it? His presence wouldn't alarm her although she might have been puzzled or even worried if he was carrying the sort of weapon we think he used.'

'Right. So we can place the firing point within a more compact area, Jack. I'll get my teams to concentrate their searches within a radius of a hundred yards of the body's position, then extend it to two hundred.'

'Right. The ejected shell must be around, Mark, unless our killer was especially meticulous in clearing up afterwards.'

'A professional hitman might do that, but hardly an amateur. So what's the theory about these stepping stones?'

'I've had words with Lewis at the path lab and I've had another look at the corpse, the bullet and the wound. First, the bullet is a large one, .303 calibre. Lewis was going to call you this morning to confirm that.'

'I must have left before he rang. So it was a .303 after all!' Pemberton expressed some surprise. 'A military rifle.'

'An odd weapon for a modern murder, Mark. It's quite an old bullet, a wartime relic, perhaps fired from a souvenir of the Second World War. A Lee-Enfield rifle probably.'

'Our list of firearms certificate holders will throw up the name of anyone with permission to keep such a weapon, but if it's held illegally, we'll have difficulty tracing the owner.'

'It would be an heirloom, handed down through a family. Even though it's more than half a century since the war ended, those kind of trophies do keep turning up – and so does their ammunition. And most of that stuff is not held on certificates. It could be anywhere.'

'Where do we start to look?' Pemberton spoke almost to himself. 'There are hundreds of possible hiding places, it'll take years to search everywhere but we've got to find it, Jack. We need a lead, a starting point.'

'Seek and ye shall find!' chuckled Preston. 'Wherever chummy's hidden it, he'd have to carry it there without anyone seeing him. If you've just committed a murder, the first thing you do is get rid of the weapon. Even though this is shooting country where the sight of men with guns is quite normal, a .303 would stick out like the proverbial sore thumb. He'd not risk being seen with it. I'd bet my pension he's hidden it, but where? I need a starting point for a search, Jack, some kind of guidance instead of wasting valuable man-hours on a fruitless hunt in this huge patch of countryside.'

'I wish I could suggest somewhere. It'll help if I can determine the place from where the shot was fired,' suggested Preston. 'That's as difficult as finding the gun. However, I do believe it was fired by someone standing erect. I don't think it was fired from the prone position at ground level. The angle of entry suggests otherwise.'

'You'd need a very steady hand to hit a target with a rifle of that weight and size, Jack, especially from a standing position.'

'I agree, but that's what I think he did.'

'I find that very disturbing,' admitted Pemberton.

'Exactly. I think he'd need a support.'

'He wouldn't carry a tripod or a stand around with him if he was going to commit a murder!' Pemberton's eyes flashed.

'Why not? If he was going to commit a pre-planned murder, he'd make sure he did the job properly. He'd take a tripod or he'd use a rest, something like the branch of a tree, a wall or even a window ledge.'

'How about Mill House? Or Cam Beck Farm?'

'We must consider Mill House but there is no sight-line from the farm; all the farm buildings are out of sight from the place she fell. But a riverside tree is a possibility, or one on the edge of the field. And a tree would provide cover or concealment. I'm here to eliminate as many sites as I can. And once I've eliminated all the impossibles, that will leave us with a selection of possibles.'

As Pemberton looked around, he noted several dry stone walls, some in a ruinous condition and others well maintained. There was a high one between the bluebell field and the farm. The likelihood of the wall providing a firing point would be borne in mind.

'Sir, do you want us to search the river bed for the ejected shell?' Detective Sergeant Fenton, listening to the conversation between these two senior investigators, decided to make his contribution.

Dr Preston replied, 'It won't require your frogmen, Mark. Wellies and good eyesight should be sufficient but yes, we'll need the stream to be searched unless the shell turns up elsewhere. I don't think it will have washed far in this current because it would lodge among the stones. The beck does have a bed of pebbles.'

Pemberton nodded towards the sergeant.

'Take your cue from Dr Preston, sarge. Now I'm heading for Mill House. Alicia went there for reasons I'm not too sure about and I'm concerned that she took children with her. I'm not sure whether she was ever alone there with a child, that's something else I'd like to establish. But I want to see the place and get the feel of it before our teams get cracking.'

'You're thinking black thoughts, Mark, but do you mind if I come along?' asked Jack Preston.

'I'd welcome that – I was going to ask Sergeant Fenton to join me in any case,' confirmed Pemberton. 'The key's in the outside loo.'

As the three men approached the old house, its sturdy outline materialised through the trees. It was a long, low building of dark granite with a blue slate roof. Two storeys high, it was rooted among large boulders and the wall abutting the beck bore the disused millwheel. Tall brick chimneys rose from each end of the building and the roof seemed in good repair, but the woodwork was in dire need of fresh paint. A profuse growth of moss clung to the northern walls while the millwheel had not turned for decades. Its base was hidden among weeds which in turn concealed the still waters of the former mill race. This deep man-made channel had been excavated years ago to carry water diverted from the passing stream, its purpose being to turn the huge wheel. Having driven the millwheel, the diverted waters rejoined the beck a few yards downstream, and thus a small island had been formed. It was covered with trees and a tangle of under-growth; there was a small wooden foot-bridge in a poor state of repair leading to it from near the grounds of the house.

'You'll be searching that mill race, sarge?' Pemberton asked.

'Yes, sir, every inch of it. It's deep, a good hiding place for a rifle!'

Pemberton, Preston and Detective Sergeant Fenton explored the exterior, noting the small-paned ground-floor windows, the front door overgrown with moss suggesting it had not been used for years, and stonework which needed repointing. Miniature trees and weeds of all kinds were sprouting from the gutters. What had once been a garden was now an enclosure of rampant undergrowth, briars and nettles growing over the flagged paths and surrounded by a dry stone wall. The remnants of a sundial could be seen while the paved footpath to the back door showed signs of regular use. Near the back door was the outside toilet with bare stone walls and a disused earth closet. Pemberton entered, screwed his eyes against the darkness and felt among the beams above his head. He found a large mortice key and unlocked the heavy door with a solid 'thunk'. They were assailed by the distinctive aroma of an old house with no damp course. There was more than a hint of dry rot, wet rot and ancient furniture. Greeted by a cool and crushing silence, they entered a greenish gloom, the effect produced by the canopy of trees which obliterated most of the daylight to make lights a necessity, even in summer. Heating would be needed too; electricity was supplied, Pemberton noted.

They found themselves in a long, narrow rear lobby with coat hooks along the whitewashed wall. With a stone-flagged floor, it ran the length of the house and doors opened to the right into several rooms. As their eyes adjusted to the gloom, they saw lines of colourful hunting prints along the lobby wall.

There was a rack containing several walking-sticks, another containing fishing rods, gaffs and nets, while several pairs of black rubber wellington boots and waders stood against the outer wall in a range of sizes, some with dried mud around their soles. Waterproof clothing hung further along the wall. There was a clock whose pendulum hung immobile, the pointers showing three thirty. Judging by the cobwebs and grime on the glass, it had been stopped for years. Pemberton led the way into the first room on their right, a kitchen with a Welsh dresser full of crockery, a mugwump bearing half a dozen white mugs, a scrubbed wood table and six chairs, a black Yorkist fire range, complete with kettle and pans, and a red-tiled floor in need of a polish.

There was a kitchen sink with hot and

cold taps below the window, which over-looked the distant bluebell field; the stream could be seen across to the right. The kitchen must have been used occasionally because an open shelf bore a jar of instant coffee and a box of tea-bags, each half used. There were two unopened bottles of orange squash too.

'This window hasn't been opened for years, just ask those spiders!' remarked Pemberton. 'The shot didn't come from here.'

'Those mugs might bear fingerprints,' said Fenton.

'Exactly,' responded Pemberton. 'This place needs a thorough going-over, sarge, every inch searched, every hiding place found. Constance's prints should be on the telephone wherever that is, and, well, the rest are anybody's guess. We should find some from visiting schoolchildren, and some from Alicia.'

Along the front of the house, each with windows overlooking the bluebell field, were a lounge, dining-room and small study. All were gloomy, all had small-paned windows which had not been opened for years and all were furnished with antiques, a little tatty in their neglected age. The telephone was in the lounge, a black handset with an old-fashioned dial; it was on an occasional table near the fireplace. A staircase led to the first floor from a lobby at the woodland end of the house, beyond the lounge.

There was a window half-way up, also rich with spiders' webs, and then they were on a long landing which ran along the rear of the house, directly above the downstairs lobby. The first two doors revealed a bathroom and a toilet, then a small bedroom with a single bed bearing an uncovered mattress, a dressing-table with a mirror, a chair and a small cheap wardrobe. The middle bedroom was larger with a double bed, this one being covered with a purple eiderdown. There was a dressing-table with make-up bottles and boxes on a glass tray, a mirror, a large wardrobe and two easy chairs. The room was cleaner than the others and appeared to be in regular use. The windows of all the rooms were closed and had not been opened for years, but this room appeared to have been used fairly recently.

The third bedroom was quite different. Larger than the others put together, it had two Yorkshire sliding windows, side by side, and they overlooked the stream above the millwheel. These were draped with lush purple velvet curtains with tie-backs but bore the familiar cobwebs. The light purple walls were hung with curtains of the same style and colour, all edged with gold braid.

Against the rear wall stood a huge ornate chair on a dais with steps, a throne in fact.

It was embossed with gold, red, white and blue and was positioned beneath a canopy bearing a splendid arrangement of expensive silk curtains. On the throne was a deep cushion covered with green silk. An ornate multicoloured silk carpet was spread upon the floor at the base of the throne, with another on the floor of the bedroom.

'A throne room!' Pemberton was accustomed to strange sights in houses he had raided or visited but he'd never encountered a throne room. There were built-in wardrobes along one wall, the doors of one standing partially open. Without touching anything, he peered inside.

'Royal regalia,' he muttered to Fenton and Preston. 'Coronation outfits, or copies of them. Queen's clothing, or princess's. Page boy uniforms. Lots of them in different colours, blue, green, white, red... Amazing... So what happened in here, I wonder?'

'It's her theatrical streak,' grinned Jack Preston.

'So this is where she rehearsed her pantomimes! Well, sarge, we need this place photographed in full glorious Technicolor and it needs a very thorough search. God knows what you'll find.'

'No problem, sir, it'll add colour to our day!'

'We need the names of everyone who came here,' Pemberton said to no one in

106

particular, 'children or adults, and we need to know what they did here. How far back do we go? Two years? Five years? Further? What do you make of this, Jack?'

'Once I had to examine a corpse in a bedroom fashioned in the style of Captain Cook's cabin on the *Endeavour,* and on another occasion a bedroom was done out like Robin Hood's cave, complete with bows and arrows hanging in the roof and a picture of the Sheriff of Nottingham on the wall! We see all sorts – this one's not likely to hold too many surprises.'

'Well, I asked for that,' grinned Mark Pemberton.

'This confirms Alicia's fetish about being a princess,' said Preston. 'Maybe when she was a little girl, she played here all alone? Or brought friends in to join her games? It's a bit like an adult-sized doll's house, isn't it?'

'A stately playhouse?' smiled Fenton.

'Somewhere to keep the kids out of father's way!' smiled Preston. 'I must say this room does look as if it's been used regularly. There's not a lot of dust about, or spiders' webs. This is surely where she brought those schoolchildren, Mark.'

'So what about the house being used as the firing point?'

'I'd say not,' said Preston. 'None of the windows give a suitable view and they haven't been opened for years.'

'We haven't found the mill room,' Pemberton reminded him. 'I thought there'd be a room full of millstones and huge gear wheels.'

'I think this throne room was part of the operational area,' said Preston. 'It's in the right place, overlooking the mill race. If that is so, the kitchen below us would house gears and millwheels. I'd say they were stripped during the modernisation but the old wheel was left as an adornment, it's no longer functional.'

'What's this say about Alicia, then?' Pemberton put to the forensic scientist.

'It appears she enjoyed playing out some kind of fantasy and used this place as a vehicle for her wishes. A place to retreat into her childhood.'

'And the page boy outfits?'

'She might have worn them when she was a child. Or other children might have taken part in her play-acting, even with an adult queen or princess or king on that throne. When she grew up, she might have sat on the throne with children taking part in her play-acting, wearing those page boy outfits.'

'Do you think there was anything unhealthy going on?' Pemberton asked.

'Play-acting like this doesn't necessarily mean she was abusing children, Mark, if that's what you're thinking, but nothing's impossible,' admitted Preston. 'Lonely woman, unmarried, probably having difficulty attracting a man, no hint of lesbianism, a bit of an odd existence outside her work ... it might add up to something rather less than savoury.'

'That could explain the villagers' reluctance to talk, couldn't it?' Pemberton mused. 'To voice that kind of suspicion could threaten a job or a home and besides, no parent will want their child appearing in a court of law to testify, especially during a murder hearing or at an inquest on Alicia. I think this is a case for the softly-softly-catchee-monkey type of approach.'

'I'd go along with that,' agreed Preston.

'I've seen enough for the time being – how about you two?' Pemberton asked.

Preston and Fenton agreed they could do no more until their detailed search.

'I wonder how much Constance Farrow knows about this place?' Pemberton was speaking almost to himself at this point. 'Could it hold a clue to the family secret she doesn't want the press to know about?'

'Sir?'

'I'm going to see her this morning,' he said in a louder voice. 'I wonder if she came here to do the dusting and cleaning? But I'll begin with our farmer friend.'

'Has he a son who might have been one of her page boys?' smiled Preston.

'I'll soon find out,' said Pemberton. 'Come

on, time to go. We'll secure this place. Sarge, I'm making you responsible for the key. I don't want people entering the house until we've finished with it, so don't return the key to its usual place. Keep it in the incident room. Maintain contact with me and Dr Preston as you go about your examination and remember we need evidence to identify the people who've used this house over the years.'

'But the killer won't have concealed the gun here, surely?' said Preston.

'He might have taken it from here,' said Pemberton with no further comment. 'He might have known where the key was, he might know the house inside out. He might have been here with Alicia. She might have shown him secrets, he might be grown up now. There might be a rifle among all those theatrical props, hidden by velvet curtains and robes, or packed in the loft! And the shot could have come from somewhere in or around the building. So, sarge, the next stage in the history of Mill House is down to you.'

'Yes, sir.'

They returned to the bluebell field where Pemberton lingered to observe progress before bidding the others farewell. He returned to his car, replaced his wellingtons with gleaming black shoes and walked to the farmhouse. The kitchen door was open so he knocked and called, 'Hello?'

A woman's voice responded with, 'Come in, the door's open.'

He entered to find a stout brown-haired woman pummelling a pile of dough on the table, her sleeves rolled up and her arms white with flour. With her flowered apron and round, red face, he estimated she would be in her mid-forties but she looked like a lady from a past generation.

'Oh,' she said, ceasing her labours and wiping her hands on a cloth. 'I thought it was the insurance man.'

'I'm not after your money,' smiled Pemberton. 'I'm Detective Superintendent Pemberton, from Rainesbury CID.'

'If it's Geoff you want, he's in the machine shed, summat to do with fixing a grass-cutter, he said.'

'Thanks.' He paused, then asked, 'You've heard about Miss Milverdale?'

'I have,' she said stiffly with no further comment.

'I just wondered if you or your husband saw anyone in this area yesterday morning? Around seven and eight o'clock?'

'I'm not out of the house at that time of day,' she said. 'Too busy with breakfast and household chores. You'd better talk to him.'

'You knew Alicia Milverdale?'

'I did, and a good landlady she was. Most considerate, very kind and helpful, but

111

that's all I'll say.'

'What else is there to say?' Immediately, he felt she was concealing something.

'I'm saying no more, Mr Pemberton,' and she floured her hands before recommencing her work on the bread-making. 'She's dead and that's it. Finished.'

'You're tenants, aren't you?' He refused to shift his position until he had obtained something from this stubborn woman. 'You and your husband.'

'Aye, we have been for years, and Geoff's dad before him. We've never fallen behind with our rent even if it has been a struggle at times. It's been a good life – not an easy one, mebbe, but a good one.'

'I'm told there's an opportunity for tenants to buy their properties, now the Milverdale line has ended. That would give you more security, wouldn't it?'

'I can't say it would affect us. Me and Geoff can't afford to buy this spot, Mr Pemberton, and if the new owners put the rent up, we might consider taking early retirement. Geoff could allus get a little job gardening or something to tide us over but we've no wish to buy this place. If Geoff died, I shouldn't want to carry on alone, and neither would he if I died.'

'Your family doesn't want the farm then?'

'Nay, we've one lad who's in Australia, working with computers, and another in

Canada working on a forestry project for a university. Neither wants this farm, Mr Pemberton, it's too much like hard work and too restrictive for them, seven days a week with no time off, so we've no reason to hang on to it.'

'How old are they, your lads?' he asked.

'Our Matthew's twenty-six and Daniel's twenty-three. Neither's married yet. They said they wanted to see the world before they settle down. Are you married, Mr Pemberton?'

'I was. She died recently – it's the anniversary soon. She was too young to die ... I was devastated.'

'Oh, I'm sorry, I shouldn't have asked.'

'No, I don't mind people asking, it does me good to remember the good times we had. We had no children. I regret that,' and at that point an image of Lorraine flashed through his mind.

'Aye, they make a family, Mr Pemberton.'

'They do indeed.' He paused a moment and took a deep breath. 'Now, can I ask you this? Did your boys ever visit Alicia, over there in Mill House?'

The woman's face clouded over. She began to pummel the dough with all her strength and he thought he detected moistness in her eyes.

'I shouldn't ask that sort of question if I were you, Mr Pemberton, not in this village.

113

Good day to you!'

He lingered a few moments in the doorway, wondering whether to exert pressure on this woman in an attempt to make her explain her comments and attitude, but decided against it. He needed more information before following that line of enquiry and he might want her further co-operation. He decided to leave.

'In the machine shed, you said? Your husband?'

But she did not reply; she was weeping softly as she pounded the stubborn dough.

6

Pemberton located Geoff Midgley in his spacious machinery shed. The heavy farmer, clad in overalls and sweating from his exertions with the huge grass-cutter, straightened up with a groan, put one hand on his aching back and laid his spanner on the workbench. Then he faced Pemberton, his grey hair thinning on top and his cheerful round face oozing health and contentment.

'Them blades need adjusting and there's allus one nut that defies all attempts to loosen it. You can bet your bottom dollar it'll be t'last one an' all. So what can I do for you, Mr Policeman?'

'You know about Miss Milverdale?' was Pemberton's opening gambit.

'Aye, we do,' said Geoff Midgley. 'Nasty job, no matter what you've done, nobody deserves to die like that, shot down like a rabbit.'

'What had she done?' Pemberton did not miss the farmer's quick and perhaps unintentional reference to something unsavoury in Alicia's life.

'Nay, you'll not catch me out like that!'

and the farmer's grey eyes twinkled as he spoke. 'I can't say why anybody would want to kill Alicia and I wouldn't want to say summat that might cost me my house. She did nowt wrong by us. She was a good landlady, she kept that estate running just fine and made sure our house and buildings were allus well maintained. You couldn't ask for more than that.'

'I'm told every tenant has an opportunity to purchase their property if there is no Milverdale heir.'

'We shan't be doing that. We don't want to be landed with a big mortgage at our time of life. We've a rent that'll be well below whatever repayments would be necessary and our lads don't want to take up farming, so I'm not in the market for buying this place. Me and my missus are very happy the way things are.'

'I've just seen your wife.'

'Then you'll know we're of one mind. If the estate is sold and the new owner makes the rents too high, we'll just pack it in. We'll sell up and rent a cottage somewhere. We'll get by. It's as simple as that. Is that what my missus said?'

'Yes, she did,' agreed Pemberton.

'So if you've had words with her, why come and see me?'

'I wondered if you'd seen anybody yesterday morning, sometime after seven and before eight. Shooting rabbits perhaps, hikers, village folks out walking, poachers...'

'Never saw a soul. I fetched the cows in just after seven, but never saw Alicia. She comes down here for her morning walk and usually checks Mill House, but I never saw her yesterday. Or anybody else for that matter. Mind you, by the time she generally got to the bluebell field, my cows were in the byre being milked, so it wasn't often I set eyes on her.'

'The cows were in the bluebell field yesterday morning, were they?'

'Aye, they were but they're not always that far away, they tend to queue at the gate as milking time gets closer, but yesterday they didn't.'

'Would there be a reason for that change in their habits?'

'No idea, cows are funny things. They've minds of their own. Mebbe there was somebody about early, mebbe my cows had seen 'em and were watching, you know what cows are for being curious.'

'If Alicia had been lying among the bluebells when you were there, would you have seen her? Did you go into the field?'

'No, I didn't. And it's doubtful I'd see her, not unless I happened to be looking specially, which I wasn't.' He shook his head. 'To get the cows in from the bluebell field, I usually stand at our gate and shout 'em. Cush, cush, cush and all that. It works, you can call cows as easily as hens or dogs. Besides, that field is pretty well grown this time of year, tall grass and weeds, you'd have a job seeing anybody lying among it even at close quarters. You could get a lad and lass going at it hammer and tongs in that long grass, and you'd never see 'em. But I never saw Alicia, alive or dead, if that's what you're asking. Or anybody else.'

'How long does it take to get your cows in from the bluebell field?'

'Ten minutes, quarter of an hour, summat like that.'

'So the field would be empty of cows by, say, quarter past seven or thereabouts?'

'Right, it would.'

'And Alicia's usual timing meant she'd arrive a bit later, about half past?'

'Right, but those times I did see her was when I'd be running late for some reason,' said Midgley. 'That's when I might see her, but I never saw her come yesterday.'

Pemberton continued, 'If you saw nobody yesterday, how about hearing shots? If someone was shooting rabbits, you'd hear them, wouldn't you?'

'Not always, no. It's funny, a lot depends on which way t'wind's blowing, sound can travel a long way on a wind, but while I was fetching them cows in I never heard any shots. Nor afterwards. Mind you, a twelve-bore makes more noise than a .22, and some folks do use .22s for potting rabbits. Or even air guns, but they make less noise. But I heard nowt all morning.'

'And did you return to the field after milking?'

'No, I just loosen their halters and them awd cows wander back in their own time, they know the way. Clever things, cows, they've a good sense of direction.'

'Thanks. Now, do you know anyone who might have a grudge against Alicia?'

Midgley pursed his lips and expelled a long sigh, then shook his head. 'No, I don't,' he said shortly.

'She liked children to visit her in Mill House.' Pemberton intensified his questioning as he began to sense reluctance in the farmer's attitude. 'I think they played dressing-up games.'

'Did they, by gum?' was the farmer's non-committal response.

'She helped with the pantomimes as well. And art classes. I thought you might know about that – I'm sure you knew her fairly well.'

'She was younger than me by five or ten years. We had nowt in common.'

'Did you play with her as a child?'

'You must be joking! We didn't mix with posh folks, I was just a farm lad, living with my mum and dad. They were gentry types and we weren't. The two just did not mix.'

'Things have changed, haven't they? With people of her background tending to mingle more with ordinary folk.'

'Not round here, they haven't. Folks still keep themselves to themselves.'

'Did your sons ever go to Mill House, Mr Midgley?'

'I hope you're not suggesting I shot the bloody woman because of summat she did to my lads!' he snapped.

'No, I'm not suggesting that at all. But Mrs Midgley got upset after our talk.'

'She'd be upset at the way Alicia died. She thought a lot about that woman.'

'We do need help with our enquiries, Mr Midgley. I need somebody to tell me what went on in that house when she had children to visit her.'

'Then I reckon you'll have a long wait. Nobody knows what went on, except Alicia, and she's dead.'

'Some child might know; it's important that we find out.'

'Nobody else will tell you, I can assure you of that. We shan't speak out of turn. Remember we've our jobs and houses to think about. And I have no idea who killed her. I couldn't begin to guess. Except it wasn't me or my missus. That makes sense, doesn't it? Us not killing her. We might have to pay higher rent now she's gone, so I'd want her alive, wouldn't I? That makes sense to a Yorkshireman.'

'I take your point,' agreed Pemberton.

'And my lads didn't bump her off because they're abroad. You'll have to look somewhere else. Sorry, but I saw nowt, heard nowt and know nowt.'

There was an air of finality in his manner and words, and this was emphasised as Midgley turned around, picked up his spanner and returned to his work on the grass-cutter. 'Now, if you don't mind, I must get this damned thing working. Time's money for us farmers, you know. We can't stand around all day talking.'

It would be futile to make any further attempt at questioning Midgley so Pemberton thanked him for his time, albeit adding that he would return if further questions were required. From the depths of the grass-cutter, Midgley grunted a reply and Pemberton left.

A quick examination of the dry stone wall bordering the bluebell field showed no depression or disturbance of the vegetation and he concluded that the gunman had not crouched there to fire his rifle. If he had, the chances were he would have been noticed by Midgley or his wife.

Mark Pemberton drove back along the quiet lane into Campsthwaite and halted on the summit of a hill to call the incident room on his mobile phone.

'Pemberton here. I've completed my visit to Mill House and have interviewed Geoffrey Midgley of Cam Beck Farm. I don't think we should put him in the frame; he didn't see anything that would help, nor did he hear the shot. Now, I'm *en route* to Milverdale Hall for another chat with Constance Farrow. Any messages?'

Inspector Larkin responded. 'Larkin here, sir. There's a call from DC Cashmore. Constance Farrow has formally identified Alicia's body. I've informed the coroner. Miss Cashmore has gone to the Hall with Miss Farrow.'

'We can release her name and arrange the opening of the inquest.'

'There are no other messages, no developments. It's all very quiet here.'

'Too quiet, you think?'

'Well, sir, there's too little information flowing from our house-to-house enquiries. I would have expected something for us to pursue, some names to check. I've sent teams to trace the commuters who use that early train – it leaves Campsthwaite station at 7.22 a.m. and heads up the line past the bluebell field. It would actually have passed the scene of our crime around 7.25 a.m. yesterday, and it's usually about half full of passengers. You'd think at least one of them would have seen something. I've more teams tracing the postman, newspaper lad and milkman who delivered yesterday morning, and we're checking to see if there are any ex-military personnel living locally. If we find any, they'll be asked to account for their whereabouts at the material time.'

'That should produce something, Paul! Thanks. I'll return to the incident room when I've completed my enquiries at Milverdale Hall.'

Constance Farrow had prepared a light lunch of sandwiches, fruit and coffee, sufficient for him as well as Lorraine and herself. It was beside two decanters of sherry and three glasses on a side table in the drawing-room and he was directed there by Miss Farrow, now firmly in control of herself and the situation.

For the moment, she was mistress of Milverdale Hall. 'Perhaps a sherry before lunch, superintendent? We can enjoy it while we talk?'

Constance looked very relaxed, far more at ease than yesterday. She welcomed these officers as if they were honoured guests. At her offer of drinks, Pemberton hesitated, wishing neither to drink alcohol while on duty nor to accept gratuities from a murder suspect, but he caught Lorraine's eye. She nodded almost imperceptibly, her way of saying this woman was in a delicate frame of mind and needed subtle encouragement if she was to talk freely. Being nice to her would be beneficial, Lorraine was indicating. He produced a smile of appreciation. 'That would be nice – a dry one, please.'

'Do sit down, both of you... Dry, Miss Cashmore?'

'Thank you, yes,' acknowledged Lorraine.

In a plain black dress with no jewellery other than a watch on a black strap, Constance organised the sherries as Pemberton spoke to Lorraine.

'You had no problems with the formal identification?'

'No, sir.' She spoke so that Constance could hear. 'Constance did very well.'

'But I cannot yet go ahead with the funeral arrangements, can I?' Constance put to them without facing them. She was pouring the sherry while listening to their conversation.

'Not yet, I'm afraid,' Pemberton told her. 'That depends on the coroner. He might release the body once the inquest has been opened. I'll keep in touch with you but you'd also be wise to maintain contact with Alicia's solicitors.'

'Yes, of course. I do want to give her a decent funeral and it would be nice to have a date – she had lots of friends, they're all asking,' and she turned to indicate a collection of sympathy cards on the mantelshelf.

'Now that she has been formally identified, it means we can release her name to the press,' Pemberton explained. 'I'll do that at this afternoon's news conference.'

'Is that really necessary, superintendent?' Constance turned towards them, now bearing three glasses on a silver tray.

'Yes, it's vital we confirm the identity of the victim as soon as possible, the public has a right to know who she is,' he told her. 'The press have established her identity – that's inevitable – but they won't publish her name until I issue my confirmation. It's something that has to be done and it does prevent lots of other people, living at a distance, from worrying that the dead person might be a relation of theirs.'

'I can understand that but I hope they don't start digging into her family background, superintendent. Is there any way you can stop them?'

'Sorry, no. But surely there is nothing in Alicia's history that would be hurtful? Or do you know something that might help with this investigation?'

'Oh, no, it's nothing like that, nothing sinister. It's just that her life was very private, she would be horrified if she thought people were being intrusive or inquisitive about her way of life, her financial affairs, family matters. I think it is dreadful when the press dreams up low-life headlines. Some of the tabloids are reprehensible, Mr Pemberton.'

'Most editors are very responsible and they do exercise a good deal of discretion, Miss Farrow. Much of what is discovered about people who are in the news is never published.'

Constance's attitude reinforced Pemberton's suspicion that there might be a Milverdale family secret. Could it be associated with Alicia's interest in children? If so, how did Constance Farrow know about it? And how much did she know? After all, she was the housekeeper, not a family member. He watched as she settled down after attending to them. Sipping the sherry, she said, 'Well, Superintendent Pemberton, I hope they respect her in death, that is all I can say. So what can I do for you today?'

'It is a continuation of yesterday's chat,' he began. 'I need to find a reason for Alicia's death, Miss Farrow, and I need as much help as I can get.'

'I'm not sure I can be of any great assistance, superintendent. Miss Cashmore and I have discussed this and I will be happy to present my rather limited knowledge to you. I was not privy to the family's personal matters, or Alicia's, nor was I close to her business contacts and friends. I rarely met them, unless they came to the house, of course. Then I would greet them, as I have done with you. I am just the housekeeper after all.'

'I understand. Can I start with this house? Did she have many people in? For dinner perhaps? For the weekend? Or just as visitors? Business meetings? People from the village popping in for a coffee or a drink?'

And so began Mark Pemberton's deeper questioning of the one person who might shed light upon the life of Alicia Milverdale. As the interview continued, with Lorraine taking an active part, it became evident that Alicia had led rather a lonely life in the spacious luxury of Milverdale Hall. She had no close friends but did have lots of acquaintances, chiefly through the business of running a country estate. That had apparently occupied most of her time. The sympathy cards were from people connected with the estate or from village people who'd had dealings with her – the shopkeeper, the schoolteacher, the chairman of the village institute committee, the chairman of the parish council, the vicar, the garage proprietor. Pemberton noted the names of the people who'd sent the cards – he'd ensure they were interviewed during the house-to-house enquiries.

Very occasionally, people did come to the Hall for dinner. They were usually tenants or members of staff with whom she wished to discuss estate matters or to share a celebration. One couple in an estate cottage had celebrated a silver wedding, for example, and so Alicia had invited them to the Hall for a dinner, her way of celebrating with them. She'd hired a cook, just as she'd done to celebrate the golden wedding of a couple who'd retired after a lifetime working for the estate. On another occasion, she'd allowed the Hall to be used for a small wedding reception by a bride from the village. She held an annual Christmas party for the estate workers and tenants, and carol singers from the village came to sing in the spacious entrance hall where she erected a decorated tree, lit a log fire and refreshed them with hot mince pies and punch.

Through the verbal picture which was gradually emerging, it was clear that Alicia's life-style had been somewhat mundane, albeit with one or two bright spots. She did go to London once in a while, for reasons not known to Constance Farrow. Inevitably, she travelled alone and, to Constance's knowledge, none of her trips had resulted in follow-up calls, letters or visits from new friends.

She had no idea where Alicia stayed during those trips, or whom she met in London, and Constance could not name any of the venues patronised by Alicia. What did emerge, however, was that Alicia ran a very efficient estate with contented tenants and a happy staff. She had never made any enemies and in the short time Constance had been employed here, she had never known anyone come to the Hall in anger for a confrontation with Alicia.

Pemberton then turned his attention to Mill House. Dating from the sixteenth century, it was formerly a walk mill, the term used to describe a mill which produced cloth from the wool of sheep which inhabited the surrounding moorland. It had belonged to Milverdale Estate since 1825 but, during the estate's ownership, had never been used for its original purpose. At one stage, it was a shooting lodge for visitors and later an overflow guest house for Milverdale Hall. Alicia's parents had liked entertaining, so it seemed, but as the disposable wealth of country house owners had dwindled following two world wars and the advance of socialism, so the atmospheric old mill had fallen into disuse. The Milverdales had not sold the property because it would have allowed strangers to live in the midst of the estate.

This brief history was supplied by Constance who added that Alicia had told her she began to use it as a playhouse. As a little girl, she had been allowed to take friends there for tea parties, birthday parties, games on wet days and all the things that small girls like to do. Those early friends came from similar country houses in the locality or from parents whose social status was considered suitable.

'Did she spend much time there in recent weeks?' Pemberton asked.

'Not really. You know she popped in most mornings during her walk?'

'Yes, that was sensible. People could get in without a great deal of trouble, if they wanted to,' Pemberton put to her.

'The key has always been kept in the outside toilet, so anyone could find it. Lots of villagers knew where the key was – through the children, that was – but no one abused that knowledge.'

'She was a very trusting lady!'

'She was. She was very nice, very nice indeed. She did tell the children they could use it to play in, just as she had done, but I don't think many of them did. It was a long walk from the village, and that wood could be quite frightening on a dark night or gloomy afternoon.'

'Do you know whether Alicia's activities with children produced any unsavoury rumours, Miss Farrow?'

'She would never harm a child, superintendent. I thought I made that clear last time you came. She would never harm anyone!'

'Some parents told the schoolteacher not to let children visit Mill House alone with Alicia.'

'I've heard the rumours, one does in a small community, but there was no substance to them, I'm convinced of that. Pure gossip, superintendent. Surely the parents' concern was for other reasons, walking alone in the wood, for instance?'

'You could be right. Now, were you a regular visitor to the mill?' Pemberton changed the direction of his questioning.

'No, I wouldn't say I was a regular visitor. She took me to see it when I first arrived and sometimes I was invited to join her for a picnic on a Sunday afternoon. We would take a hamper and sit by the river with a bottle of wine or flask of coffee. But I didn't go very often, it was her special place, you see, private and very personal.'

'Did you ever visit Mill House when the children were there?'

'No, I didn't. That was part of Alicia's time, her private time.'

'As housekeeper at the Hall, were you responsible for Mill House in any way?'

Constance shook her head. 'No, never.' She sipped at the sherry. 'I never worked there, she looked after it herself. Or got the children to clean up after themselves when they came. I think I'd have needed to spend hours there to get the place clean and tidy ...

with all due respect to Alicia.'

'I noticed you do keep the Hall in pristine condition.'

'It's what I have always been taught, superintendent. Cleanliness and tidiness are so important to the smooth running of a home, large or small.'

'So when was the last time you went to Mill House?'

'Apart from yesterday? Oh, it's hard to say. I rarely bothered in the winter months or early spring, the walk could be very muddy. Easter, I think. I went on Easter Monday, just for a walk, alone in fact. Alicia stayed at the Hall, she was tired and wanted to sit in front of the fire in here. I went there alone. I walked down, had a look around the house to check it over, and came home. It took about an hour, perhaps a little more. I walked briskly because it was a cool day.'

'You refer to the Hall as "home"?'

'I do, yes. It is my home, superintendent. I have nowhere else.'

'Tell me about yourself,' he invited.

'Oh, there's nothing interesting about me,' and she shook her head as if failing to understand why this man should be interested in her. 'I'm just a hired help.'

'I would like to know more about you.' He was firm now. 'I must eliminate you from our enquiries and the more we know about you, the easier that will be.'

'I've told Miss Cashmore a good deal. I've had such an ordinary life, Mr Pemberton. Boring really and lacking in adventure. I've never been abroad, never owned a car, never bought a house, never got married or had a family, never qualified in anything or developed a skill, never been to university ... really, I am nobody.'

To his gentle probing and with Lorraine making discreet written notes, she said she had been born at York on 6th September 1947 but both her parents were now dead. Her father had worked on the railways in York and her mother in Rowntree's sweet factory, Her mother had died unexpectedly from a heart attack when Constance was twenty-two, and her father died of cancer just over eight years ago, shortly before reaching his seventieth birthday. He had secured her first job, a holiday position in a sweet shop in Micklegate at the age of fifteen. She added that she had never been particularly bright although she did attend York High School for Girls, leaving when she was sixteen to work full-time. By her late twenties, she'd had a succession of boring jobs in shops and factories and decided to expand her horizons.

Without qualifications, there were few opportunities, but she'd answered an advert for a domestic post in a country house. It had been a maid's job, she said, with Lady

Consate at Holfield House, Holfield near York, and she found she liked the work, in spite of the long hours.

'Lady Consate?' asked Pemberton. 'Spelt, C-o-n-s-a-t-e?'

'Yes, that's right,' confirmed Constance, adding that she loved the atmosphere of historic country houses and had worked there from 1987 until 1994. In 1994, upon the death of Lady Consate, she'd secured a housekeeper's post with Lady Featley at Hoveton Hall, near Harrogate. That was from 1994 until 1996 when Lady Featley had been admitted to permanent care in a residential home prior to her death in 1997. In 1996, Constance had answered Alicia's advertisement for a housekeeper and so she'd come to Milverdale Hall.

That was just over two years ago and she was completely content here, happy to work for Alicia until reaching pensionable age – but now her future had been thrown into complete disarray.

'I have no idea what's going to happen to me, superintendent, I just don't know what I am going to do...' and the beginnings of tears came to her eyes. 'I shall just have to wait and see what happens to the estate and the house, I suppose...'

'I am sure the estate's solicitors will advise you,' was all he could suggest. 'I'm equally sure you will not be thrown out without anywhere to go. It does take time to settle these matters. Mr Milverdale suggested at least three years and the Hall will have to be looked after during that time. Now, let's go back to the time you first came to Milverdale Hall. Was Alicia alone then? I am thinking of her parents.'

'Oh, yes, she was alone except for Georgina Wallace, her secretary. Her father died before I got the post, the earlier housekeeper remained a while after his death but retired before I was appointed.'

'Where did the former housekeeper go?'

'Mrs Frankland? She went to join her daughter in New Zealand, she had no home of her own, you see. She is still there, I believe.'

'Did you and Georgina get on?'

'Oh yes, although we did not become close friends. She was much younger than I and married, although without a family at that time. She had her life and I had mine. I'm like Alicia, really, I suppose, in that I don't seek a busy social life. I have few close friends but lots of acquaintances. I prefer it that way. My work was my life; in a place like this, there is all the space I want, my own suite of rooms, free use of any of the estate vehicles for private purposes, plenty of space out of doors – and I could make my own hours provided the work was done. Alicia never nagged or complained – she let me get on with my duties as I thought best so long as I kept the place in the manner she expected. Which I did, of course.'

Pemberton realised that both Constance and Alicia appeared to have been living self-contained lives in this big handsome house, with very little outside contact. Not quite reclusive, but almost.

'You have been happy here?' Pemberton asked.

'Very.' She smiled briefly. 'Yes, it has been the happiest of positions. I'm so miserable now, so devastated by all this, I don't know how I shall cope...'

'Let's have lunch, shall we?' Lorraine stepped across and put a comforting arm about Constance's shoulders.

'I know this is harrowing,' Pemberton admitted to her. 'But I do have to press for this kind of background detail. Let yourself cry and shout at us if you have to. We shall understand...'

She sniffed and produced a small white handkerchief from a sleeve, wiped her eyes and her nose and made a great effort to compose herself.

'I'm sorry.' She took a deep breath and accepted a sandwich from Lorraine. 'You must think I am very silly and emotional...'

'Not at all,' Pemberton sympathised. 'Now, let's eat and have a break from questions...'

'No, please, do continue,' she invited them. 'I would rather you proceed and get it over, than stop and start all over again.'

Their conversation over the light lunch was little more than a catalogue of facts elicited by Pemberton's questions – the precise dates when she was employed by Lady Consate and Lady Featley, the names of her parents, their place of burial, the dates of their deaths and details of their work, the names of shops she'd worked in as a youngster, where she could remember them. Dates, times, places and names were all jotted down by Lorraine to be subsequently checked. Pemberton apologised several times for this apparent intrusion but justified his actions by saying it would help to eliminate her from the enquiries.

Once lunch was over, it was time to examine the papers in the estate office. Pemberton had the key and unlocked the door, knowing that Constance had had ample time to dispose of anything she wished prior to yesterday's visit but his immediate requirements were modest.

'I'll need a list of tenants,' he said to both Constance and Lorraine. 'And the names and addresses of the estate workers, a look at the Deed of Trust which lays down the future of this house and the estate, a copy of Alicia's will if she made one and a list of people with permission to enter the estate's

137

grounds for shooting, fishing and so forth. I think all those will be filed in here somewhere.'

'I can help if you wish,' offered Constance. 'Thanks to Alicia, I do have a rudimentary knowledge of the office system.'

'Thanks,' said Pemberton. 'You might enable me to find things more speedily and I might need photocopies of some documents. Is there a copier here?'

'Yes, there is, you can use it.'

The estate office was a spacious room which had been established during the Hall's construction. At the north-eastern corner of the Hall, it housed all the estate files and records in a series of modern metal cabinets. The office was computerised complete with colour monitor and a modem to enable email facilities. There might be information in the computer, Pemberton realised, and he suspected the office, or perhaps the computer, would contain Alicia's personal details too. He set to work, his attention being first drawn to the files of tenants and estate properties. There was a master list, he discovered quickly.

'I need copies of this list,' he told Lorraine. 'Two, I think, would be enough.'

After only a few minutes of rifling through the files, Pemberton had succeeded in producing a list of all tenants, with their addresses, details of their tenure, the rents they paid and any conditions attached to the property in question. There was a list of people granted fishing and shooting rights and he also found a list of employees, currently five working full-time and two part-timers. Only one appeared to have anything remotely like a motive for wanting rid of Alicia – a man called Neil Potter rented Hagg End Farm on the southern edge of Campsthwaite, and his tenancy included the former ironworks. He had made an attempt to buy his farm four years ago. Aged thirty-five but with no known military experience, he had taken over the tenancy upon his father's death and almost immediately had written to Alicia to explore the possibility of purchasing the farmhouse and surrounding land. Alicia had learned that Potter's farm was not generating much income from livestock or crops and that he intended to create a caravan site beside the beck at Hagg End. The field in question was scrubland with no future as a grazing area or as a productive agricultural patch and, with easy access from Campsthwaite, Potter had recognised its alternative commercial potential. There was no doubt the site would generate a regular income over the long term and it would also provide some employment because a site shop was proposed as well as a toilet block and shower complex. Assistants on a seasonal basis would be needed for the shop and cleaners for the toilet/shower block.

Potter's plan was overruled because it was estate policy that none of the Milverdale land would be utilised for caravan or camping sites. The estate's solicitor felt that if Hagg End was sold to Potter, it would herald future requests of a similar kind. The most suitable response was to refuse the request. It was pointed out that upon Alicia's death without issue, a future owner might take a different view; furthermore, he would be given the opportunity to purchase his property when Alicia died. But Potter had wanted immediate action – he was not prepared to wait until she died, that could be years away. He had written to her and to the estate solicitor, suggesting the estate change its policy and allow him to create the caravan site, with the estate taking a share of the profits.

But in whatever form his requests were presented, they were rejected. Pemberton noted Potter's name for an early inter-rogation. If the files were to be believed, the other tenants, including Farmer Midgley, were quite content with their contracts. Pemberton's search did produce a copy of the Deed of Trust and will made by Alicia's father in which the future of the estate had been determined pending her death without issue. He read the Deed of Trust quickly, not absorbing the minutiae at this stage, although he did note the constant references to blood relations. There was one other item of interest. He did not announce it aloud, but noted that Hall Cottage, occupied by the Breckons, had to be gifted to them upon Alicia's death. A brief note added that, because several generations of Breckons had worked for the estate over the years, always living in that house, the family must not be denied a home if the estate ceased to exist. It was another of old Mr Milverdale's generous gestures. Pemberton's search also revealed Alicia's will. That was simple – she had left £1,000 to 'my housekeeper' (not named), with smaller bequests to members of her staff, and she stated she wished to be buried in the family vault in Campsthwaite parish church. Her personal belongings including Mill House and its contents had to be incorporated in the eventual sale of Milverdale Hall. There were no other provisions and no other named beneficiaries. Pemberton did find her personal file but it revealed nothing of interest to the enquiry. It consisted chiefly of school reports, some letters written by her parents when she was at university, her birth certificate giving her date of birth as 8th August 1953 and other documents such as her driving licence and a blood donor's card. There was no passport, he noted –

perhaps she'd never had a desire to go overseas? Her address list was included and catered for such things as Christmas cards and the names of possible guests for events at the Hall. She did not appear to have any special friends, male or female, but the people on her various lists would be traced and interviewed. Her papers contained nothing about her dressing-up parties at Mill House, nothing about her visits to London and nothing about her past friendships at school or university.

Abstracting all this had taken three hours or so, and he finished with a pile of photocopied documents, for which he gave a receipt to Constance. Then he said, 'I'm afraid there's more – my officers must search the entire house and check it for fingerprints, Miss Farrow.'

'Fingerprints, superintendent?'

'My officers will dust the whole place to see if there are any prints not accounted for. Yours will be here, of course, and so will Alicia's and those of other members of staff. What we seek are prints from someone whose presence cannot be accounted for, it's all part of our careful process of elimination.'

'I think I understand, superintendent.'

'Now, Miss Farrow, guns. Is there a gun room in the house? Most estates have one.'

'Yes, we've always had a selection of

weapons here, but Alicia never used them. Her father did, he was a good shot, so I am told, a keen grouse-shooting man and he also shot pheasants and did a spot of fishing in the beck. Shall I show you?'

'Please.'

Taking a set of keys from the safe, she led them out of the office and along a narrow corridor to halt at a door beneath the staircase in the huge hall. She fitted the key, pulled open the door and switched on the light to reveal a surprisingly large window-less cupboard, the size of a small room. It contained a collection of fishing rods, gaffs and nets along one wall and an array of shotguns and rifles along another, the latter all secured as the law now demanded. Pemberton examined the contents noting that gun covers and fishing rod covers were hanging towards the rear of the cupboard while taking care not to touch any.

'Who has access to this cupboard?' he asked.

'Just Alicia – oh, and me. And that secretary, Georgina, used to have access. We didn't replace Georgina when she left. Georgina would sometimes come to work during busy periods but she never went into the gun cupboard. The keys are kept in the office safe, only the three of us knew the combination of the safe but we changed it when Georgina left. Then only Alicia and I knew the combination. Alicia never used any of the guns, superintendent, but she did ask me to keep them clean. I would clean them periodically, every three months or so, inside and out. With pull-throughs and oil. She insisted, she said the guns were valuable and would benefit a museum in due course. They belonged to her father, like the rods, but she never used those either. She was allowed to retain the guns when he died, all held on certificates in the name of the estate.'

'All the guns will be listed in our records,' he said. 'Now, what have we? Four double-barrelled shotguns, twelve-bores. One .410 single-barrel shotgun. Two .22 BSA rifles. Take a note of them, Lorraine, and we'll do a check against our files. Miss Farrow, were there any other weapons here?'

'Oh, no, superintendent, that's the lot. They've been here since I came to the house and I don't think they've been out of the building since then.'

'Right. And the ammunition?'

'Here in the bottom of the cupboard, in a locked container.' She located a stout metal box, opened it with the second key on the ring in her hand, and showed it to him. The contents included several boxes of twelve-bore cartridges, some for the .410 and a few boxes of .22 bullets.

There was no .303 ammunition, he noted

without mentioning the fact aloud in the hearing of Constance Farrow, and no sign of a .303 rifle having been stored here.

'I shall have to confiscate those weapons,' he told Constance. 'We will need to have them all examined by our ballistics people.'

'For your elimination purposes?' She smiled wryly at him.

'Yes,' was all he said, taking the key from her, albeit knowing that none of these weapons had been used. But they might bear the fingerprints of persons other than Constance, their keeper and protector. 'Are there any other weapons in the house?'

'No, this is the lot, superintendent.'

'Thanks. Now, can we have a look around the rest of the house?' he asked. 'I'd like to examine it in daylight.'

Then he turned to Lorraine and said, 'Lorraine, while we're looking around, can you ring the incident room and get SOCO to send four teams here as soon as possible? To fingerprint and search the Hall as I've suggested, and to examine those guns. I'll brief them when they arrive.'

'Sir,' she said, and he handed over his mobile.

Lorraine made her call while Constance began this more detailed tour of the house with Pemberton, who wondered what would be revealed, first about Alicia, and then about Constance Farrow.

And as Lorraine caught up with them, he recalled the name of Lady Consate. It had cropped up earlier in his career – he remembered it because of the curious spelling, at first wrongly associating it with Consett in Co. Durham. He struggled to recall the circumstances but failed, which meant it was probably not in connection with any major incident. But he knew the name from somewhere.

7

The tour of Milverdale Hall produced no surprises and some useful information. With the necessary upgrading, it would make a splendid country hotel but was too small and lacking in history to be considered a stately home. The downstairs rooms were spacious and beautifully appointed while a minor wing extended north from the main building. This contained the former domestic servants' quarters, comprising three small rooms on the ground floor with six bedrooms and a shared bathroom above. The ground floor was still utilised as staff rest rooms and storage space but the bedrooms were superfluous. The only resident member of staff was the housekeeper who had her own suite in the east wing. Around the rear was a range of outbuildings including a coal shed, wood shed, potting shed, greenhouse, garages, implement shed and other sundry places used for a variety of purposes.

The family's upper-floor rooms, all beautifully furnished, lacked modern amenities such as *en suite* facilities and up-to-date bathroom and toilet fittings although the five main bedrooms overlooked superb views of the dale with the parkland of the house and the former ironworks in the foreground. The two lesser back bedrooms were equally well furnished but lacked the extensive views. The entire building was immaculately clean and the crisp paintwork told them it was well maintained both upstairs and down.

'My men will want access to all rooms, including yours,' Pemberton warned Constance as they walked along the landing. 'First, I'd like to see Alicia's bedroom.'

'It's the one directly above the drawing-room.' She pointed to a large white door sporting an ornate brass knob.

'Have you been in since yesterday morning?' Pemberton asked.

'Yes, I made the bed as usual and tidied the dressing-table as I do every morning, then later, before going to look for her, I hoovered the place. It was due to be hoovered, you see. I clean it twice a week, superintendent, after morning coffee.'

'You do the work yourself?'

'Yes, we could not afford a maid. I don't mind. I like being busy.'

'Have you been in since you learned of her death?'

'Yes,' she said. 'Last night. I put some flowers on her dressing-table, a sort of token, I suppose, and this morning I went in to check the water in the vase. But that's all.'

'Can we see it now, please?' He stood back as she opened the door, then stepped inside, going no more than a couple of paces into the immaculate room.

'What do you hope to find, superintendent?' asked Constance.

'Who knows?' was his reply. 'Clues to her life, answers to queries. A bedroom can provide a gateway to a person's life, Miss Farrow. Sometimes, it's the only truly personal place in a household.'

'She liked hers to be very tidy.'

'So it seems. It reminds me of those bedrooms one sees when touring stately homes. So neat and clean.'

'She wasn't killed in here, superintendent. I thought you'd pay more attention to the bluebell field...'

'Every place which is closely associated with the victim has to receive very detailed attention,' he told her. 'We are as interested in Alicia's life as in her death.'

Lorraine and Constance stood behind him as he surveyed the room. It was a complete contrast to the throned bedroom of Mill House, even if some of the colours were complementary. But not a thing was out of place in this room. The huge bay window was in three sections, all hung with thick purple velvet curtains enhanced with tiebacks and tasselled pelmets. The wallpaper was very pale green with a slight white-based pattern, and the polished wooden floor was covered with several expensive Persian rugs in bright colours. Purple and green dominated the rugs and the bedcover. The bed was a double, a four-poster with purple drapes and a dark green cover reaching to the floor. Its head was against the west wall and a teddy bear lay on the pillow. The dressing-table, antique mahogany by the look of it, bore a selection of bottles and make-up jars, while a set of mahogany drawers stood just inside the door bearing two glass candlesticks and a statue of Venus de Milo. There were sepia photographs on her dressing-table too.

'Her parents?' Pemberton asked Constance.

'Yes, she kept their pictures beside her.'

Portraits of ancestors adorned the walls, and one was a full-colour copy of the well-known representation of King Charles II by Peter Lely. It showed the sovereign's mass of curls and his strong face as well as his ornate costume.

'She was proud of her ancestry?' Pemberton observed.

'Very,' Constance confirmed. 'I think the family originated in the Leicester area but she didn't mention it very frequently, except the links with Charles II.'

'Was he very significant to her?'

'She claimed descent from him through Lady Castlemaine – she was one of his mistresses,' said Constance. 'Alicia genuinely believed she was of royal blood.'

'Was that ever substantiated?' asked Pemberton.

'I don't know, I don't want to pry into such things,' said Constance. 'I do know it was a source of some pride to her – and a little sadness.'

'Sadness?'

'Sadness that she had no title, nothing to show for the royal blood in her veins, not even a tiny keepsake from her royal past. No lock of hair or scrap of clothing.'

'I think a lot of people could make similar claims,' smiled Pemberton. 'The blue blood of our nobility can be found in many ordinary people, with a fair smattering of royal blood among it. Even though Alicia's claim might be valid, it is not unique.'

'I've never delved into that sort of thing,' said Constance. 'It's never interested me.'

'Maybe Alicia did not want the press to delve too deeply in case her claims were false?' suggested Pemberton. 'Maybe she had investigated and found the truth lacking? That would be a deep embarrassment for her, would it not? Perhaps that is why she didn't welcome any press interest?'

'That is possible,' acknowledged Constance. 'She was very proud of her royal ancestry and her facial features were very like those in the portrait of King Charles. Sometimes, in a certain light, the resemblance was uncanny.'

'Well, even if this is a royal bedroom with some great-great-great-great and many more times great ancestor on the wall, my officers will need to examine it in some detail,' he warned her.

'Yes, I see,' was all Constance said.

'Did she use this room?' asked Lorraine. 'It doesn't look as though it has ever been slept in... I wish my dressing-table was as tidy as that!'

'She was very meticulous and insisted the room was kept like this,' said Constance. 'That was part of my job. It was her parents' room and they were just as careful. Hers used to be the one next door. To the west. I suspect that was rather more casually kept,' and there was a quick smile. 'Something like Mill House.'

'We'll have to examine that one too, her former room,' he told her.

If Constance had cleaned and polished the main bedroom since Alicia's death, she might have destroyed some valuable evidence although the average dusting session was not too destructive.

Alicia's childhood bedroom proved to be very plain and simple with a single bed, a chest of pine drawers with a mirror on the top, a narrow pine wardrobe and a chair made of cane.

'There's nothing in this room,' Constance told him. 'It's been empty for years.'

'It reminds me of boarding school!' grimaced Lorraine.

'My officers will examine it along with the others,' Pemberton reminded Constance. 'Now, Miss Farrow, I would like to peep into your flat, please.'

She led them through the upstairs corridors and opened her door; this time there was little need for his scrupulous care because she was living in the place. His first impression was of a very plain suite of rooms, with little colour on the walls. It was equipped with modest and rather cheap furnishings.

'Your own furniture?' he asked.

'No, it is all supplied,' she said. 'Rather like in the services, even the knives, forks and spoons don't belong to me, but the bed linen does. I can decorate it to my own taste, though, and bring in my own pictures and ornaments.'

The small kitchen, with views up to the moors, had magnolia emulsion on all the walls and so had the adjoining lounge which boasted superb views over the parkland. The single bedroom, coloured the same, faced east with a moorland view across the roofs of some outbuildings and there was a combination bathroom and toilet next to it, also in magnolia. It was a quiet flat some distance from Alicia's quarters – but it was home to Constance Farrow.

Some of the walls bore framed photographs in black and white. Among them he noticed a Scottish ski scene, a street near York Minster, a view of the North York Moors showing Ralph's Cross, and a shot of Scarborough's North Bay.

'Yours?' he asked, indicating the photographs with a general sweep of his hand.

'Most were here when I arrived. That's mine, though, an old school photograph.' She pointed to one hanging above the fireplace. It depicted four rows of teenage girls in school uniform but the picture was printed in black and white.

'Your old school?' he asked.

'Yes, York High School for Girls, 1961. Form 4b. We won the tennis championship that year, and the hockey. That's me,' and she pointed to a tall thin figure in the back row. She was one of two very tall girls standing together. In their 1960s uniforms and hair-styles, they looked like twins, but the quality of the photo was too indistinct for him to recognise her now. Besides, the picture was thirty-seven years old.

'You enjoyed school?' he asked.

'I wasn't very academic, although I did manage to get a place there, but yes, I did enjoy it. Being an only child, I was lonely at home and school meant I had friends around me. That was nice. I left at sixteen, though, I didn't stay on for A levels. I wanted to earn some money.'

'Do you keep in touch with your school friends?' Lorraine asked her.

'I used to, but not now. We've all moved on. Some got married, some moved away for their careers, others went overseas. We intended to keep in touch, to have reunions, but we never did. So, superintendent, this is all I have. Do you want to search the flat now?'

'No, I shall leave that to my experts.'

'They'll be here soon.' Lorraine looked at her watch and, almost on cue, the house filled with the sound of a doorbell.

Constance hurried downstairs to answer the front door as Pemberton and Lorraine followed at a more leisurely pace. He looked at Lorraine as she moved down the sweeping staircase, gliding with all the poise of a trained model, so graceful, lithe, smart and beautiful. People like her couldn't get cancer, could they?

'You're watching me!' she chided him without turning round.

'Of course I am!'

'I'm still in one piece, I can still walk and talk and use my brains...'

'And I like the piece I see,' he chuckled.

'Nice to see you keeping so cheerful.'

'I enjoy being with you,' she responded with a kick of one of her heels. 'That's what keeps me cheerful!'

A group of eight detectives had arrived in the foyer and Pemberton asked them to assemble in the main hall where he would address them. While he was doing that, he suggested that Lorraine and Constance gather the estate workers together for a preliminary chat. As the two women disappeared, Pemberton addressed his teams on their own grand tour of the Hall.

'Alicia's two bedrooms are important.' He indicated the doors. 'I've no idea what you might find, except I need the weapon that killed her – a .303 rifle of some kind – and anything else that would suggest a killer or a motive. Think blackmail letters too, threats from any of the tenants or staff, someone in the village.'

'You think the housekeeper used the rifle, sir?' asked Detective Sergeant Fenton who was in charge of the group.

'She's my prime suspect at the moment, even if I can't find a motive.'

'Could a woman handle that kind of rifle, sir?' asked Fenton. '.303s are heavyweights.'

'I can't see why not. Women join gun clubs and some are very capable shots with rifles just as ancient and heavy. Don't forget she could have hired a professional. It goes

156

without saying that I want Constance's flat searched with extra care. Take as long as you need, but do it properly. And, sergeant?'

'Sir?'

'See if you can get a sample of hers for DNA analysis. From Constance's flat, without her knowing. A piece of hair would do, from her dressing-table. I'm sure her comb or brush will have some.'

'Right, sir, will do. Come on, lads, it's time for our stately home tour.'

Leaving them to their task, Pemberton went outside and found Lorraine in the courtyard talking to four men, then Constance appeared through the archway accompanied by a fifth, a fair-haired youngster in jeans and a battered sweater.

'They're all here now, superintendent.' She was slightly out of breath.

'Thank you,' and he moved in front of the little group. 'I won't keep you long. My name is Detective Superintendent Mark Pemberton and I am investigating the unfortunate death of your mistress, Alicia Milverdale.'

They stood before him, uncomfortable and nervous, all silent and brooding with none knowing how to react to the situation.

'Miss Milverdale was found in the field of bluebells, near Mill House.' He felt he should provide some facts in case they'd been fed rumours. 'She'd been shot; it wasn't suicide, we're sure about that, but we can't rule out a tragic accident. My job is to find out who fired the fatal shot. For that, I need your help.'

After watching their reactions for a few seconds, he continued, 'She left the house at seven o'clock yesterday morning to go on her daily walk but she failed to return at eight, her usual time. Miss Farrow went to look for her around noon and found her but we think she died between seven and eight. You all work here so I wonder if any of you noticed anyone yesterday, say between half past six and half past eight. In particular, I want to know about people on the path between here and the bluebell field, that's over the railway viaduct and down the fields, or even in the Hall grounds and old ironworks.'

One man, the most senior judging by his age and appearance, raised his hand. Short and rather slender, he would be around fifty with thin fair hair, a weathered face and strong hands. 'I saw Miss Milverdale leave the house. At seven it was. She was walking along the lane towards the viaduct. I usually see her set off, sir. I'm in my kitchen, getting breakfast, and can see out of the window.'

'Was she carrying anything? A rifle, for example?'

'No, nothing. Nothing at all.'

'And was she alone? Did anyone follow

her or even go ahead of her?'

'I never saw anyone, sir, not in the time I was having my breakfast.'

'Thanks, and you are?'

'Jim Breckon, I live in the cottage behind the house, an estate house. Hall Cottage. I'm the caretaker. Well, general handyman really.'

So this was the lucky Mr Breckon. 'We'll talk at length later, Mr Breckon, but you've a good view of the back of the Hall, have you?'

'Yes, very. My kitchen looks right over to the back yard of the Hall.'

'And what time do you start work, Mr Breckon?'

'Half seven, Monday to Friday. Days off Saturday and Sunday although I go in sometimes if things need doing.'

'Did you see Miss Milverdale return after her walk?'

'No, but it's not often I do because I'm at work by then. I'm usually in the buildings or fixing things in the house by the time she gets back for breakfast. I never saw anybody else, either before or after she left the house.'

'What about other days? Were there people knocking about before yesterday? Strangers? Hikers? Anyone following her or observing her routine? Watching the house from a distance?'

Breckon shook his head. 'No, I never saw a soul.'

'Right, so think back to yesterday morning, all of you. Did you hear gunshots? Someone rabbiting or just loosing off shots for the hell of it, especially between seven and eight.'

'We don't get here till eight, sir,' said one of them.

'And you heard nothing or saw nothing as you came up the drive?'

They all shook their heads, then Pemberton spoke to each in turn. The estate gardener worked in the greenhouse, potting sheds or extensive parkland; his assistant tended hedges, pruned trees, cared for the domestic garden and looked after the orchard. The estate carpenter spent a lot of his time fixing fences and maintaining buildings while the mechanic, who chauffeured Alicia in her old Rolls when necessary, driving her to Rainesbury to catch trains to York and on to London or to appointments in the locality, maintained the estate vehicles and even fixed the lawnmower if it developed a fault. The fifth was a stonemason who kept the estate walls and buildings in good repair, along with assisting in the maintenance of the main house. None had noticed anything out of the ordinary yesterday morning nor had they seen anyone hanging around the estate grounds or nearby landscape. The two part-timers had not been to work this week; they'd be interviewed by his house-to-house teams. Their whereabouts at the material time had to be determined.

'What are your feelings about Miss Milverdale?' He changed the direction of his questions now. 'As an employer, I mean. Was she good to you?'

'The best,' said the gardener. 'She paid the best wages round here and was always kind, she knew our names and our wives' names and even our kids' names.'

Another added, 'And if the kids were sick, she'd give us time off to see to them, and she'd come and visit the house. She was the best, Mr Pemberton, the very best.'

'Is that the feeling of you all?' He felt like a judge checking that members of a jury all agreed with the verdict.

The mutterings of consent and the general feeling of sadness which radiated to him told Pemberton that these men loved their work and respected their mistress.

'Thanks, but I have to ask this,' he told them. 'Can you think of a reason why anyone would kill her? Or do you have any idea who might have done this?'

'We've talked about nowt else since it happened, Mr Pemberton, me and the lads,' said Jim Breckon. 'But we've come up with nowt. I mean, whoever's done this has put our jobs at risk, and homes. We've no idea what's going to happen. Have you?'

'The estate will be administered by a trust until everything is sorted out. That will take time, three years at least, I'm told; I'm sure you'll all keep your jobs during that time and I would hope the new owners will keep you on. But that's speculation on my part.'

'We know the estate will be sold and we've the chance to buy our own places, but none of us here can afford to. We're happy as we are, in our tied houses, so long as we've got jobs,' said the gardener.

Breckon did not refer to the special situation regarding his own cottage, but Pemberton would interview him later, in private. He thanked them for their time and asked that they contact him or any of his officers if they recalled anything useful. They all assured him they would and he believed them.

'Miss Farrow,' he said. 'I have a news conference very shortly so I must leave you. My officers will be here for some time but I'm sure they will not make too much of a nuisance of themselves.'

'Thank you, Mr Pemberton. You will keep in touch, won't you? About any developments, and especially with the funeral arrangements in mind.'

'Of course. Now before I go, have you a recent photograph of Alicia? I'd like one to distribute among my men, it will be an enormous help in their enquiries, and I would like to copy it for the press as well.'

'The press?'

'It's the kind of thing they will ask for, and if we arrange distribution through our press office, it will save you a lot of time and worry. It could help us determine whether Alicia had been seen away from here, for example, talking to someone who might be of interest to us.'

'I'll find you one before you leave. I will respect your judgement about releasing her personal details to the papers. I had some calls yesterday, late last night in fact, but I didn't tell them anything. I just hope you find her killer, that's all I ask of you.'

'We'll do our best,' he said. 'Now, I'll take those firearms with me. I think they'll be better examined on our premises. Can we get them now, please?'

'Yes, of course.'

Pemberton unlocked the gun room door and then released each of the securing chains which led through the trigger guards. Constance stepped forward to help and he watched her in action. She had done this many times when cleaning the weapons and in spite of their size and weight she handled them with ease, even breaking the shotguns for safety reasons before passing them to him, one by one.

'I'll give you a receipt,' he said as he stood

the guns on the floor near the wall. 'And when this is over, the estate can apply for their return, with the certificate suitably amended due to Alicia's death.'

'I'm not sure we'll need all those guns in the future, but I will await your decisions in due course. Now, let me find that photograph of Alicia.'

She went to the office and returned with a coloured print of Alicia in fancy dress taken at one of her pantomimes. It was in a silver frame, a clear picture some two years old, and Constance said it was a good likeness. There was no one else in the photograph which depicted her holding up a string of coloured balloons.

'That's just what I wanted,' and he thanked her, thinking that Alicia did resemble King Charles II, especially in her pantomime outfit.

He took his leave and left Constance Farrow to a lonely vigil in the Hall, soon to be empty for another long night. He wondered how she tolerated the silence and loneliness, but she did not appear to have any worries or fears about remaining.

Pemberton and Lorraine drove to the incident room in separate cars, he with the guns in his boot, and consequently there was no opportunity for him to talk privately with Lorraine or to seek her impression of that visit.

In the incident room, several detectives had returned to record their work in the incident log and to have the salient facts programmed into the HOLMES computer. Larkin spotted Pemberton and followed him into his tiny office. Lorraine arrived a few minutes later, but did not join Pemberton at this point.

'Any joy, sir?' Larkin asked.

'Nothing substantial, Paul.' He shrugged his shoulders and provided a resume of the visit, adding, 'I've got a photo we can use, it's Alicia in party mode, and there's a chap called Breckon, the caretaker, who gets the gift of his house now that Alicia is dead. I don't think he's a prime suspect, but he'll need interrogating – I'll do that. Of more interest is that tenant farmer called Potter, Neil Potter of Hagg End Farm. Alicia's rejection must have cost him a lot of money and her death might enable him to make a lot! Maybe that's given him a motive? I'll have words with him later today as well.'

'And if he's a farmer, he'll know how to handle a gun,' said Larkin.

'And he'll get up early on a morning,' smiled Pemberton. 'First, though, it's time to see Mr Browning.'

Richard Browning, a partner in Snowdon and Hurst, Solicitors, of Finklegate, Rainesbury, was in his mid-forties, a neat man with dark curly hair and dressed in a smart suit enhanced by a rather gaudy tie. He welcomed Pemberton with a cup of tea and biscuits. Pemberton enjoyed them as he provided an outline of the case, stressing his vital need to be sure there were no heirs who might want Alicia out of the way.

'If there are any, Richard, they're all suspects!'

'There aren't any, Mark. We've done rigorous checks. It's something of which we have been acutely aware ever since it was clear that Alicia would not produce a family. None of us likes to see the end of a dynasty or the breaking up of a good estate but sadly that is the case with Milverdale. Over the years, we have endeavoured to trace any blood relatives, however distant, but have found none. Alicia was the last – the very last. The Milverdale name and estate died with her.'

'It's a blood relationship rather than kinship through marriage that is the key factor,' said Pemberton.

'That was Mr Milverdale's condition. Any heir had to be a blood relation; blood ties were important to him. He stipulated that after Audrey's death.'

'He was a sincere man, was he?' asked Pemberton.

'A thoughtful person, I'd say. He liked helping others, as Alicia did. He was conscious of the public role he was expected to adopt – he was chairman of the parish council, for example, a member of the county council, commanding officer of the local contingent of the Home Guard during the war, warden of a home for sick children, a real public-spirited man.'

'So the lack of heirs would have been a blow to him?'

'I think it was. He placed great hopes on Alicia, he did not want the family to die out or the name to disappear, but, well, she did not produce any offspring.'

'So the murder is not a means whereby someone hoped to acquire the estate?' said Pemberton.

'I can't see that it is,' admitted Browning. 'I can't point you to anyone who might have a vested interest in inheriting the estate, and to my knowledge there has never been any hint of impropriety, no illegitimate children hidden away. Mind, I might not have known if there was!'

'There is one matter I'd like to investigate, Richard. We've learned that Alicia went to London occasionally, but don't know why, where she went or who she met. Have you any idea?'

'She told me in confidence, Mark. She wanted someone in a position of trust to be aware of the destination of her money! She donated cash, substantial sums, and drew cash from her private account for the trips. Now she's dead in such awful circumstances, I can tell you, if only to ease your mind. She went to a foundation established to help deprived children. She worked as a volunteer when she could spare the time. She helped at all levels and I do know she specialised in art and pantomimes, although she would also wash the pots or clean the floors if necessary.'

'And she paid her way in cash?'

'Yes, she was generous with financial help to the foundation, Mark, and liked to keep her donations secret, even from her bank manager. She paid her rail fare, her accommodation, her food – everything – in cash, and gave large sums to the foundation. The cash payments helped to keep her movements secret.'

'Did the foundation know who she was?'

'I doubt it, she told me she never used her real name. She called herself Audrey. Just Audrey, no surname.'

'After her aunt, no doubt,' Pemberton said.

'Her aunt?'

'She had an aunt who died young, Richard. Audrey, her father's sister, Audrey Milverdale.'

'Of course, I've seen that name in the file. I didn't catch the connection with her pseudonym. One of our senior partners always called her Honest Audrey. It seems she was very religious and claimed she would never tell a lie. A sad case, dying at such an early age.'

'That honesty business explains the inscription on her memorial. It says, "It's good to be honest and true."'

'It's the sort of thing the family might do,' smiled the solicitor.

Pemberton continued, 'Did Alicia bring any of her London children to Mill House or Milverdale Hall?'

'No, she merely went off to London to do that work just as some people disappear at weekends to their hideaways in country cottages, or on retreats at monasteries.'

'And where was this children's foundation, Richard? Do you know its name or whereabouts?'

'No, I don't, she never told me.'

'Well, if we need to trace it I'm sure we could,' Pemberton said. 'Now, back to Audrey. Alicia's aunt. You said her name is in the family files.'

'Yes, I've seen it.'

'She died suddenly, Richard. In 1947. Do you have details of her death?'

'Oh, I'm sure it wasn't suspicious in any way, Mark. You're not thinking of links with Alicia's death, are you?'

'I'd just like to know how she died, Richard. Consider it part of my investigation.'

169

'You chaps work in mysterious ways,' the solicitor smiled. 'But hold on while I have the file brought to me.'

It took a few moments for his secretary to locate and deliver the file, but soon it was on Browning's desk. He turned to the relevant section then said, 'Audrey died in Hove, Mark. Sussex, that is, on 7th September 1947. In hospital. The cause of her death is not given – there is no hint of suspicion, however, no mention of a police investigation. Her body was brought home for burial in the family vaults at Campsthwaite. I do not know why she was in Hove nor how long she spent there, there is very little about it in these papers.'

'No cause of death given?'

'No. You can examine the papers if you wish, you might know what you are looking for.'

Browning passed the file across and allowed Pemberton to read it but it was very brief. Too brief, felt Pemberton, without saying so to the solicitor. There was nothing to describe how Audrey had died, no doctor's report, nothing to say where she had been staying or whether she had been ill and was recuperating or why she was in Hove. It was almost as if some key papers had been deliberately omitted. He read the few that remained, making notes where he felt appropriate, and then passed the file back after thanking Browning.

'So Audrey's death – unmarried as she was – meant Roderick alone was left with the responsibility of ensuring the future of the family?'

'Yes. He married, rather late in life, but he did produce Alicia – she was the only child. His wife was an only child too, Emmeline Spurnet. There are no relations on that side of the family either, they're all dead. That's the end, Mark. The estate will function for another three years, I can confirm that, and we shall keep all the staff and tenants in their existing houses and jobs until the matter has been finalised. That was Mr Milverdale's wish.'

'Well, thanks for all your help. I'll keep you informed of developments and perhaps, if you think of any reason why Alicia might have been killed, you will inform me?'

'Of course, Mark, I'll do what I can.'

Pemberton left the solicitor's office for it was now time to prepare for his afternoon news conference. There was a half-hour drive back to Campsthwaite, time enough to consider his next moves.

8

While Pemberton prepared for the after-noon news conference, Lorraine concen-trated upon the background of Constance Farrow, using the information Constance herself had provided. Pemberton asked if, during her enquiries, she could discover more about Lady Consate and Lady Featley. Perhaps they had relatives who might remember Constance? But he asked Lorraine not to leave the office until she'd been acquainted with Pemberton's latest theory.

The news conference was a low-key affair because there was little to add, other than confirmation of Alicia's identity. This prompted questions about Alicia's family history but Pemberton declined to comment, saying it was not a police matter. However, he did confirm that no heirs were known and the police were not seeking one as a murder suspect.

When the journalists had departed, Pemberton said to Larkin and Lorraine, 'Come into my office, both of you. I want you to hear what I'm going to say to Hove Police.'

Pemberton rang Hove in Sussex and was connected with Detective Inspector Lindley. After identifying himself and supplying details of the present investigation, he said, 'I'm interested in a death which occurred in Hove, Inspector. Sadly it was a long time ago – 7th September 1947. The dead woman was Audrey Milverdale. She was brought back to North Yorkshire for burial in the family vaults at Campsthwaite. Her niece, Alicia Milverdale, is the victim of our crime, but I'm interested in Audrey's death. She was only thirty-two and her death is described as sudden, so there might have been some police involvement. A post-mortem or inquest, perhaps.'

'Most of our records are destroyed after ten years, Mr Pemberton, unless it's a major crime.'

'I appreciate that. Audrey was a member of an important family in this area, there might have been a photograph in your local paper or something in hospital records, or in the registrar's office. It would help enormously if I could learn anything about the circumstances – is there any way you can research it for me?'

'I've a detective constable in my department who's keen on family history. It'll be a good task for her! Detective Constable Karen Warner, sir.'

'Thanks, I appreciate your help. I'll await

her efforts with interest.' He replaced the phone, turned to Larkin and said, 'Right, Paul, if you get a call from Hove, you know what it's all about.'

'You must think it's relevant, sir, but I can't see how Audrey's death is of any interest to us.'

'She died on 7th September 1947,' Pemberton reminded him 'Suddenly, according to the memorial in the church. Aged thirty-two.'

'Yes, I got that.'

'So could it have occurred during childbirth, Paul?'

'Childbirth, sir?' Lorraine chipped in. 'She wasn't married. Anyway, if so, where's her child now?'

'Those are exactly the sort of questions for which I want answers, Lorraine. Let me remind you that Constance Farrow was born on 6th September 1947.'

'The day before Audrey died!' Paul Larkin breathed.

'Right, Paul. Coincidence or not, do you think? Could Constance be her daughter about to claim her blood-linked inheritance?'

'But if there was a child, sir, illegitimate or otherwise, surely it would have shown up in the family records?'

'Not necessarily. In some sections of society, it was customary, even after the war, when an unmarried woman got herself embarrassingly pregnant, to send her away for the birth, to some place where she was unknown so that it could be kept a secret. Audrey went to Hove for some reason. Might she have gone there to give birth? But she died there, Paul, not at home. Perhaps she was sent there because complications were expected by the family, to get her away in case of a scandal...'

'So if the child was not wanted or recognised by the Milverdales, it would be adopted, wouldn't it? Or fostered? Or brought up in a home?' Lorraine said.

'Yes, there were plenty of options. But if Audrey *did* give birth, there should be a record somewhere – a birth certificate at least. If the birth was in Hove, the record will be there.'

'You've reason to think she gave birth, sir?'

'It's no more than a hunch, Paul. I can't see any other motive for this murder except a secret heir waiting in the wings. And remember, Alicia's death has all the hallmarks of a skilled execution. Organised by that heir, perhaps?'

'I can't see how Constance Farrow fits into the scheme of things. Her family background is based in the York area,' Lorraine reminded him. 'She had working class parents, dead end jobs and all that. That's what she told me.'

175

'It's something to look into very carefully, Lorraine – discreetly too, I suggest, without Constance knowing of our additional interest. It might be that Constance was adopted and her parents moved to York. Farrow might be her adopted name, but Milverdale blood might be in her veins.'

'Might this be associated with Constance's worries about the press digging too deep, sir?' Lorraine continued.

'It could explain that. I do believe there is some mystery in the background of the Milverdales – maybe that's why the villagers are so reticent. If there has been a cover-up about an illegitimate or embarrassing birth, it might explain her concern about press enquiries, especially if she is Audrey's child. She does show a level of concern that's higher than I'd expect from an employee.'

'You have been thinking deep, sir!' Larkin commented. 'So would DNA help establish the truth?'

'I've already asked the pathologist to ensure he takes a sample from Alicia's body, and I've asked the Scenes of Crime teams to recover a piece of hair or something from Constance's dressing-table. They might help to establish a family link – or otherwise.'

'But if Constance is the heir, why would she commit murder? Once she makes her claim, suspicion is focused immediately upon her.'

'It is already, Paul, she found the body! She's in the frame.'

'*Touché!*' smiled Paul Larkin.

'I'll ask you to bear this in mind as you make your enquiries. I'm going to see that landlord now, and after that, I want words with the schoolteacher.'

'School will have finished now, sir,' Lorraine reminded him. 'But I could interview Mrs Donaldson – I've some phone calls to make, local police and employment agencies that might help with Constance, but once I've done that, I could fit her in. Mrs Donaldson might still be marking books or something.'

'Right, Lorraine. You talk to Mrs Donaldson. I want the names of children, now and in the past, who've been to Mill House with Alicia, or who've taken part in any of her schemes. We need positive leads, Lorraine, leads that will take us to a child and then to a parent who is willing to talk to us. Now I must go.'

Mark Pemberton found Andy Nelson working in his office at the Miners Arms.

'Paperwork! I hate it, Mr Pemberton. VAT returns, income tax, orders and invoices, it never stops!' The bulky man eased himself out of his chair. 'Folks think all I do is stand behind the bar, serve drinks and put the world right! But come through to the lounge, it's more comfortable. A drink? Tea?'

'A cup of tea would be most welcome.' Pemberton realised he was thirsty. 'Milk, no sugar, please.'

'Coming up, I could do with one myself.'

Sitting in the comfortable bar lounge which overlooked the dale, Pemberton faced the formidable crew-cut landlord over a small round table bearing a tray of tea and biscuits. Pemberton presented the facts so Nelson would be in a position to relay the truth to his customers. The murder would be the chief topic of conversation for weeks to come, something which Pemberton welcomed because it might produce worthwhile gossip.

'Now,' Pemberton said eventually. 'Last night, I got the distinct impression you didn't want to talk about Alicia Milverdale. Was that because the pub was full or was the reason more complicated?'

The big man studied Pemberton for a few moments, as if contemplating some kind of deep and meaningful response to the smart detective, then he said, 'There's nothing I can say, superintendent.'

'But you live in the village! You must know something!'

'I hardly knew the woman, Mr Pemberton, she wasn't a customer of mine, she never came in for a meal or a drink, we didn't mix in the same social circles. She was virtually a stranger to me. And this pub is not part of Milverdale Estate, the brewery owns it. It's not mine, I'm just the landlord.'

'Someone had a reason for wanting her dead,' said Pemberton.

'I can't think who,' muttered Nelson, sipping from his tea. 'No one has ever said they wanted to harm her, not in my hearing anyway. Most of the locals thought the sun shone out of her.'

'If she wasn't killed deliberately, it might be a tragic accident. I've got to look at all possibilities.'

'That wouldn't surprise me. This is shooting country, Mr Pemberton, but I'd say all our local shooting folk are responsible with their guns, they wouldn't loose off a shot without knowing where it was going to finish up. I can't speak for strangers, of course, or idiot youths.'

'My thoughts also, Mr Nelson.'

'Andy, everybody calls me Andy. There's no bloody-minded heir wanting her out of the way, is there?'

'Not that we know, we're sure she's the last of the line, Andy. No brothers or sisters, no siblings, no distant cousins so far as we can tell. All those negatives leave another alternative,' and Pemberton watched Nelson closely. 'Last night when we talked, you said that when it involved Alicia Milverdale, you knew nothing and could tell me nothing. I know that people were listening to us and you've got to be careful what you say in public but I thought that was a rather curious thing to say.'

'No, it wasn't. It's what I've just said now, in private. I know nothing so I can't tell you anything.'

'It was your terminology that intrigued me, Andy. You said, when it involved Alicia Milverdale, you knew nothing. Why her in particular?'

"No reason, it was just something I said, you were asking about her.'

'I get the impression there is something that the villagers know about Alicia, something that is not known to other people perhaps, maybe not even known to her closest friends or to family when they were around, something that is certainly not known to the police and something the villagers – or some of them – don't want my officers to know about. And I feel that that something, whatever it is, might have led to her death. I am wondering if that reason, whatever it is, is behind the reluctance to be open with my detectives, Andy.'

'I've no idea what you are talking about.' The big man took a long drink from his cup. 'Are you saying there's a conspiracy of silence in the village?'

'Put it this way, my officers have gained

the impression that some villagers are reluctant to talk about Alicia. She seems to be the problem even if she is the victim, and I find that intriguing. In most cases of murder, people are willing to help us trace the killer, but here I find the opposite. And yet there seems to be a curious contradiction because the people liked her...'

'You're accusing the people of Campsthwaite of shielding a murderer, are you?' demanded Andy.

'They are shielding something, Andy, and I'm not sure what it is – but why would they do that? Why keep quiet about something that might solve our murder?'

'I'm sure no one knows who killed Alicia, so how could they shield the killer?'

'Then why won't they talk about Alicia Milverdale?'

'Search me!'

'You won't talk either, Andy.'

'I'm talking now, but I'm not much help because I know nothing. Other than the fact she was a bloody good estate owner, I know nothing about her.'

'It's gossip I'm interested in,' said Pemberton. 'The "no smoke without fire" syndrome.'

'It's mainly man's talk in here.' Andy Nelson produced a quick smile. 'Not gossip, not women's talk about kids' toilet achievements. Football, cricket, gardening, hunting, shooting, fishing, that sort of thing. And women, of course! Men will talk about women, their conquests mainly. Half of that's fiction, though, pure imagination!'

'So those conversations didn't feature Alicia Milverdale? Wasn't she an object of their passions, or supposed passions? A wealthy spinster with a big estate?'

Nelson grinned suddenly. 'She didn't appeal to my customers,' he said. 'I never heard her name mentioned in that context, Mr Pemberton. She wasn't a target for any of them, not a challenge, if you understand.'

'I'm going to dwell on her sexual proclivities for a moment,' Pemberton began. 'Or her possibly sexual proclivities, to be precise.'

'I know nowt about that!' chuckled the big man. 'I can't say she's the sort of woman I'd want to chase. And I've a good healthy appetite, just ask my wife.'

'Alicia took children to Mill House, Andy,' Pemberton began. 'We know that. We know she organised functions like the annual pantomime and she took children there to rehearse. And art classes too. What interests me is whether she had any other reason for inviting them to her very isolated home in the woods.'

'No idea,' said Andy Nelson. 'I've no kids of my own, so I wouldn't know about that sort of thing.'

'Is that the aspect of Alicia's life that the villagers won't talk about? If it is, I can sympathise with them,' he went on. 'That's if she was interfering with youngsters, abusing them to use the fashionable word. I have to say that from what I have learned so far, the indications are there, signs that she might have had a rather unhealthy interest in children.'

'I never said that!' Nelson looked uncomfortable now. 'I never said she abused children, nobody has said that.'

'But is that what the villagers thought?' Pemberton was quick to sense Andy's discomfort. 'Is it more than just a rumour? Do they know she was abusing them?'

'Look, Mr Pemberton. Suppose your little lad was being abused by a grown woman, would you want him to go to court to tell the world about it? No, you wouldn't. You'd want it stopped, that's all, without a fuss, and the way you'd stop it would be to keep him away from the bitch, wouldn't it? You might even leave the village with your kids to get away from it all, like the Robsons did.'

'Robsons?'

'Nine years ago, before I came here. The whole family cleared off to Scotland. Some said their little lad had claimed Alicia had touched him. Mind you, they were a funny lot. The dad was the type who'd make all sort of accusations against folks, so you

183

couldn't place much weight on what he said. He didn't like authority and he hated the gentry. He could have put the kid up to it.'

'But there's no smoke without fire?' smiled Pemberton. 'I'll try and trace the Robsons. So were the police involved?'

'No, the whole thing fizzled out, so I'm told. But that's how parents like it in that kind of situation. No police involvement, no publicity. And you'd warn other parents to keep their kids away from her, wouldn't you? Getting the police involved only makes it worse, especially for the bairns. And don't forget a wrong accusation against Alicia could cost you your job and your home – she had a lot of power round here, good as she was to her tenants.'

'Point taken. Like you, Andy, I have no children and to be honest, I'm not sure how I'd react if that sort of thing happened to a child of mine.'

'If she was doing things to little lads, why drag it up now? You can't prosecute her, she's gone, Mr Pemberton, it's all over. Finished.'

Pemberton did not respond for a few moments, then Nelson continued, 'I need a drink!'

He went to the bar counter, opened the flap and helped himself to a double measure of malt whisky, a Glenmorangie. 'How about you, Mr Pemberton?'

Normally, Pemberton would not have agreed to an alcoholic drink but in these unusual circumstances, as during his chat with Constance, he accepted. 'Same for me,' he said.

He waited as Nelson produced the drinks, saying nothing until the landlord had returned to his seat. 'I think you've told me all I wanted to know. You've put your finger on what I feared. So what changed your mind?'

'I'm not behind the bar now, I'm speaking to you, man to man, because I don't want your men stirring up dirt in the village, Mr Pemberton. Think of those kids, generations of them, who've been in her grip. Little lads who've lost their childhood, kids living in the village even now, then that new school-teacher encouraging them to visit her. The people have told Mrs Donaldson not to let the bairns visit Mill House without parents being there but Mrs Donaldson thinks they're lucky to have a tutor with such wonderful imagination and flair. That upset a lot of parents. Some are talking of taking their kids to other schools... Anyway, it's all over now. Alicia's dead. Problem solved. Parents can breathe a sigh of relief, I'd say.'

'So that's why the villagers won't talk to us?'

'There's their jobs as well, but they don't

185

want their little kids dragged into this, Mr Pemberton. Surely you can understand that? That's why I'm talking to you like this, man to man, even though I've no real idea what the parents have been suffering.'

'I appreciate it,' said Pemberton.

Nelson sipped at his whisky. 'If the folks out there knew I'd told you this, I'd be blackballed, I'd lose my custom overnight, but my reasoning is that if you know what's been going on, you can deal with it better, cope with the villagers, understand them maybe. Well, understand their reluctance to talk. They're protecting children, not shielding a murderer. We all want your help to make sure that continues.'

Pemberton nursed his drink in both hands. 'I thought there was something like this behind the scenes. I'll not betray your confidence. I'll promise you that. But my men will have to continue their house-to-house enquiries – perhaps one of the parents will decide to talk to my officers?'

Nelson shook his head. 'I doubt it. It was something everybody agreed years ago, they'd not involve the authorities, they'd simply keep their kids away from Alicia and they'd warn incoming families about her. All they want to do is protect their bairns, you see. And that still applies, Mr Pemberton. But even if one of them does decide to talk to you, I hope you won't go dredging up the muck that went on in that old house...'

'Even after listening to you, Andy, I must admit I'm still not sure whether it was all rumour.'

'Pretty strong rumours if you ask me!'

'Right, but we can't prosecute her now, and I still have to find a murderer.'

'Whoever it was, he's done a service to the kids of this village, Mr Pemberton, even if that's not the reason for killing her.'

'Would you know any adults who might have been abused by her when they were children?' was Pemberton's next question.

'I'm saying no more, Mr Pemberton. I've said more than I should. I've made you aware of the situation. I've done enough.'

'All right, but one final question. Which of the parents would be so angry and upset that they'd shoot her?'

There was another long pause while Nelson sipped at his whisky, then he said, 'I don't think any of them would, Mr Pemberton. They'd not do it because if they got caught, the whole story would emerge, and their little lad would be involved. That's no way of protecting a child. No, the locals would simply keep their kids away and warn others off. They'd not kill her, Mr Pemberton. I'd bet my life on that. You'll have to look somewhere else.'

'I need to know, for certain, that she did abuse the children.' Pemberton spoke quietly. 'I need to know that the abuse was real, I need evidence, I need to be sure that the parents did not imagine it. I know how rumours can spread and how they can develop into what becomes reality, when in fact it's all fiction. False memories and all that, misunderstanding what children are saying.'

'I think it was real enough,' said Nelson.

'But who can testify to me that it was true?' Pemberton asked. 'I can't base my investigation on rumours...'

'You asked for gossip, Mr Pemberton. Now you've got it! Find those Robsons for starters – if you can trust them, that is. But I'll tell you something else – so far as I'm concerned, this conversation never took place. I'll not make a written statement but I felt you ought to know all this, for the kids' sake.'

'I've promised to respect your confidence, and will instruct my officers to do likewise. Some of them will be coming here tonight, for their suppers.'

'I'll behave as if I've not told you any of this, and if anybody else asks, I'll say I do not wish to discuss the murder,' he said.

'That's fine by me,' said Pemberton, draining his glass.

'Just think of those children and their parents who have to live here when you've finished your enquiries,' said Nelson, rising to follow Pemberton from the room. 'Just think of them. That's all I ask.'

'I will,' promised Mark Pemberton.

Margaret Donaldson was small and rather plump. In her late forties, she wore a brown tweed skirt, a dark green jumper and brown low-heeled shoes. With thinning brown hair turning grey, and horn-rimmed spectacles, she looked older than her years and was almost like a rural grandmother as she led Lorraine into her office at the village school. High on the moor above Campsthwaite, the handsome school was built of local granite and roofed with blue slates; the spacious playground had been created from open moorland and the views across the dale were stunning. The school's catchment area included several communities which meant it had survived when others of comparable size had closed. It catered for around 120 pupils of primary school age.

'I've already spoken to one of your detectives, you know,' she told Lorraine as she bade her be seated. 'There is so little I can say, I did tell her everything I knew.'

'Yes, and thank you for that.' Lorraine settled on a chair beside the desk. 'But our enquiries always generate further questions as we go along, and that means returning to the people we interviewed in the initial stages.'

'So how can I help now?'

'We're interested in the children who went to Mill House with Alicia Milverdale,' Lorraine said, going straight to the point of her visit.

'As I told your colleague, I've discontinued those outings,' said Mrs Donaldson. 'The parents did not want the children to go there. They never told me why, Miss Cashmore, but a deputation came to see me, only last week in fact, and asked me – well, told me more like – to stop the visits to Miss Milverdale's old house.'

'Was any reason given?'

'No, that was the odd thing. They said they were speaking for all the parents of children in the school, and requested I stop the outings. That's all.'

'And what was your reaction?'

'Well, I was taken aback, I must admit. I think it's a good thing for children to experience things outside school, and outside the home, and Miss Milverdale was very artistic, a natural teacher, and clever with her hands.'

'I believe she wrote her own scripts, usually featuring a princess?'

'They were good, Miss Cashmore, those I've seen. The children loved them. But I was unaware of any complaints about her, until that deputation turned up.'

'So how long have you taught in this school?'

'Only since last September,' was the answer. 'The start of the new school year. I took over when Miss Baines retired.'

'And did Miss Baines take the children to Mill House?'

'According to Miss Milverdale, she used to take them, years ago, and then she stopped for some reason. When Miss Milverdale came to see me about helping at the school, on a voluntary basis with art and theatre, she said Miss Baines had ended the association without giving a reason. Miss Milverdale thought it might be something to do with new rules governing primary education, and so when I was appointed, she arrived one afternoon and put the proposal to me. I saw no reason why the children should not enjoy the occasional trip to Mill House, to rehearse a pantomime or enjoy an art class or anything similar like a natural ramble. Miss Milverdale said she would collect the children and return them to their homes or to the school afterwards.'

'What sort of numbers are we talking about?' asked Lorraine. 'The whole school or just a handful of children?'

'Oh, very few. Seven or eight perhaps. Even fewer. Mainly those in the intermediate class, the eight to nine-year-olds.'

'Not the older ones?'

'No, they would be preparing for secondary school, you see, the ten to eleven-year-olds that is, and the little ones were too young for the work Miss Milverdale expected of them – remembering lines, dancing and so on, performing on stage.'

'Boys and girls went, did they?' asked Lorraine.

'Oh, yes, Miss Milverdale wanted to encourage boys to become involved with the theatre. She maintained that too often they were encouraged to go into offices or the professions or even into manual labouring for builders or farming jobs when really their inclinations were towards more artistic pursuits.'

'She could be right,' smiled Lorraine. 'So the pantomime at Christmas was the first and last occasion when your own pupils went to Mill House? And the art classes?'

'I started the art classes after Christmas to occupy the children once the pantomime season was over. Miss Milverdale said I could use Mill House on Saturday mornings, for extra classes out of school. I liked the idea, I'm not a nine to three thirty teacher and I felt it gave the children something constructive to do on a Saturday morning, something outside the home.'

'And how many went to those sessions?'

'Two or three, these were the older ones. Ten or eleven-year-olds.'

'Did you go with them?'

'For the first two or three weeks, yes. I

enjoyed it, Miss Milverdale was good with children, she could persuade them to produce work I'd never be capable of doing – she was a natural artist, Miss Cashmore. And such a good teacher. Anyway, I had a family event one Saturday, the wedding of a niece, so on that Saturday the children went on their own.'

'Did the parents know where they were going?'

'I don't know, to be honest. The children came to the school first, perhaps they did not tell their parents they were going on elsewhere? I ferried them to the entrance to Mill Wood in my four-wheel drive. It carries eight, ideal for a teacher. Then we walked through the wood, the path is not suitable for vehicles.'

'Perhaps Alicia told them not to tell their parents that they were going to Mill House? Perhaps she hinted at a secret of some kind? Perhaps that secrecy continued until their parents found out and put an end to the visits.'

'Yes, the parents did not seem worried if the pantomime or art classes were in the school, even with Miss Milverdale there, provided they were always in my presence. The children did enjoy the pantomime and of course, the parents always came to collect their offspring after rehearsals.'

'It can't have been easy for you, coping

with them and Alicia. Now, Mrs Donaldson, can I have their names, please? The children who went to Mill House, either for art classes or pantomime rehearsals. I would like to speak to them.'

'Well, I am not sure I should, I would have thought that sort of thing was confidential to the school.'

'In a murder investigation, Mrs Donaldson, in fact in the investigation of any crime, every citizen has a duty to help the police with their enquiries. If we find people are obstructive, we can either issue a subpoena to compel them to give evidence in court, or we can obtain a search warrant... Now, we never like to do that and I would remind you that we are engaged in tracing a killer, Mrs Donaldson. He has killed once – he might repeat his crime if we don't stop him.'

'Only last night, I got a telephone call from one of those parents – I don't know who – to say I should not give the names of any of those children to the police. They do not want their children involved in this enquiry.'

'That suggests something very sinister, Mrs Donaldson. We must have those names. To protect others. Surely you can see that?'

'But I am here with the consent of the parents, through the school governors, and I cannot afford to lose my post...'

'We are talking of murder, Mrs Donaldson. Not some petty local squabble.'

Lorraine waited as Mrs Donaldson fought to make her decision, and then she said, 'Yes, you are right. Of course you are right. I'll get the names.'

'And I would like the names of all the children who visited Miss Milverdale,' said Lorraine. 'Past and present if the records are available.'

'Yes, yes, of course, I'm sure they're in our files. Miss Baines was very good at record keeping.'

'Where is Miss Baines? Any idea?' asked Lorraine as Mrs Donaldson busied herself with the filing system.

'She retired to Northumberland, a village near Hexham. I have her address. Do you want that?'

'Please, we'll have to talk to her about the children from her classes who visited Miss Milverdale.'

'Miss Cashmore, forgive me for being stupid or naïve. I have no desire to be obstructive or awkward, but is there something sinister about Alicia Milverdale? I've always found her to be utterly charming and pleasant, both to me and the children.'

Lorraine was not sure how much Pemberton wished to reveal about his own suspicions, but she was aware that she was dealing with a mature woman who had a responsible position in the village.

'There is a suggestion – and it is no more than that, Mrs Donaldson – that Alicia's interest in children, probably young boys, was not entirely wholesome. We are trying to establish whether or not there is any truth in these suspicions.'

'You mean she was abusing the children?' There was a look of horror on the teacher's face. 'You mean she was using me as a means of gaining their trust?'

'We don't know,' admitted Lorraine. 'I might be guilty of perpetuating a vicious rumour, but none of the villagers will talk to us. We believe they are shielding their children – which is understandable – but it doesn't help us catch a murderer. Maybe the rumours are wildly out of control and totally false. We need to find out and I need to talk to someone who has first-hand knowledge of what went on at Mill House when Alicia was alone with the children – or with just one child.'

'Oh, I see. Well, that makes it all very clear. I had no idea... I do wish the parents had told me what was worrying them, they were very guarded about it.' Mrs Donaldson was flicking through a file of papers as she talked.

'Perhaps they do not have any firm evidence, Mrs Donaldson, perhaps it is all conjecture and rumour, but they see themselves as doing their best to protect their children. I respect that but we have a job to do. We have to catch the killer before he kills again.'

'Well, now that I understand, I shall be as co-operative as possible, but I do not wish to antagonise the parents.'

'There is no need for them to know what has transpired between us, Mrs Donaldson. We shall not reveal our sources of information.'

'Thank you, that helps. Now, here's a list of the children who took part in the last pantomime, and the art classes. Back files will contain earlier names, going back, oh, ten or twelve years. Shall I photocopy them for you?'

'Thank you, yes. And I need the names of the parents who formed that deputation.'

And so it was that Detective Constable Lorraine Cashmore left the school bearing files containing dozens of children's names, pupils past and present, all of whom would-have to be interviewed. She was also clutching a list of three names, the deputation of parents. There were two women and one man. She read the names – Mrs Gill Austin, mother of Adrian, Mrs Anita Riley, mother of Henry, and Neil Potter, father of Daniel. The addresses were given; all were in Campsthwaite – and Neil Potter's was Hagg End Farm. He was the man who'd tried to buy his premises from Alicia, Lorraine recalled. He wanted to buy the farm so that he could build a caravan site and increase his income.

And Alicia had turned down his application.

She thanked Mrs Donaldson for her co-operation and left the school.

9

Lorraine hurried to the incident room but Pemberton had not returned.

'He's out doing interviews.' Inspector Larkin was brewing himself a mug of coffee. 'Is it urgent?'

'Important rather than urgent,' she told him.

'Look, get yourself a coffee and come into the office.'

Minutes later, Lorraine was sitting in Mark's chair as she explained about her discussions with the schoolteacher and Neil Potter's role as spokesman for the parents. She concluded with, 'Has anyone been to interview him yet?'

'Not yet, that action's awaiting allocation.'

'In view of this development, Mr Pemberton might want to do it,' Lorraine suggested.

'Or he might want you to do it,' Larkin smiled. 'That's if you're up to it.'

'Up to it, sir? Yes, of course I am.'

'I thought you looked a bit under the weather this morning, worried, under pressure of some kind. I don't want to overload you with work, this kind of enquiry can become quite demanding.'

She had no intention of telling him about her visit to the doctor, but did appreciate his concern; she had no idea that her condition was so evident to others.

'It's nothing a good night's sleep won't cure!' She produced a light response with all its veiled suggestiveness.

'You're getting on with your colleagues, are you?' Larkin put to her. 'I know that sometimes they might not include you in their conversations and parties and so on, thinking your loyalties are to the boss rather than to them.'

'It's not easy,' she admitted, realising that Larkin was not prying. He was a very experienced manager; the welfare of his staff was of deep concern to him. 'I think everyone knows I'm living with Mark and I suppose it does set me apart from the troops. Rank differences are a funny thing in the police service – that's why I always call him "sir" when I'm on duty, although I must admit there are times I forget!'

'He's a good boss, Lorraine, and a nice chap, you're very lucky – and so are we. And I'm not just saying that because you're sitting here!'

'He's good to be with, sir,' Lorraine said easily, relieved to have the focus taken off her. 'I thought I might find things tough, working with the man I'm living with, especially in a job like ours, but he has the knack of switching off at home. He never wants us to talk about work when we're alone, and I've got him persuaded to take up walking in the countryside. He likes that – well, we like that, I should say.'

'I must say he looks better since you joined him! The death of his wife did knock him back a lot.'

'I thought he might have caught me on the rebound, as they say, or even a second rebound, but I know he didn't...'

'I know that,' Larkin said kindly. '*We* all know that. But look, if there are problems of any kind, work or otherwise, you can always bend my ear!'

'Thanks, that's reassuring, sir.'

'And now to business. You said you've got the names of children who've been to Mill House with Alicia, as well as the names of two parents who formed the deputation with Potter?'

'Yes, I managed to persuade Mrs Donaldson to provide them!'

'Well done. I'll make sure they're interviewed; it might need someone with a sensitive touch and I don't care if that is politically incorrect! I'll let Mr Pemberton decide. Now, where's Potter live?'

'Hagg End Farm,' Lorraine said.

'Let's find it on the map. It'll be interesting to see how his land relates to the bluebell field.'

A large-scale map of Campsthwaite hung from a wall in the village institute and they left the tiny office to examine it. Those houses already visited by detectives, and whose occupants had been eliminated from the enquiry, were marked with green. Midgley's farm bore a green dot but most of the others bore no markings, indicating they were yet to be visited. Those houses known to contain primary school children bore blue dots while any with occupants who were regarded as firm suspects would eventually be marked in red. Houses occupied by people with a military background, however slight, had a yellow dot. There were two at the moment – one containing a retired seventy-five-year-old colonel and another with an ex-RAF National Serviceman; both had green dots to show they had been eliminated from the enquiry. Currently, the only house sporting a red dot was Milverdale Hall, although the homes of the estate workers did carry pink dots. That meant they had not been totally eliminated and might be reinterviewed depending upon the enquiry's progress. Lorraine noted that Neil Potter's farm already bore a pink dot.

'So,' mused Larkin as he studied the map, 'my first impression is that Potter could have walked from his farmland, across

Bottom Road and through the old ironworks to the viaduct without crossing any public place – except the road, of course. He'd not be seen during that trek and, near the viaduct, he could join the route taken by Alicia to the bluebell field and Mill House. It's possible he could have either followed her or gone ahead to lie in wait.'

'Would he know her route and timing?' asked Lorraine.

'Most of the village seems to have been aware of it, but if he didn't, he could find out,' said Larkin. 'And, being a farmer, he would know how to handle a firearm.'

'Don't forget the murder weapon was a .303,' said Lorraine. 'I doubt if any farmer would have one of those on the premises.'

'It could be a war trophy kept by his father or grandfather, even illegally,' suggested Larkin. 'Or an old Home Guard issue that was never reclaimed. We can't rule that out. And farm outbuildings are ideal for keeping or hiding a gun.'

'He's had two hefty slaps in the face from the lady of the manor – it might be more than a red-blooded fellow could tolerate,' suggested Lorraine.

'Let's place Mr Potter well and truly in the frame,' smiled Larkin. 'Well done. Now, Lorraine, there was a phone call for you. The police at Harrogate rang about Lady

Featley. Her son now occupies Hoveton Hall – Terence Featley – and he remembers Constance Farrow. She came to look after the house after Lady Consate died in 1994. Later, Lady Featley went into a home so Constance wasn't needed any more; at that point, the son moved in with his own small staff. Constance joined the Milverdale household from there. It seems she was highly regarded.'

'Thanks, sir. Anything about Lady Consate? Mr Pemberton seems to think he knows the name from somewhere.'

'Not yet. I wonder how Mr Pemberton is getting on with his enquiries?'

Georgina Wallace was in her early thirties, a charming petite woman with long blonde hair, blue eyes and a fine set of pure white teeth. Her husband was a stonemason and they lived in a terrace house near the Methodist Chapel in Campsthwaite. Upon being told the purpose of his visit, she invited Pemberton into her small but comfortable lounge which was strewn with toys.

'Sorry about the mess.' She began to move things. 'It's Stephanie, mum's just taken her for a walk.'

'Don't worry about that!' He settled in an armchair. 'You've just the one little girl?'

'Yes, just one at the moment. She's

eighteen months old. We can't afford another, so my husband says. There's no overtime these days, we can just manage without me working.'

'It's good of you to see me. I won't keep you long,' Pemberton assured her. 'You've heard about Alicia Milverdale?'

'Yes, it's terrible, who could do such a thing? I was expecting you, I'd heard the police are visiting everyone.'

'You used to work for her, I'm told.'

'Yes, as the estate secretary. I left when I had Stephanie. Miss Milverdale would have kept me on, but I wanted to be a mum at home. We could use the extra money, who couldn't! She didn't replace me and I did return sometimes, for a few hours' work when things were hectic like the financial year end. Miss Milverdale said I was always welcome to return full-time if I wanted. I thought I might go back one day, maybe part-time when Stephanie starts school ... then this happened. It's dreadful, Mr Pemberton, who could do such a thing? And why? Why do that to the Princess?'

'Those are the questions I must answer,' he smiled. Under Pemberton's gentle questioning, she explained her duties, saying that Alicia was a very good employer and that she had enjoyed her work with Milverdale Estate. They discussed Constance Farrow, with Georgina saying she had never grown close to the housekeeper in the short time both worked at the Hall, probably due to their age difference and the fact that their jobs had little in common.

Georgina worked for the estate and Constance kept the house.

'I've got to ask you this,' Pemberton put to her. 'Was there any animosity between Alicia and Constance? Any shouting matches? Angry moments, jealousy?'

'No, not a thing, Mr Pemberton. The Princess was such a good employer, everybody liked her, she was so kind and lovely. They all called her the Princess, you know. I keep referring to her like that ... not that I did to her face, though.'

'I had heard the nickname,' smiled Pemberton.

'Miss Farrow liked her work at the Hall, she told me so. She said it was the happiest place she had ever worked in. And she did keep things so nice and clean, everything ran like clockwork, she kept things so tidy and smart and if the smallest thing wanted doing, like a new washer on a tap or a lick of paint on a window ledge, she always made sure it was done straight away. She really did make sure the men did their jobs, outside as well as in. You'd have thought it was her own home, the way she cared for it.'

'And the estate's regular staff? They all seem very happy there.'

'Yes. Part of my job was to put up their wages on a Friday, and I never had grumbles from them. We had a very low turnover of staff, Mr Pemberton, none of them wanted to leave and if we did want to increase the staff, we never had any trouble recruiting local people.'

'Was the staff increased while you were there?'

'Just the once, we advertised for an assistant gardener. We had loads of applications. He's still there.'

'It makes it all the more puzzling why anyone would want to kill such a good mistress. Now, though, I'd like to mention the tenants, Georgina,' he went on. 'I know about the trust which allows the tenants to buy their homes and farms in the event of there being no heir.'

'I was told about that when I started work,' she confirmed.

'One of the tenants tried to buy his farm in advance,' he said. 'Did that happen while you were working there?'

'Yes, it was Neil Potter. The Princess told him to put his request in writing, then she'd talk to her solicitors about it.'

'Did he strike you as being a reasonable man?' Pemberton asked.

'Oh yes, very. He was most polite and when the Princess talked to him, she asked me to take notes in shorthand, and write them up for the file. She was very nice to him.'

'And when the decision went against him? Was he still as reasonable?'

'She wrote to him with the decision but he came to see if she would change her mind. He was quite forceful, Mr Pemberton, but never nasty, he never lost his temper or raised his voice, but he did persist for some time, writing letters to see if she would change her mind or even take shares in his schemes. He couldn't see why she couldn't let him buy the farm when he and his family would be allowed to buy it later.'

'I've seen the file,' he told her.

'I thought you might,' she smiled. 'The solicitors felt that if an exception was made in his case, it could lead to a break-up of the estate prematurely and, of course, the estate does depend upon the revenue from its rented properties. It has to pay its way – wages, running costs, maintenance and so on. Besides, such a sale was contrary to estate policy – to be honest, there was no way the Princess could allow it. Mr Potter wasn't very happy, and I do know he tried to get permission for his caravan site while still renting the farm, but both the estate and the planning authority turned him down. He never tried again.'

'Do you know Neil Potter very well?'

'Not really, he's older than me. By the

time I started primary school, he'd gone to secondary school, and when I went to secondary school, he was in the seniors, nearly ready to leave. We never went to the same places or had the same friends, even though we lived in the same small village.'

'His parents had Hagg End before he took over the tenancy. I believe?'

'Yes, and I think his grandfather had the farm before that, the family goes back a long way in its association with Milverdale Estate. It was Neil who suggested taking over the old ironworks for cultivation – it had been left as wasteland until he took it on. He got it for a very low rent.'

'That's another positive sign of the good relationship between the estate and its tenants, and it does show something of Potter's ambitious nature. Now, to change the subject – on the topic of primary education, Georgina, did you attend the village school?'

'Yes, when Miss Baines was headmistress. I liked it.'

'Was Alicia, Miss Milverdale, involved with the school while you were there?'

'No, it's about twenty years since I left Campsthwaite school, Mr Pemberton, when I was eleven. I think the Princess was at university then. It was when I was at secondary school that she returned and started to work on the estate.'

209

'So you weren't involved in any of her pantomimes?'

'No, although I know she did start them, using children from the primary school.'

'Did you ever come across any rumours about her? Her activities with children, I mean.'

'I was aware of tales, Mr Pemberton, I first heard them at school, tales about goings on at Mill House between the Princess and her obedient page boys. Most of us were aware of them. Some of the village lads thought it was hilarious and made fun of it. They couldn't understand anybody getting worried about it.'

'Were the stories true?' he asked.

She shook her head. 'I don't know. I never knew anybody who'd actually had anything done to them by the Princess, but everyone was wary of letting their children be alone with her. Some parents weren't happy about their children going to Mill House, and I did wonder what I would do if she asked Stephanie to go. I think it was all rumours though. False rumours, I mean. I worked with her and never suspected her of anything untoward, either with children or anyone else. I know she never got married but that was her choice. I don't think she was a lesbian either.'

'Did you come across a family called Robson?'

'I heard about them from my dad, he said they'd left the village after the little lad had said something about the Princess. But I don't think anyone believed him.'

'Do you know where they are now? The Robsons?'

'Sorry, no. I don't think they were here long and from what I hear, it was a case of good riddance.'

'It was unfortunate if they were lying about Alicia. Now, you liked working with her?'

'Yes, I did. I liked the work and I liked her, Mr Pemberton, I'll be honest about that. I would speak up for her anywhere – even against parents who think she did nasty things with their children. I'm sure it was all malicious gossip.'

'Fine, I respect your views. Now, it appears Miss Milverdale took regular trips to London. You were her secretary, so did she tell you anything about the trips?'

'No, she would go off for a few days, not regularly because of her work on the estate, but when things were quiet she liked to have a break.'

'In her old Rolls?'

'Not all the way. She'd be driven to Rainesbury station to catch a train to York, then she'd change at York for London. Our local trains through Campsthwaite mean a long wait for the right connection.'

'And what did she do in London? Any idea? Meet friends? Go to the theatre? A restaurant for a fine meal? See the sights?'

'I don't know, Mr Pemberton. She'd just say she was going to London and I'd make sure she had enough cash for the trip.'

'I understand she drew considerable sums of cash for those trips. Her solicitor told me.'

'Yes, she never used cheques or credit cards on those trips. She paid her rail fare in cash and all her expenses.'

'Where did she stay?'

'I don't know, she never told me and it wasn't the sort of thing I could ask.'

'So how much cash did she draw?'

'A thousand pounds for every trip, she always said London was expensive.'

'A thousand? So how long were the trips?'

'They varied, depending on how busy we were, but she'd often go on a Monday afternoon, stay in London Tuesday, Wednesday and Thursday, then come home on a Friday afternoon.'

'So, although she said she was going to London, she could have gone anywhere? There were no receipts, hotel invoices, tickets or anything to show where she'd really been.'

'No, Mr Pemberton. Nothing. They were private trips, you see, not part of the estate's business, so she didn't keep records. That's what the Princess told me. She kept her private matters quite separate from estate matters.'

'And for business trips, she kept a record of her expenses?'

'Oh yes, she was very careful about that. She believed in keeping very accurate records.'

'She's made sure there are no records of her private outings, other than the fact her driver took her to the station and collected her when she came back?'

'That's right, Mr Pemberton.'

'Well, I suppose everyone needs a bit of personal space and privacy. Thanks for being so helpful, Georgina.' Pemberton was genuinely delighted with this young woman's response. 'Now I must leave you.'

'Mum should be back soon with Stephanie,' she smiled, leading him to the front door. 'I do hope you catch the man, Mr Pemberton.'

'If everyone was as co-operative as you, we'd have no problem,' he thanked her. 'And if you can think of anyone who might have a motive, I'd appreciate a call. Your work as Alicia's secretary might have introduced you to someone with a festering grudge of some kind. Call me if you recall anything, however minor.'

'Yes, I will. I'll miss her,' and Georgina closed the door behind Pemberton. Now it was time to return to the incident room.

The moment he entered, he was met by Lorraine who was very excited. She led him into his tiny office, first relating the result of the call about Lady Featley, and then asking Paul Larkin to join them.

'What's all this about?' he smiled at her. 'Have I won the lottery?'

'I don't know about that, sir,' and she remembered to use the formal address. 'But we've a prime suspect for you.'

'Really? Who?'

'Neil Potter, the man who tried to buy his farm.' She explained her theory, adding, 'He acted as spokesman for the parents when they ditched Alicia's schemes for art classes and the pantomime.'

'He's certainly been to the forefront of things so far as battling with Alicia was concerned,' Pemberton commented. 'But is that a strong enough motive for killing her?'

'He has a little boy at school, he attended her classes,' Lorraine told him. 'Maybe the child said something after one of those visits. If that happened, Potter might have erupted, particularly if he was still smarting over his failed farm purchase.'

'That was four years ago,' Pemberton reminded her. 'That's ample time to calm down.'

'You don't sound very enthusiastic, sir. I thought Potter was right in the frame now, at the very top in fact, well ahead of Constance Farrow. He's got two motives against her nil!'

'Point taken,' he told them. 'Funnily enough, I've just been talking about Potter. I've been to see Georgina Wallace.'

He provided details, stressing Georgina's view that Potter had reacted without anger or resentment; he also said Georgina believed Alicia was not abusing children although she had heard strong and enduring rumours to that effect, including those surrounding the rapid departure of the Robsons. He then told them about his conversation with Andy Nelson, stressing its confidential nature and adding that Nelson had a point about the care required by the detectives when dealing with the alleged child abuse by Alicia. Nelson was quite sure Alicia had been abusing children but suggested the Robsons' version of events be treated with caution. 'So we have two local but very opposing views,' he sighed. 'Nelson thinks she was abusing children, Georgina doesn't.'

'Rumour or not, it does provide a possible motive for someone, sir,' said Larkin. 'For lots of people, in fact. Even if the abuse stories are all based on rumours, we can't ignore them.'

'Right, so we need a witness if we are to substantiate them. Paul, see if you can find those Robsons. Put a team on to tracing them. Someone living locally might know where they've gone and why, and don't forget that Robson himself, if there is a man of the house, or even the child himself, would be a suspect. He – or they – will need to be eliminated.'

'Tracing them shouldn't be too much of a problem, sir.'

'No, but getting them to talk might be! We need to be discreet about all this, Paul. Imagine what the press would make of it if they knew we were conducting our enquiries on the basis of child abuse by the lady of the manor! God, I can imagine the tabloid headlines! For the sake of the children, we can't let that happen.'

'We've no names of other children who have been abused, have we?' Lorraine pointed out.

Larkin said, 'None. I ran a check for any cases of child abuse reported to the local police over the past ten years. There's none. No prosecutions, no reports, no allegations, no disproved complaints. Not even one from the Robsons.'

'There never will be any complaints from this village if the parents decide to remain silent,' Pemberton reminded them. 'If we persist with that line of enquiry, we'll get nowhere and we'll alienate potentially co-operative witnesses. Let's keep abuse-linked interviews on the back burners for a while.'

'You will resurrect them though, sir, when all other possibilities have been exhausted?' suggested Larkin.

'What other possibilities? There are none!' remarked Lorraine. 'It's the only motive we've got!'

'If Georgina Wallace is right, then Alicia was not an abuser,' stated Pemberton. 'And if she was not an abuser, then it's not a motive. We must look elsewhere, we must find other possibilities.'

'Where?' demanded Lorraine.

'Neil Potter for starters,' Pemberton acknowledged. 'Let's keep those two mums out of things for the time being. I don't want to involve children if I can help it. Potter does seem ambitious – he's already expanded by taking in the old ironworks. If we can get him thinking he's under suspicion, who knows what dirt he might reveal while trying to wriggle off the hook.'

'Does that mean we're keeping the entire child abuse line of enquiry out of contention for the moment?' asked Larkin. 'I need to know our policy if I'm to allocate actions.'

'Yes, Paul. I'd prefer to concentrate on finding other motives; keep the abuse theory as a second option. I am aware that if child abuse is the motive for her death, her killer might be someone she abused years ago, someone old enough to take his revenge in this way, someone not living in this village any more. But I want to concentrate on the village first.'

'I have a list of children who've left the school,' said Lorraine. 'It goes back several years and it includes those who've left the area – without their forwarding addresses, I might add. I didn't see the name of Robson there.'

'The family left some time ago, but it does provide some actions for your teams, Paul,' smiled Pemberton. 'Remember TIE – Trace, Interrogate and Eliminate. Have those former pupils interviewed starting with those living hereabouts. There's no need to mention child abuse. Just trace them and find out where they – or their parents – were yesterday morning, for purposes of elimination.'

'Right, sir. It'll be up to them to refer to any abuse if they think it relevant.'

'Exactly,' smiled Pemberton. 'I'm pleased that's settled. Now it's time for words with Neil Potter. Come on, Lorraine. This one's for both of us – oh, Paul?'

'Sir?'

'I might need SOCO to search Hagg End Farm, Potter's place. It sounds like a good spot to keep a rifle, or to hide one. Can you arrange for them to stand by, just in case?'

'They're still fingertip-searching the

scene, sir, and some are at the Hall.'

'Those at the scene could take a break if I need them for this. A change might do them good. Right, Lorraine. To Hagg End Farm we go – and then it's time I had words with that engine driver.'

Hagg End farmhouse was a traditional building of dark grey granite with blue tiles; it was known as a long house because the domestic quarters occupied one end of the long, low building, while the cattle and other livestock used the other. In days gone by, that system ensured a warm house in winter because the cattle were kept indoors. The warmth they generated permeated the entire building. The north-facing windows were small for the same reason – to limit the chill factor – while the south-facing windows enjoyed panoramic views across the dale and distant moors. Lying low to the north was the spread of fields, mainly arable and grazing but with two planted with oil seed rape and one with flax. As Pemberton drove into the yard he was impressed by the tidiness of the premises; all the buildings were clean and freshly painted, machinery was arranged in orderly lines with no discarded items left to rot and rust, and there was even a disused stone horse trough full of colourful spring flowers. A nice welcome.

'It's cleaner than some town houses I've

been to!' he commented to Lorraine as he eased the car to a halt. 'Come on, let's find our man.'

Pemberton rattled the brass knocker of the crisp white-painted back door. It was answered by a woman in a T-shirt and jeans; she was in her early forties and almost as tall as Lorraine, a big woman with dark hair held back with a red ribbon.

'Yes?' she asked.

'CID.' Pemberton showed his warrant card. 'I'm Detective Superintendent Pemberton and this is Detective Constable Cashmore.'

'It'll be about Miss Milverdale, is it?'

'Yes, we're members of the investigative team.'

'Do you want to see me or Neil?'

'Both,' Pemberton told her. 'We're interviewing everyone in the village.'

'You'd better come in. Excuse the mess in the kitchen but I'm in the middle of ironing.'

She led them into the sitting-room which had pleasing views to the south and was furnished in a rather old-fashioned way with dark-coloured furniture standing on a floral patterned carpet. There was a smell of old houses and Pemberton gained the impression the room had not altered since Potter's father lived here, or even his grandfather.

'Is your husband in?' he asked.

'He won't be long. He's gone to pick up Daniel – he visits a friend after school on Thursdays – then he's going to get some petrol and I asked him to pop into the shop for some washing-up liquid while he's out. You can wait if you want. Can I help?'

'We're interested in the whereabouts of everyone in Campsthwaite yesterday morning, Mrs Potter, especially between seven and eight o'clock. Alicia was found on the bluebell field, near Mill House, and we think she died between those times. We're anxious to establish if anyone was around at that time, or perhaps a little earlier and a little later; they might have seen a stranger or they might have seen Alicia.'

'Neil goes out early most mornings, Mr Pemberton, he likes to check his fences before he brings the cows in for milking. He can do a quick check while the cows are making their way into the buildings. He didn't say he'd seen anybody yesterday.'

'What time does he go out?'

'Just after seven, he's usually back by half past. By then, the cows have filed into the byre ready for milking.'

'Did he follow that routine yesterday? Is that something you would know?'

'He was back late yesterday, just a fraction. He said he'd found a hole in the fence, in our bottom field. He fixed it while the cows were coming in. There's a public footpath through our fields, it leads from the road outside here, down across our field to join Bottom Road near the wooden bridge over to the ironworks. Our fences often get broken by ramblers, they don't seem to respect anyone's property.'

'So what time did Neil return?'

'Getting on for eight, I think. It doesn't make much difference, the tanker doesn't come for the milk until mid-morning so we don't have to have our quota ready very early. The cows don't like being late, though.'

'Did he mention strangers? Or seeing Miss Milverdale?'

'He'd never see her from our bottom field, Mr Pemberton, nor strangers walking on her land. You can't see her land from there, or even from up here.'

'Did he say what had damaged the fence?'

'Ramblers almost certainly. That's what he said. Climbing over and putting their weight on the rails. They're a menace, Mr Pemberton, leaving gates open, dropping litter, running dogs among our livestock ... and they're so nasty if we remonstrate with them. They seem to forget we have to work in what they see as a playground or a theme park. Neil's very particular about keeping his fences in good order, he doesn't want any livestock to stray. The damage must have been done during Tuesday, otherwise he'd have seen it earlier.'

'Tuesday?'

'Yes, he would have checked his fences first thing on Tuesday morning and if there'd been a problem, he'd have fixed it straight away. So this damage must have been caused sometime later on Tuesday.'

'That suggests there were visitors in the village on Tuesday.'

'That's how I see it,' she agreed.

'Alicia died on Wednesday morning,' he reminded her. 'It might or might not be relevant, but thanks. Your husband is obviously a careful man and I noticed your premises are remarkably tidy, Mrs Potter.'

'We do our best – Neil's good like that. Miss Milverdale often complimented him on keeping such well-maintained fences and such a clean farmyard and buildings.'

'I understand Neil tried to buy the farm from the estate,' Pemberton continued.

'That was four years ago, Mr Pemberton. He had this idea for a caravan site on some wasteland and because the estate has a policy of not allowing caravans on to its property, we thought we could buy the farm. You do know, I would think, that with Alicia's death the tenants will be given a chance to buy their properties?'

Pemberton nodded. 'Yes, I know that. Will you buy yours? You also rent the old ironworks, don't you?'

'I'm not sure whether the ironworks would be included in the sale but if we can afford to buy the lot, then yes, we'd like to. Without a caravan site to generate extra cash, though, I doubt if we could raise the money. The snag is our local planners don't favour touring caravan sites because caravans clog up the country roads, generate queues and hamper emergency vehicles such as vets and doctors tending patients, not to mention the delays they cause to working farm vehicles and so on. The nuisance value has to be considered so we'll have to think about it all very carefully – we don't want to upset the villagers.'

'You've three years to make up your mind. Were you very upset when that first request was turned down?'

'Neil couldn't understand why we weren't allowed to buy it when it would be offered to us in due course, but he saw the reason eventually. Estate policy was behind the decision. He wasn't too upset, we hadn't set our hearts on owning the place, it was just an idea that came along when somebody said there was no caravan site in Campsthwaite.'

Pemberton was about to ask her views on Alicia and children when they heard a door bang, followed by a clatter of feet and then the sitting-room door burst open and in dashed a red-headed boy aged about nine. He was wearing long brown trousers and a small green cagoule.

'Mam, Stephen's got a new bike... Oh,' and he halted at the sight of the two visitors.

'It's expensive bringing up a child as well as running a farm! He's been wanting a new bike for ages, a mountain bike with umpteen gears,' grinned Mrs Potter. 'Is Daddy there, Daniel? Can you tell him there's someone to see him.'

The little boy turned around without a word and ran away, shouting, 'Dad, there's somebody to see you.'

'I'll make a cup of tea,' said Mrs Potter, rising to leave them now. 'Would you like one?'

'Not for me, thanks.' Pemberton did not wish to accept hospitality from a family who might find one of its members accused of murder.

Lorraine followed his example and declined. Then they heard a man's voice: 'In here, are they?' and both stood up to greet the arrival. A tall, powerful red-haired man materialised in the doorway and halted for a moment, looking at his visitors. In his mid-thirties, he wore corduroy trousers, a checked shirt and heavy shoes, but his thick red hair dominated the room. He was a man of striking appearance, fresh-faced from his outdoor work, clean-shaven and with dark brown eyes. That he was a strong man was not in doubt – he'd be strong in personality and strong in the physical sense.

'Potter,' he said, striding into the room. 'What can I do for you?'

Pemberton made the introductions when Potter indicated they should return to their seats. Pemberton then outlined the purpose of his visit with a brief account of Alicia's death.

'You've talked to Helen, have you?' he asked. 'She'd tell you all you want to know, I expect.'

'Most of it, yes, thanks. We'd like to know if you saw anyone when you were out yesterday morning. Fixing a fence, she said.'

'Damned ramblers, they claim to follow the country code but half of them have no idea what that means. If I had a pound for every gate they've left open and every fence they've damaged, I'd be a rich man!'

'Did you see the people responsible?' asked Pemberton.

'No, you never do! It wouldn't be so bad if they'd tell me they'd broken a rail, then I could fix it straight away. But they just cause the damage and clear off! Not even an apology.'

'When do you think it happened?'

'Tuesday afternoon, I reckon. If I'd seen them, I'd have asked them to pay for the timber and mebbe my time...'

'I'm trying to trace any strangers who might have been in the village yesterday morning.'

'Sorry, Mr Pemberton. I think this lot would have gone by then. But I never saw them so I can't help you anyway.'

'How long did it take to fix the fence?' Pemberton asked.

'Half an hour or so. I did it while the cows were heading for the byre, they go alone, you know, Mr Pemberton, at a very gentle pace once you've got 'em started. They find their own stalls and wait there until I arrive. While they were doing that, I had to go and find a hammer and some nails, and then get myself down there.'

'So you'd be there from what? Seven thirty?'

'About that, yes, till around eight. I can't be exact. It wasn't a long job.'

'Did you see anyone while you were working? On Bottom Road perhaps?'

'No, when you've got your head down determined to finish a job as fast as you can, you're not aware of folks passing by.'

'And shots? Did you hear a shot or shots while you were in the field?'

'No, never heard a thing, not with all my hammering and banging. But I doubt if I'd hear a shot from the bluebell field, we're a long way from it; unless there happened to be a north wind, which there wasn't.'

'Thanks.' Pemberton changed the direction of his questioning. 'Now, I understand you tried to buy your farm from the estate.'

'Helen explained all that, did she? And how we got the old ironworks. The estate was neglecting it, they've no staff for something that size, so I took it on. I'll grow corn there eventually. We've no secrets. You can't run a successful business if one partner keeps the other in the dark. We're partners, Mr Pemberton, good ones.'

'So you weren't too upset when you couldn't go ahead with your plans?'

'I was upset for a while, of course I was. I could see the potential for a caravan site even if I hated the bloody things; I'd make caravanners pay for bringing them into the countryside! But I've got over all that, it was four years ago. I hope you're not thinking it would make me take a pot shot at Alicia?'

'You keep guns on the premises?'

'I do, and you can examine every one of them if you want. I've three twelve-bores and a pair of .22s. Your records will show that anyway, and there's nothing hidden. Search the place if you want. I know we're all suspects, Mr Pemberton.'

'Everyone's a suspect until we eliminate them, Mr Potter, and I can tell you that we're not interested in shotguns, .22 rifles or air guns. Have you any other firearms on the premises? War trophies perhaps? Or is one missing, stolen by someone prowling in the area...?'

'No, nowt like that. I've never had any other gun and my dad didn't fight in the last war. Reserved occupation, you see, being a farmer. So he never had a soldier's gun. Have a look round if you don't believe me. And I do take care of my guns, I keep 'em securely locked like I'm obliged to, so nobody could pinch one.'

'Thanks. Now to another aspect of our enquiries. I understand you led a deputation to the school, to ask Mrs Donaldson to end her practice of allowing children to visit Miss Milverdale at Mill House.'

'I did, Mr Pemberton. Somebody had to. We've no parent-teachers' association so I did a ring-round of parents, got their opinions and decided to do summat about it. There's nothing sinister in that, is there?'

'We're interested in every aspect of Miss Milverdale's life.'

'Well, I know nowt about her private life, Mr Pemberton. She was a good landlady, I will say that, but as to what she got up to in private, well, that's nowt to do with me.'

'So why were the children's visits stopped?'

'There's been rumours, Mr Pemberton, for years, very unsavoury rumours. I know the local folks respected Miss Milverdale and most had a lot of time for her – them without children mainly – but that doesn't give her licence to mess about with our kids. We decided not to give her the chance. Keep the kids out of harm's way, that's our way of thinking. It's a simple answer. It's what we've always done.'

'Are you talking about child abuse?'

'Mebbe that's putting things a bit too strong, Mr Pemberton, but larking about with kids, taking liberties, well, that might be a better way of putting it.'

'The village people don't want to talk about it,' Pemberton said. 'I can understand that, they don't want their children involved in anything unsavoury.'

'Our aim is to stop problems before they start, like not letting your kid play with fireworks or not allowing them too close to deep water. My lad did go to Mill House, just once, then I stopped him going. I had talks with him and can assure you nowt happened but I can't say things didn't happen to other bairns. Mebbe it's all rumours, Mr Pemberton, I wouldn't know, but I'm not prepared to take that risk. And if kids have been interfered with, it's the sort of thing folks keep to themselves, family secrets, and if my lad had got into her clutches, I wouldn't be talking to you now. I wouldn't want Daniel involved in a police matter of that kind, not when parents can stop it ourselves, like we did.'

'Have you any proof of her paedophile activities, Mr Potter?'

'Nope, not a thing. Not a jot. I've never come across anybody who's actually been abused by Miss Milverdale. One family did leave in a bit of a rush a few years back, some said their little lad had said something about Alicia fondling him or touching him, but nothing happened as a result. Not to Alicia, I mean. Mind you, they were a queer family. Best out of the way, most of us reckoned. Mebbe it is all gossip, long-term gossip over many years, but it's better to be safe than sorry. Mind you, even though we stopped our bairns going to Mill House, the parents did say she could teach them pantomime and art at school, in school hours or afterwards, but always with at least one parent or teacher present. We never stopped her altogether, Mr Pemberton, we just thought of a way of keeping an eye on her.'

'Would any of the parents kill her if she interfered with their child?'

'No way, Mr Pemberton. I'd swear to that. If you want to find her killer, you'd be better looking somewhere else. We've dealt with our side of things in a civilised way without dragging our kids through the newspapers and courts. That's how we do things in Campsthwaite. We take our own action early on, like keeping weeds under control. But

we'd never kill the bloody woman, she had
her good points, you know, some very good
points. And she owned a fair portion of this
village. You've got to take all that into
account.'

'So you didn't kill her?'

'You know very well I didn't,' said Neil
Potter.

10

'Where are we going?' Lorraine asked when Pemberton drove from Hagg End Farm in the direction opposite to the one she expected.

'Along Bottom Road,' he told her. 'To see if Potter fixed that fence. He said the broken bit was at that end of the path, at the other side of the field near Bottom Road.'

As Potter had indicated, there was a gate and a length of wooden fencing near the public footpath sign. Judging by the marks around it, it seemed more people climbed over the fence than bothered to open the gate. Pemberton could see the new section. It was very distinctive against the older wood with shining new nail heads and clear evidence of someone having worked there very recently.

'He could have done this any time, but I think he was telling the truth. It was being done about the time Alicia died. I wonder if anyone saw him working?' Pemberton said as he returned to the car. 'That's a job for our teams – ask the early birds if anyone saw Potter and if so, what was he doing?'

'You don't think he's guilty, then?' she

asked as they drove up the steep hill to the incident room via a different route.

'I don't think so, but I could be wrong. He's provided an acceptable reason for being out of the house at the material time and he's satisfactorily explained his attempt to buy the farm and his part in ending Alicia's work with the children.'

'So what about searching his farm, Mark? For the rifle or whatever else we might turn up?'

'I have no grounds for doing it at this stage; besides, if Potter wanted to hide a rifle, he wouldn't do it on his own premises. If he'd shot Alicia with it, he'd have disposed of it long before he got home. On the other hand, I do think he's quite capable of handling something like a .303. He's very positive, Lorraine, and clearly ambitious but he's not angry, not the sort who'd lose control of himself. At least, that's my opinion. I won't activate our search teams, not yet anyway.'

'So he's not in the frame?'

'I don't think so, but let's keep him in mind – with a pale pink dot!' he grinned. 'What we need is a sighting of him yesterday morning, a witness who saw him fixing his fence would be useful. That would exonerate him altogether. Now, I must visit that train driver, he's the only witness we *know* to have been anywhere close to the murder scene around the material time.'

'I'll do more work on Constance's background.'

'Yes, don't be frightened to jump into a car and go to York or wherever you think is necessary. And don't ignore Alicia in all this – or the possibility of a connection between Alicia and Constance.'

'I'll do my best to dig deep,' she smiled.

'You're all right to take this on, are you?'

'Mark, for heaven's sake! Of course I'm all right ... I've told you, I'm not an invalid...'

'Just asking!' he smiled. 'Now, let me put something to you. Do you think we've been led off-course by rumours of child abuse? It might have no connection whatever with her death, a clever red herring to divert our attention from the real motive. Should we be concentrating more upon her tenants? Or is there another reason for her death? Something connected with inheritance? I'm going to have to rethink this right from the start. I need to establish where the key players were at the material time – and by that, I mean her staff. The snag is I don't know precisely when Alicia died. I think I know *where* she died even though Forensic haven't confirmed it yet. I'm sure she was shot where she fell. I'm sure her killer has great skills with a firearm, a professional ability, the sort you might acquire from military training. So why would such a person kill her? I *think* she died between seven and eight yesterday morning but I can't be absolutely sure. I don't know whether she died before or after visiting Mill House. All those uncertainties are no good in a murder investigation. There are too many imponderables. A lot of time is unaccounted for, Lorraine. Just one hour is enough for the killer to drive forty miles, enough for a hiker to be four miles away! We need to narrow down the time of death, we need to establish exactly where her staff members were at the precise moment she died. But that's an impossible task because we can't pinpoint the moment of death. It might even have been later than we think.'

'Later? How much later?'

'To be totally honest, I don't know.'

'I thought the pathologist had expressed his opinion about the time of death?'

'It was just an opinion, Lorraine. It was an approximate time. It's never an exact science unless someone saw it happen.'

'You did mention a reconstruction? Someone to walk the route she took and being timed along the way. Would that help?'

'Yes, it would, but it would be wise to stage it exactly one week after the death. Just in case there were people on the train who use it weekly or people who come through the village on a weekly basis, on Wednesdays.'

'I would agree with that. You seem to think

her estate workers are important?'

'I think they are. Take Jim Breckon. He was the last person to see her alive – apart from her killer. That puts him into the frame – he saw her leave at seven but not come back. And he gets his house as a gift now she's dead.'

'You've not interviewed him yet? As a suspect, I mean?'

'Not as a suspect. I need to get a better overview before I tackle him.'

'Overview? What do you mean, Mark?'

'Everyone says she did not come back to the Hall at her normal time of eight o'clock. But she might have done, Lorraine. She might have returned, gone inside for some reason and gone out again immediately, without anyone seeing her. And she might not have been trying to hide from them. At eight o'clock, each one of them would be doing his or her own work. It was often the case she was not seen actually returning to the Hall – she was seen *after* she had returned.'

'Breckon was working in the Hall when she was due back, the others were all due to start work at eight, except for Constance. She had her own hours. You're suggesting she might have come home and returned immediately to the bluebell field without anyone knowing?' Lorraine sounded surprised.

'It's not impossible.'

'I appreciate what you're saying. Constance rarely saw Alicia actually return to the Hall, did she? She'd be organising breakfast. I agree with you, Mark, it's quite possible that Alicia could come and go without being seen. She'd know where every member of staff was at any given time too, useful if she wanted to *avoid* being seen.'

'Right. Constance said Alicia was good at informing her about any change to her routine. But on this occasion, she didn't do so. Why?'

'Go on. Mark.'

'I wonder if Alicia was trying to do something secretive? Trying to avoid being seen by her staff? What sort of routine do the staff members have at that time of day?' he mused. 'I'm thinking of what they do minute by minute.'

'That's something we'll have to establish, Mark. They're the only people who might have seen her in her usual haunts, or not seen her as the case may be.'

'This supports what I said earlier, doesn't it?' He concentrated on his driving and changed down a gear as the gradient grew steeper. 'I'm beginning to think Alicia's rumoured antics are of secondary importance or even totally irrelevant. Instead, we need to establish, minute by minute, the time and place of every stride of Alicia's final walk, and the minute by minute position of all her staff.'

'You need a choreographer. It'll mean interviewing them all again, to establish that.'

'That's not a bad thing to do, pin them down to where they were at any given moment, and I include Constance in that equation.'

'She'd be devastated if she knew what you were thinking, Mark.'

'I think she's a very clever and cunning person – she needs to be out-thought by us, Lorraine. Even the cleverest killers make mistakes.'

They were cresting the rise of this quiet back route through Campsthwaite and their road emerged on to the main street, almost opposite the Miners Arms. Pemberton completed his drive to the institute. It was ten minutes to six and Detective Inspector Larkin was at his desk when Pemberton and Lorraine entered.

'We've two things to report, Paul,' Pemberton said. 'First – I don't think Potter is our man. He could have done it, I can't argue with that. He had the time and opportunity, he might even have had a motive, but he's not a killer. Forthright, blunt even, but not a killer. Give him a pink dot, we might want to talk to him again, then we'll search his premises. But not now.'

'Right, sir. And the second thing?'

'The movements of Alicia. There's a possibility – a slight one perhaps – that she could have returned from her walk around eight o'clock unseen by any of her staff, and then returned to the bluebell field at a time we've not considered. She could have died later than we thought.'

'I thought the pathologist had stated the time of death? Between seven and eight.'

'He was not specific, Paul. We know she was alive at seven, two witnesses say so. We don't *know* whether she was alive or dead at eight, an hour later. I'll talk to the staff again, Paul. And Constance Farrow.'

'It's always worth double-checking times, sir,' Larkin agreed.

'I'll talk to Jim Breckon at the same time, he's got to be eliminated from the enquiry. And another thing – I need sightings of Neil Potter yesterday morning. He was fixing a fence on Bottom Road around seven thirty; I've seen the repair but it would help if someone actually saw him working on it.'

'I'll include that in the next batch of actions, sir.'

'Right. So have you got a time chart running?'

'Yes, sir, on the computer.'

'Has it revealed anything worthwhile?'

'No. The statement readers have been asked to abstract any reference to people's whereabouts between seven and eight yesterday morning, and half an hour either side of those times, but nothing much has emerged. The only person near the bluebell field at the material time was Geoff Midgley; he was there just after seven to bring his cows in for milking. Constance Farrow got there around twelve, looking for Alicia. No one else was there – except for the passing train.'

'The driver's next on my list of interviewees,' said Pemberton. 'I'm off to see him now. Lorraine, what are you doing?'

Larkin said, 'There is a message for Lorraine, sir. From York police. Lady Consate died in 1994 – no suspicious circumstances. She was ninety-seven years old. A neighbour, still living next door to Holfield House, remembers Constance Farrow but is rather vague about it all. She thought Constance left some time before Lady Consate died.'

'Thanks,' smiled Lorraine. 'And now, sir,' she addressed Pemberton, 'I want to continue enquiries into Constance, I've several lines of enquiry. Then there's Northumbria police to contact about interviewing Miss Baines. She lives at Hexham.'

'Right, you concentrate on Constance, Lorraine. Paul, you could ask Northumbria police to interview Miss Baines.'

'Right. I'll see to that.'

'Good, and now I'm off. I'll be on the mobile if I'm needed, Paul, but I should be back before you close the shop.'

Eric Morgan lived on an estate of smart Victorian terraced houses called Turnbull Park at Rainesbury. His home was number 27, Harbour Street, a clean, well-maintained house of three storeys with a splendid bay window overlooking the street, but lacking a garden or parking space.

Pemberton eased to a halt outside, mounted the steps and rang the doorbell. Morgan answered and Pemberton introduced himself. Grey-haired, balding and in his early fifties with a slight stoop, he bade a welcome to Pemberton. He was wearing a pale blue open-necked shirt, grey trousers and carpet slippers.

He invited Pemberton into his front room. Warmly furnished, it was very comfortable, a family room with a caged budgerigar in one corner.

'The wife has put the kettle on,' he said slowly. 'So, Mr Pemberton, what can I do for you?'

As Mark Pemberton outlined details of the investigation, Mrs Morgan appeared with a tray of tea and scones, placed them on a table and vanished without a word. Morgan poured a cup for himself and his guest, handed him a scone thickly covered with butter and waited for Pemberton to begin his questions.

'You leave Rainesbury at seven every morning, I believe?' began Pemberton.

'Yes, except Sundays. It's a two-coach diesel, we run from Rainesbury to Long Barfield, it's the up line, we call it the commuter run. Arrive Long Barfield at 7.50. It's that new town, full of offices, supermarkets and shops. We carry lots of workers into Long Barfield, specially from villages along the line such as Campsthwaite. Then we do the run in reverse, leaving Long Barfield at eight on the dot and getting back into Rainesbury at 8.50, in time for commuters to get to work.'

'So what time do you pass through Campsthwaite?'

'On the up run, we arrive at 7.21 and leave at 7.22; return or down run, 8.28 arrival, leaving 8.29.'

'Our officers will be visiting stations *en route*, Mr Morgan, to talk to regular commuters, especially those on the up line. We might put some on board to catch those travelling in both directions. Are you the only official on board?'

'Yes, we did away with guards a few years ago. Folks get their tickets locally, some have season tickets, and the station staff are responsible for checking tickets. So I'm alone.'

'Good, now cast your mind back to yesterday. We have reason to believe our victim died between 7 a.m. and 8 a.m. It could be later but we'll concentrate on that hour for the moment. Every morning, she went for a walk, Mr Morgan, leaving home at seven. She lived in a big house, it's on your right, on a hill, as you leave Campsthwaite station. Milverdale Hall. Her name is Alicia Milverdale.'

'The Hall, I know it by sight. She walked across the viaduct, didn't she? Some mornings. That lady. Over the viaduct which crosses the line near the Hall? Then down the fields towards the stepping stones. If she was on the bridge while I was passing under, I'd give a toot and she'd wave back. Most mornings she'd be well down the fields by the time I passed and I'd give a toot there. That's where I mostly saw her, down near the beck.'

'Which side of the beck, Mr Morgan?'

'My side, the railway side.'

'Did you ever see her at the other side, where the bluebells are growing?'

'No, Mr Pemberton. Never.'

'Thanks. Go on, Mr Morgan.'

'Well, she was one of my regulars, that's what I called her, people we pass on the trip and hoot at.' Morgan spoke wistfully. 'Is it her, then? Who's been murdered?'

'Yes, I think we're talking about the same

lady, Mr Morgan.'

'Good God, how terrible...'

'So did you see her yesterday?'

'Yes, on the viaduct like I said. Walking across, quite briskly I thought, rushing back to get something maybe? This is terrible, Mr Pemberton. To think I knew somebody who's been murdered ... well, I never knew her, not even her name, but you know what I mean.'

'Rushing back, you say?'

'Yes, going towards the Hall.'

'Not heading for the stepping stones, then?'

'No, that's why I thought it was funny.'

'Always alone was she, when you saw her?'

'Yes, always. I never saw her with anybody else.'

'And yesterday? Was she alone?'

'Yes, same as usual. I didn't see her every morning, Mr Pemberton, sometimes we missed each other. Mebbe she'd be a bit late or a bit early, and mebbe I would be. In fact, I was a bit late yesterday.'

'How much late?'

'Only a minute or two. There was a horse on the line just out of Rainesbury and it made me four or five minutes late, no more. I did see her, though. Around half seven it would be, mebbe seven thirty-two or three.'

'How much of her could you see?'

'Well, in the fields, most of her. She often

wore jeans and waved. On the viaduct, it was head and shoulders.'

'So, yesterday, could you see if she was carrying anything?'

'I'd say not, Mr Pemberton. Her arms were swinging, like she was marching.'

'And can you be sure it was the same woman you saw each time?'

'Tall, middle-aged, dark brown hair...'

'Sounds about right,' said Pemberton.

He realised that Alicia could have shortened her walk, omitted a visit to Mill House perhaps, and hurried back to the Hall for some reason – the timing was about right for a return just before eight. If Morgan had seen her completing her normal walk it meant she *had* returned to the Hall just before eight – without anyone else seeing her. That meant she must have returned to the bluebell field and been shot on the second trip. She could have been back in the field by eight thirty or so. An hour's discrepancy in the estimated time of death was not out of the ordinary. But *had* she gone straight back? And why make the second journey?

'Did you notice anyone else, Mr Morgan? Either on the viaduct or in the fields or beside the beck and stepping stones?'

'Never saw a soul, Mr Pemberton. Not that I gaze around very much. I have to keep my eyes on the line but when she was directly above me on that viaduct, well, you couldn't miss her. Not that I've ever had time for a close look at her, I wouldn't know her if I met her in the street. She was just a figure I happened to see once in a while.'

'A friendly figure on your lonely trip?'

'Yes, she was. She was nice, waving at me like she did, especially if she was the lady from that big house.'

'Did you ever meet her? In town, or at the station or anywhere?'

'No, never.'

'So if another person was there around the time you expected Miss Milverdale, would you know the difference?'

'Not really, unless there was summat striking about them, like a bright orange cagoule or something.'

'So the person on the viaduct yesterday might not have been Miss Milverdale? It might not have been the lady you normally saw near the beck?'

'Oh, I'm sure it was, Mr Pemberton. There's never been anybody else about at that time of day. Who else could it have been?'

'Who indeed? So let's think about your return journey yesterday morning. You'd pass the bluebell field and go under the viaduct just before half past eight, wouldn't you? On your way back to Rainesbury via Campsthwaite station.'

'Yes, I'd made up my lost time. I never saw anybody then. I've never seen the lady on that return run, Mr Pemberton.'

'Mr Morgan, if she died at the time we believe, between seven and eight, she would have been lying in that field of bluebells when you passed by. She'd have been there during your return run around half past eight.'

'Oh, that's dreadful ... really awful ... to think I was so close and had no idea...'

'So were you aware of anyone in that field when you returned? Either lying there, walking, standing, alone or with someone else?'

'No, I never saw anybody, Mr Pemberton. The snag is with me approaching the station on the down run, looking out for signals and things on the line, I couldn't stare around but even if I had, I don't think I'd have seen anybody lying in the grass or among those flowers. There again, if she'd been wearing one of those bright coloured waterproofs, then I might have seen her. But I didn't, I saw nothing. Nothing caught my eye. But, as I said, I didn't look at the field.'

'You've been very helpful, Mr Morgan. Thank you for your time.'

'I've not been much help, have I? I saw nothing suspicious, Mr Pemberton. Sorry. I hope some of my passengers can help you. But I can't get over this, me seeing that lady on those daily runs and now she's been murdered...'

With daylight fading, Pemberton returned to the incident room before it closed for the day and reported his interview with Morgan.

'Paul,' he said to Larkin afterwards. 'Tomorrow morning, I need a few teams on the 7 a.m. train out of Rainesbury. I don't want to wait until next Wednesday. They should ride with the commuters and talk to them; if I know my commuters, they'll sit in the same seat every morning and it's quite possible someone was gazing out of the window as the train passed the bluebell field. That applies to the return journey as well. Three teams, do you think? There's only two coaches.'

'Right, sir. Consider it done.'

'And we could repeat the drill next Wednesday if nothing turns up.'

'I'll see to it, sir.'

'If the driver saw Alicia – or someone else – the chances are that a passenger also saw her. Make sure your teams check that point, Paul.'

'Right, sir. Now, our man Potter.'

'Yes. Paul.'

'I tried HOLMES. His name was on file. He did fix that fence yesterday morning. The milkman came along Bottom Road at

7.35 a.m. on Wednesday and saw Potter working on the fence.'

'Did he!'

'The milkman didn't see anyone else, he's sure about that. And he never heard any shots. Mind, he's a long way from the bluebell field, but it does provide an alibi for the milkman as well as Potter!'

'So Potter was telling the truth even if he didn't mention the milkman! If he was mending his fence, he couldn't have shot Alicia who was about a mile away at the time. Now, consider another scenario. Alicia leaves the Hall at seven – that's confirmed. She goes on her walk but for some reason hurries back to the Hall and gets there before eight. Just before eight.'

'You've a reason for saying this?'

'The train driver saw a woman crossing the viaduct, heading *towards* the Hall around seven thirty, perhaps a minute or two afterwards.'

'She could have been back in the bluebell field by eight thirty, couldn't she, if she'd done a quick about-turn?'

'Yes, Paul, she could. It means we might have to rethink it all, from the timing aspect. And, of course, it means her second trip was not planned in advance, so anyone familiar with Alicia's normal routine would have been thrown off course a little... If she was killed on the second trip, it doesn't sound as if someone could have been lying in wait for her.'

'We need further words with the pathologist, sir.'

'We do indeed!'

'Elimination, sir, it's all a question of elimination. Didn't Sherlock Holmes say something along those lines?'

'He said a lot of very profound things, Paul, but he wasn't a real detective! Even so, I must try to deduce things as he did. But I think the quote you have in mind is, "When you have eliminated the impossible, whatever remains, however improbable, must be the truth." It means that if Alicia returned to the field, at eight thirty or thereabouts, Potter could have killed her after fixing his fence and crossing the old ironworks – it's his rented land, he could cross it unseen by anyone from the village.'

'That's if he wasn't milking his cows, sir.'

'And let's not forget the footprints found at the scene. Apart from mine, Lorraine's, PC Wardle's and Constance's, only Alicia's were there.'

'Supporting the idea that Alicia was shot from a distance?'

As they talked, Inspector Brian Fowler entered the incident room; he looked tired and dirty and one of the civilian staff, Jennie, asked, 'You look as if you could do with a cup of tea, Brian?'

'I could murder one, and a sandwich!' he said, then he spotted Pemberton. 'Oh, hello, sir, I didn't see you there.'

'I wouldn't say no to a cup as well. Can you get someone to brew up, Paul?'

As the three senior officers awaited their tea, they chatted about inconsequential matters before Pemberton said, 'Right, into my office for a bit of peace and quiet. Are you ready to tell us how things went at the scene, Brian?'

'Yes, sir, I've ended the search for today, the darkness beat us again. We've almost finished, though – I reckon a good morning tomorrow should see us through.'

'Any interesting developments?' asked Pemberton, fearing a negative answer; had there been something very positive, he would have been told earlier.

''Fraid not, sir.' Fowler shook his head. 'The house first. We've given it a thorough dusting for prints, sir, inside and out, and then we searched for anything that might be evidence of the crime, or linked to it. There is no evidence the shot was fired from there. We did bear in mind what you'd told us about children using the house.'

'And?'

'We've recovered several sets of prints, sir, palm prints and fingerprints. Children by the look of them. We'll have them processed and printed out tomorrow, but we need control samples if we're to put names to them.'

'We haven't fingerprinted any children yet, but these prints do prove that children did visit Mill House.'

'Yes, sir. We found some art materials in a cupboard, easels, sheets of cartridge paper, paint, brushes, that sort of thing. Lots, of children's prints were there.'

'And that odd bedroom?'

'More prints, sir, on glossy surfaces. The mirrors on the dressing-table, in the bathroom, sides of chests of drawers, wardrobe doors and so on. And adult markings – Alicia's, we think, judging by the quantity of them and their position in the kitchen, for example, on the back door and so on. We can identify hers, of course, from prints taken from her body.'

'Anything to prove child abuse?' Pemberton asked.

'Nothing, sir. No dirty videos or drawings, no sex aids, no mucky books or photographs. Just loads of costumes, everything from the Three Bears to Snow White and the Seven Dwarfs. It's like the costume department of the Theatre Royal.'

'So we can't prove any child abuse from what's in Mill House?'

'No, sir. Not a bit of it. It shows she had children in there for dressing up and for art lessons. There's nothing sinister in that.'

'So what about the rest of the scene?'

'We've found rubbish both in the bluebell field and in the woods around Mill House and the field. Discarded household stuff, most of it, some litter dropped by ramblers like drinks cans and plastic wrappings – we can discount those because many of them have their sell-by dates on. They were dropped last year, many of them.'

'No spent bullets or shells? I'm keen to know whether you've found another of the kind we recovered from Alicia's body. He might have fired more than one shot – missed her with the first, for example.'

'We've not found any, sir.'

'So it seems the killer did fire just the one shot. A marksman, to be sure. How about the path through the wood?'

'It was sealed off by our men. We checked it from the gate that opens into the village, down through Mill Wood and all the way to the house; there were no fresh vehicle or cycle tyre marks, no fresh footprints... I'm certain chummy did not enter the bluebell field that way, sir.'

'And we're sure he didn't enter by the farmyard, aren't we?'

'Yes, we've had further words with Mrs Midgley. She works in her kitchen from about six thirty every morning, washing eggs and getting breakfast and doing a host of preparatory daily chores ... she saw nothing.'

'And her husband?'

'Him too, sir. I've spoken to both of them. They can't tell us anything. And our teams searched the rough areas of woodland, sir, where there are no formal footpaths. One of our lads has studied survival techniques, and he says no one has trampled through the rough woodland to reach the bluebell field.'

'Does that mean chummy gained access to the murder scene by the stepping stones?' asked Pemberton.

'I don't think so. There's nothing to suggest he crossed the stepping stones. The only prints we found there, at the bluebell field side of the stones, were those of Alicia and Constance. There were some cattle hoof prints nearby, but not enough to obliterate the marks.'

'Incoming marks, were they Alicia's?' Pemberton asked. 'Marks made as she was entering the field?'

'Yes, sir. Toes pointing towards the bluebells. One set of her shoe prints, that's all. Two sets of Constance's, coming and going.'

'She came that way only once, you think? She didn't pay two visits to the bluebell field?'

'I'd say not, sir, her prints look about the same age, all made by the same pair of shoes at the same time. Just one line of them, a single journey. We didn't find any prints in the field at the far side of the beck, by the way, the ground there is too solid, not soft like the bluebell field.'

'Nothing left by the killer then?'

'Nothing, sir,' confirmed Fowler.

'So there's only one conclusion,' Pemberton savoured the hot tea, 'and it's something we've suspected all along. The gunman is an expert shot and he fired from a distance. He did not enter those woods, Mill House or the bluebell field. He did not enter the murder scene, he didn't even come to the scene to check whether his victim was dead. There is no trace of him at or near the scene, Brian. You've found nothing because there is nothing. The fact he did not check whether his victim was alive or dead means he's a very confident shot. If this was the result of someone firing indiscriminately, letting off shots just for the hell of it, we'd have found more stray bullets. It's murder, I'm sure of that, murder by a trained marksman.'

'I think he fired from somewhere between the stream and the railway line,' said Fowler. 'There are alders to provide cover along the banks of the beck.'

'What does Dr Preston think about all this, Brian? You've kept him informed?'

'He's been there most of the time, sir, doing his own research. He was still there when I left.'

'Working late, was he?'

'He wanted to check a theory about the origin of the fatal shot. He said he'd contact you if there was any development.'

'He's cutting it a bit fine!' smiled Pemberton, glancing outside. 'It's almost dark now ... What was his theory, Brian, any idea?'

'I think he'd reached a conclusion about the trajectory of the shot, sir. He had based his theories on the power of a .303 rifle, the elevation of the shot, the angle of entry into the skull and the height of the victim.'

'Well, I hope he comes up with something. We've absolutely nothing,' and at that moment the door opened and in walked Dr Jack Preston, smiling broadly.

'Hi, Mark, Paul, Brian.'

'You look cheerful!' observed Pemberton.

'I've found the firing point of our fatal shot, gentlemen,' he said.

11

'Brilliant!' beamed Pemberton. 'So where is it?'

'The fork of a young rowan tree, just below shoulder height to someone your size. It's on the island formed by the mill race.'

'How did you find it?' Pemberton was both pleased and surprised.

'A bit of luck, I suppose. We all need a bit of luck in a case like this—'

'It wasn't luck, sir,' chipped in Inspector Fowler. 'It was hard work and skill, using ingenuity aided by countless geometrical diagrams which meant nothing to me.'

'Well, after taking into account all the relevant factors, I examined every likely firing site around the bluebell field. And bingo, I found this one.'

'So what did chummy do? Can we establish that?' Pemberton was delighted.

'Almost certainly, he crossed the river from the side furthest away from the bluebell field. By that, I mean he came via the field between the beck and the railway line. There's no bridge or stepping stones at that point so it's probable he waded across. It's shallow there, eighteen inches deep at the most with a rocky bed. From that island, you get a very clear view of the entire bluebell field. Once there, he waited for her, and to steady his aim he rested the barrel of the gun in that convenient fork.'

'How do you know that?'

'He removed a tiny growth from the fork. It was only an inch long, an infant branch, but it must have been in the way of the barrel as he rested the gun there. He broke it off to allow the barrel to sit securely. We found the twig on the ground. Needless to say, we've retained it for examination – it might provide some information.'

'That was careless, leaving something behind!' said Pemberton.

'It was not the sort of thing a hired assassin would do,' remarked Preston. 'A true professional would not leave anything, not even something so apparently insignificant as a broken twig. Secondly, there are footprints in the ground. Large ones, smooth soles with studs in them. We've managed to isolate two marks, a left and a right.'

'Hiking boots?'

'No, I don't think so. Waders, more likely.'

'The sort used by fishermen?' Pemberton suggested.

'I think so. And thirdly, we found the ejected shell. It's from a .303 rifle, wartime ammo by the look of it. If we can find the gun which fired it we can make a match, but I'm going to compare it with the bullet recovered from Alicia's head. I'm sure there'll be a match. In my opinion, Mark, she was killed by a well-aimed shot from that point. Just one shot, quite deliberately aimed at her head.'

'You searched for more ejected shells?'

'We did, but found none.'

'It was no accident, then.'

'Not in my opinion. I'd say it was someone who knew she would be there. The firing point could have been determined in advance, part of the preparation for the murder. It's well hidden for one thing, and it's not the sort of place you'd come across and use spontaneously. A perfect place for a sniper, in other words.'

'I'd like to see it,' Pemberton said.

'Sure, you'll need to see it in daylight, Mark. I'll be there tomorrow. What time can you be there?'

'I've two conferences in the morning, detectives at nine thirty, press at ten thirty.'

'Early rather than later would be better,' said Preston.

'Eight o'clock then?' suggested Pemberton. 'Before things get busy?'

'Right,' said Preston. 'Don't go to the island, go to Mill House, we've finished with it now. Eight o'clock it is. I'll escort you from there. There is a small footbridge over to the island, as you know.'

'What do you hope to find?'

'We won't know until we find it, will we?' grinned Preston, giving the stock answer.

'Tomorrow morning, I'll have officers on the early train which passes the site, quizzing passengers,' Pemberton told the forensic scientist. 'Can the island be seen from the railway line?'

'No,' said Preston. 'I checked that. The line runs through a cutting as it goes under the viaduct and then the cutting develops into an embankment on the up line. Between the cutting and the island, there's an elevated chunk of land. It's part of the field which rises above the beck as it stretches up to the end of the viaduct – it blocks the view so you can't see the island from the railway line.'

'Pity, but you can see the bluebell field from the embankment.'

'Yes, the passengers might have seen him before or after he was on the island, making his way to or from it.'

'We'll do our best, Jack. Right, this could be the breakthrough we've been waiting for. The teams are coming in. I'll talk to them before they leave – this could give them the boost they need as they tackle tomorrow! I take it the island is preserved?' and Pemberton glanced at Larkin.

'Yes, sir, it's secure.'

'Good, right, let's talk to the troops and see if they've anything to tell us.'

By eight thirty, most of the detectives had returned to the incident room to log their reports and file their statements. Mugs of tea and coffee appeared as if by magic and while they savoured these, Pemberton stood on the stage to address them.

'Tomorrow morning,' he said, 'I need three teams to travel on the 7 a.m. train out of Rainesbury to Long Barfield, and to remain on board as it executes the return journey. Every regular passenger has to be quizzed to see if they saw anything or anyone from the train as it passed the bluebell field on both the up and the down journeys. Don't ignore the possibility that the gunman could have used the train. Had he time to shoot Alicia and catch the train on its return journey? Also, I want to consider anyone seen later near the bluebell field. I can't entirely rule out the possibility that Alicia went back to the Hall about eight, then returned almost immediately to the bluebell field or Mill House. Now, more news. Dr Preston has identified the site from which the fatal shot was fired. I'll be looking at it tomorrow – it's the little island between Cam Beck and Mill House, and that is confidential information at this stage. For your ears only. Now, anything special to report, anyone? PC Wardle, how about you?'

'I got around most of the men who could possibly have been shooting in that field yesterday morning, sir, but they all deny being there. There's not many rabbits around, it's the close season for pheasants and partridge, and my local poachers aren't very active. Besides, these men use twelve-bores, not .303 rifles. Since I was posted to Campsthwaite, sir, I've seen every firearm certificate in the village and in the years I've been here, I've never come across anyone authorised to keep a .303. I've made more enquiries about ex-military men in the village, but they can all account for their movements and none kept a firearm as a souvenir. There's only two, as you know. If it's any help, sir, I don't think the killer is a local man.'

'I respect your local knowledge, PC Wardle,' said Pemberton. 'And why use a .303 when all those other weapons are so easily available? Now, what about the other villagers? Have you talked to any of them?'

'Yes, sir, several, but I've not found anyone who saw anyone remotely suspicious yesterday. You can't see the bluebell field from anywhere in the village and hardly anyone goes there, and I didn't overlook the approach paths and roads, sir. Nothing.'

'Well done.'

'One thing, sir. Constance Farrow was in the village yesterday – she came to the shop.

It was around mid-morning, she was doing the weekly shopping for the Hall.'

'Thanks. Now, what about a family called Robson? Does that mean anything to you?'

'Inspector Larkin mentioned them, sir. They left before I was posted here but people still talk about them. They weren't very nice folks, never paid their bills, always fighting in the street, causing strife among the neighbours, that sort of thing. They left after making some kind of complaint about Miss Milverdale, something she was supposed to have done to their son, but whatever it was, they didn't take it any further. They just packed their bags and disappeared up to Scotland, so I'm told.'

'Thanks. Keep asking around.'

As Pemberton moved from one detective to another who'd had some special task to undertake, the answers produced nothing of value. He'd now come to expect that kind of result.

'All right, time to go home,' said Pemberton. 'Those of you not going on the train journey should be here tomorrow at 9 a.m. The start of another day.'

Then the telephone rang. One of the civilian staff, Lucy Bates, picked up the receiver. 'Mr Pemberton, it's for you. Detective Constable Warner from Hove.'

'I'll take it in my office,' he said. 'Paul, you'd better listen in to this one,' and moments later he was listening to Karen Warner's story.

'I couldn't find any record of a police investigation into Audrey Milverdale's death, sir, most of our records have been destroyed anyway, but I did check the local paper and found nothing there. I went along to the Registrar's office. Her death is recorded there, on 7th September 1947 as you said. She died in St Anne's Maternity Home, sir, and the cause of death is given as 'complications arising from childbirth'. Her place of birth, which is on the death certificate, is Milverdale Hall, sir, in Campsthwaite, so we are talking about the same person.'

'Childbirth, you said?' He wanted that to be confirmed.

'Yes, sir, that's the only cause of death on the certificate and it was certified by a doctor. There would be no post-mortem or inquest, sir.'

'Right. So there was a child! I wonder what happened to it? Do you know if it also died?'

'No, sir, it didn't. I checked in the register of birth certificates. Audrey gave birth to a little girl, sir, the day before she died. 6th September 1947. She was registered as Beatrice but Audrey was married, sir, not a single woman as you believed. The entry implies she was a married woman.'

'Married? Go on, Miss Warner. Who was the husband?'

'It doesn't say husband, sir, it just names the father of the child. Roderick, Roderick Milverdale. And she was Milverdale – I assumed they were man and wife.'

'Roderick? He wasn't her husband, she wasn't married! But it could be her brother – or her father! Roderick is a family name, Miss Warner, and her brother was called Roderick. God, have we a case of incest? But why would she name him as the father even if it was true? There's no wonder Alicia didn't want any press interest... Sorry, Miss Warner. I'm waffling on and I interrupted you. Is there anything else we should know? Clearly, those certificates won't show what happened to the child.'

'No, they don't, but I followed that up, sir, being keen on family history research. Beatrice was adopted, sir. I've found a certified copy of the certificate in the Adopted Children Register. She was adopted by a family called Hammond. She became Beatrice Hammond. They lived in Hove – as you know, the address of the adoptive parents is given on those certificates. The man was called Simon Hammond and he was a railway worker – his occupation is on the adoption certificate too. His wife was called Jean and she is described as a housewife.'

'Beatrice Hammond – I wonder where she is now?' he muttered.

'The family moved to York, sir, Mr Hammond was offered promotion; I spoke to a lady who lived next door to them. She's elderly now, but she remembers the Hammonds as very nice people who adopted a baby girl and then moved to York. Beatrice was their only child, she said; they moved to York in 1952, she thinks, before Beatrice started school. She can't remember the address now. For a while she got Christmas cards from the Hammonds, but they stopped a long time ago. She's completely lost touch now.'

'Miss Warner, this is excellent. You've done exceedingly well in a very short time. You'll put this in writing, won't you? For our files. And thanks for your efforts. I appreciate the work you've done.'

'Thank you, sir,' she said, replacing the telephone.

'Now there's an intelligent young detective,' he said to Paul Larkin who had been listening on an extension. 'You got all that?'

'I did, sir. Bloody amazing, isn't it? What put you on to this angle?'

'It was because the monument in the parish church describes Audrey's death as sudden. As you and I know, that often means a police investigation, although our meaning of "sudden" might differ from the public's perception. However, we've found a possible heir, Paul, a blood relation no less! I wonder if this was incest? But whatever the origin of this child, she is a secret heir, a woman called Beatrice Hammond. And that provides a motive perhaps?'

'But if she was adopted, sir, isn't she denied any inheritance?'

'An adopted child cannot inherit a title, Paul, but if old Mr Milverdale's Deed of Trust refers specifically to blood relatives – which it does – then this Beatrice has a double dose of Milverdale blood! Talk about keeping it in the family! Audrey must have provided the father's name to keep up appearances – after all, she was in Hove, a long way from home, and she must have thought no one would know Roderick was her brother! An easy deception to make, to imply she was married without actually saying so.'

'It could have been rape, sir,' said Larkin. 'Raped by her brother, or her father ... her way of getting revenge perhaps? Keeping the record straight? Naming him in an official document? And she, being an honest woman, wouldn't want to commit a criminal offence by making a false declaration...'

'You could be right. But her father was dead by then, wasn't he? Old Mr Milverdale? It must have been her brother.

Whatever her parentage, Beatrice, wherever she is, has three years to learn about her inheritance and decide what to do. I wonder if she was a normal healthy child?'

'The solicitors didn't know about her?'

'Not according to Mr Browning. If there is nothing in the family records, it seems the Milverdales decided to reject the infant. That happened a lot, you know, in the past.'

'And she was born on 6th September 1947?'

'The same day as Constance Farrow,' Pemberton reminded Larkin.

'You think Constance is the heir, don't you, sir? But she provided details of her family background, jobs and so on, didn't she? The name of Hammond never cropped up, did it?'

'Her childhood was in York, Paul, so some discreet enquiries are needed there before we tackle Constance about this. Let's keep this to ourselves for the time being, although I will tell Lorraine; she's been delving into Constance's background. I wonder if she's turned up anything interesting?'

It was midnight when Lorraine returned home. Pemberton was waiting.

'Overtime, eh?' he smiled. 'Have you eaten?'

'I got a take-away,' she said. 'But I'm shattered...'

'Tramping around York is always tiring... You've finished there, have you?'

'No, I have to go back tomorrow. I'll go straight from home, if that's all right with you.'

'Of course, so now to bed,' he said. 'I'll bring you a cup of hot milk, shall I?'

'Please,' she sighed. 'And then I'll tell you all about my day...'

But she was in bed and fast asleep when he entered the bedroom only ten minutes later. He did not disturb her.

At seven o'clock on Friday morning, six detectives boarded the two-coach diesel which ran from Rainesbury to Long Barfield. Detective Sergeant Rogers was in charge and he had familiarised himself with its route and timing, particularly after leaving Campsthwaite and passing the bluebell field.

At eight o'clock, Pemberton, leaving Lorraine asleep in bed, arrived at Mill House and was escorted to the island by Jack Preston. They used a route approved by the forensic scientist, crossing the mill race by the narrow footbridge.

'You don't think he came this way then? Over the bridge and through the grounds of the house?'

'No,' said Preston. 'The prints we found

suggested he came from the opposite direction.'

'Out of the river?'

'Yes, by wading across. We need to search the banks for more footprints now it's daylight.'

By this stage, they were on the small island. Twenty yards long by ten yards wide with stony shores and a rock-strewn base, it was smothered with wild trees among a profusion of undergrowth such as briars and nettles.

'There's the rowan, Mark,' Preston indicated the tree. 'A young one but perfectly positioned for our man!'

The graceful tree with its ash-like leaves, clusters of white flowers and smooth grey bark stood close to the water's edge. When Pemberton approached it, under directions from Preston, he realised how perfect it was for a sniping position, ideal for killing someone in the bluebell field. He stood behind it, moving slightly to gain the killer's perspective. Anyone standing near this tree would not be visible from the railway line, the farm, the stepping stones or the viaduct – or even the track over the viaduct. The surrounding foliage and undergrowth were thick enough to conceal the sniper from anyone visiting Mill House or merely walking in the area.

'If he knew Alicia would be among the

bluebells at a particular time,' Pemberton mused, 'it seems he knew the tree was conveniently placed to serve his purpose. It adds to my belief that some careful planning went into this crime, Jack.'

'That means there must be a powerful motive, Mark. That's one for you to sort out!'

'The only one I've come up with is the inheritance issue. I wonder if someone has discovered the Milverdale secret?'

'It's as good a theory as any!' smiled Preston. 'So while you're testing theories, we'll be using scientific methods. We'll test the rowan and a few nearby trees to see if any deposits have been left – fibres from clothing perhaps, something caught on a thorn maybe. We'll examine the river bed, too, there could be marks there. It flows slowly here, and is shallow in parts with some sandy beds.'

'My men will help.'

'Thanks, I've already spoken to Inspector Fowler. Now, where will you be today if I need to call you?' Preston asked.

'The incident room until eleven or thereabouts, then Milverdale Hall. I want more words with the estate workers. I'll be on the mobile, call me on that if anything dramatic turns up.'

And so Pemberton returned to the incident room. Things were going his way at last.

After a restless night, Lorraine climbed out of bed to prepare for her day. On her way to the kitchen, she noticed a letter on the doormat. It bore her name and the hospital logo and she began to weep as she took it to the breakfast table. Switching on the kettle, she reached the table to find a note from Mark. It said, 'I love you, Mark xxxx', then, 'See you later, have a nice day in York!'

As the kettle, still warm from Pemberton's coffee-making, began to boil, she knew she must pull herself together and so, taking a deep breath, she opened the envelope. It was an appointment for her breast examination. Next Monday, 10.30 a.m.

'Oh, God...' She wished Mark was with her.

Wiping her eyes, she made herself a mug of coffee.

At the conference of detectives Pemberton confirmed that a very detailed forensic examination was under way at the sniping position, stressing that this information be regarded as confidential for the time being. He wanted neither the press nor any of the suspects to be aware that the position had been identified. He did point out, however, that the island was invisible from both the village and the railway line but that the killer had to reach it on foot while carrying a rifle.

Where had he come from? Which route had he taken? Someone must have seen him either before or after the murder, and it was such a witness that must be traced and interviewed.

There was very little further information at this stage, so Pemberton released his teams to go about their enquiries while he concentrated on finding something for the news conference. But there was nothing he could tell the press – no developments, no suspect arrested, no clues discovered, no motive ... and not even the press had produced any startling information about Alicia Milverdale and her family.

With Lorraine heading for York, Pemberton announced that he was going to Milverdale Hall for further talks with the staff. This time, he drove to the rear and parked in the yard. He decided to first visit the Breckons' house, knowing Jim would be working in the Hall. A private word with Mrs Breckon would not be amiss and he did not, at this stage, announce his arrival to Constance Farrow. After all, she was an employee, not owner of the premises.

Mrs Breckon led him into her lounge which had wonderful views across the moors. She was a large, jolly lady in her fifties who said she had once worked in the Hall as a domestic servant but much of that work had dwindled with the death of Mr

274

Milverdale. Her father had been game-keeper on the estate until his retirement. There was no gamekeeper now, she said wistfully, the estate hadn't enough moor-land and woodland to justify a full-time keeper and the tenant farmers kept down their own foxes and other vermin as well as rearing young game birds.

'I'm interested in Wednesday morning,' he told her. 'I'm revisiting everyone in the Hall because I need to establish where everyone was.'

'Oh, you don't think it's one of us, do you?' She looked terrified at the thought.

'No,' he smiled. 'But someone managed to get close enough to Miss Milverdale to know her movements and then to shoot her, Mrs Breckon. Her routine has been studied, I'm sure, and I think the killer must have either known or been able to find out where everyone was that morning, so as he could avoid them.'

'Oh, I see,' she said, not entirely con-vinced.

'You and, Jim are the only couple who live on the premises, aren't you? Other than Constance Farrow. The others travel in from the village every morning?'

'Yes, that's right, Mr Pemberton.'

'I'll be seeing Jim very soon. He told me he starts at seven thirty and he said he's in your kitchen around seven having his breakfast. That's when he saw Alicia on Wednesday. Do you have breakfast with him?'

'Yes, we have breakfast together as a rule. You can see the back entrance of the Hall from our kitchen, Mr Pemberton. Do you want to have a look?'

'Thank you.'

She led him into the small and rather dark kitchen; the window ledge was full of plant pots with new seedlings enjoying the sunlight, and he could look across the lane to the rear of the Hall. A range of brick outbuildings stood at each side of the entrance and the large wooden gates were rarely closed.

'That entrance between the buildings,' he said. 'It goes into a rear yard, I believe.'

'Yes, quite a large one, Mr Pemberton, a courtyard with doors going into other buildings and sheds, and into the kitchen block, and the back of the Hall itself.'

'And when Alicia went for her morning walk, she always came out this way, on foot?'

'She did, yes. Regular as clockwork. Seven o'clock on the dot.'

'So as we look at it from here, she would turn to her left – that's to our right – and head along the lane towards the railway viaduct?'

'Yes, striding out. She was a brisk walker, Mr Pemberton.'

'Alone? Was she always alone? No dog? Colleague? Walking-stick even?'

'No, always alone. She didn't have a dog and she never used a stick.'

'She'd be out of sight from the Hall, then? The moment she turned to her left.'

'Oh, yes, you never saw her once she'd turned that corner. You always said the mistress had gone by seven and would be back by eight.'

'She returned promptly, did she?'

'You could nearly set your watch by her coming and going. She'd always come back at eight, ready for the day, unless she had something special to do.'

'Did you see her on her return journey?'

'No, not as a rule, Mr Pemberton. I was usually busy in the house, away from the kitchen, but I know she always came back at eight because the household was ready for her, breakfast, you know, with post and papers on the dining-room table. Jim always said how reliable she was in her time-keeping.'

'I understand Miss Milverdale always walked alone, but did Miss Farrow ever go on that walk, Mrs Breckon? Either alone or with her mistress? Later in the day maybe?'

'Not at seven, Mr Pemberton. I never saw her go that early with the mistress, but they did sometimes go to the old mill together, in an afternoon if things were quiet on the estate or on a weekend if the weather was nice. Miss Farrow has been on that walk alone too, but not very often. It's nice in the bluebell field.'

'So, once your breakfast is over, what do you do?'

'Well, Jim always goes out after breakfast to check his plants. He grows our own vegetables and likes flowers, he's got a good garden.'

'Is it here or does he have a piece of the Hall garden?'

'No, it's behind our cottage. He'll be out there at quarter past seven, just for ten minutes on a morning, and then he comes back into the house, picks up his flask and goes off to work. He's always on time, Mr Pemberton, he's never been late in his life. Like the mistress he is, good at time-keeping.'

'And while he's doing all that, what do you do?'

'Well, I have to clear the table and wash up the breakfast things, he always likes bacon and eggs, then I have to make his flask, he always takes coffee for mid-morning in case he's working away from the kitchen.'

'And when Jim has gone to work?'

'I make the bed and generally do a bit of dusting, tidy the bathroom, get any bits of washing ready that might need doing, that sort of thing.'

'All before he sets off for work?'

'I try to get as much done as I can before he leaves, but he usually sets off while I'm making the bed,' and Mrs Breckon began to look rather puzzled by Pemberton's persistence in asking about such trivial domestic detail.

'And when he's gone, what do you do?' he smiled.

'Well, I must be honest, I usually sit down and read the papers. They come at half past seven, you see. I like reading and I like women's magazines, so I get them with the papers. *Woman's Realm* comes on a Wednesday and I like to read that for a few minutes.'

'In the kitchen?'

'No, the front room,' and she was puzzled again.

'Which overlooks the moors, I noticed. So you'd not see any comings and goings at the back entrance to the Hall while you were in that room?'

'No.' She shook her head. 'No, it's a nice private room, not overlooked.'

'So it's just your kitchen that gives a view of that back entrance?'

'Yes. It's usually well after eight when I return to the kitchen. Quarter past maybe, or even half past if I get my head into a good story. I prepare the potatoes and vegetables for dinner, peeling them and putting them in pans ready. Jim always comes home at twelve for his dinner, he likes it on the table when he gets in, so I do a lot of my preparation well beforehand.'

'And this Wednesday, you saw Alicia heading out along the lane as usual at seven, but did you see her come back?'

'No, Mr Pemberton, I was in the kitchen at eight, I was going to do the potatoes. I remember because I put the radio on and heard the news. I never saw her come back while I was there.'

'How long were you in the kitchen?'

'Most of the morning on Wednesday, I'd say. I might have popped out to the loo, or through into the lounge for my coffee and a look at the papers about half ten, but that's all. I never saw her, Mr Pemberton, but that's not surprising, is it? She didn't come back, did she?'

'I want to be sure she didn't,' he said. 'I wondered if she might have returned as usual at eight, and then gone back to the bluebell field.'

'No, I'd have seen her going back a second time, Mr Pemberton. I was in the kitchen, Wednesday's my baking day, you see, and then there's Jim's dinner to prepare. I'd have noticed if she'd been walking later than usual, or had anybody with her.'

'And did you see anyone else using that lane, following in her footsteps on Wednesday?'

'No, Mr Pemberton, apart from seeing her go off at seven, I never saw a soul.'

'Thanks for being so accurate with your times, Mrs Breckon, it's been a great help. Now, before I go to find Jim – I believe this cottage comes to you on Alicia's death? It was Mr Milverdale's bequest, I understand, from the estate?'

'Yes, we've no pension from the estate, Mr Pemberton, me nor Jim, so old Mr Milverdale said he'd make sure we got the house, as a gift, if the Milverdale line came to an end. He thought we might lose our home and jobs, you see, if new folks took over and he said once it was ours, we could sell it and make ourselves a nice little nest egg for retirement.'

'It was thoughtful of him.'

'He was good like that. Alicia took after him in many ways. We've been with the Milverdales a long time, Mr Pemberton, Jim and me, and our parents worked for the estate before us.'

'You would know Audrey then?' he asked.

'Oh, yes. A nice girl. Very religious. Churchy, a bit over the top.'

'She died young, I'm told.'

'She did, Mr Pemberton, away on holiday not long after the war, but she was brought back home to be buried. She's in our churchyard.'

'I saw her memorial,' he said. 'People said

she was a very honest young woman.'

'She was, she once said she was like George Washington, she could never tell a lie. It was a pity she died so young.'

'Was there any suggestion about the cause of her death?'

'Well, they said it was TB, but she'd been away a while and we all thought she must have caught something. Why are you asking this, Mr Pemberton?'

'I like to know all about the families of murder victims, Mrs Breckon.' He smiled charmingly at her. 'Now, your inheritance. The house. Will you sell it?'

'I'd say not. We've a few years before retirement, it's best to wait and see what the new owners will do. We might have the house *and* jobs for a few more years!'

'So it's a very nice "thank-you" present!'

'Aye, it is. But they were like that, the Milverdales. Good to their staff and tenants.'

'Right, well, I hope everything works out and that you enjoy the future. Now, where can I find Jim?'

'It's Friday, Mr Pemberton, and what time is it?' She glanced at her watch. 'Half past eleven. That's when he checks the boilers, winds the clocks and checks the downstairs windows, locking all those windows in rooms that won't be used over the weekend... He doesn't work weekends,

282

unless there's an emergency of some kind, and the mistress always liked the ground-floor windows closed and locked over the weekend, even in summer. I should go to the back door, Mr Pemberton, and start with the kitchen, you'll find him somewhere in that part of the house. He likes to get those jobs finished before he has his dinner on a Friday.'

Leaving her, Pemberton went to the rear door of the Hall, absorbing the detail of his route as he progressed, and found Jim Breckon in the kitchen – checking windows as his wife had calculated. Breckon hailed him, bidding him enter through the kitchen door.

'Hello, Mr Pemberton, are you wanting Miss Farrow?'

'No, Mr Breckon, not yet. I'd like a chat with you, if you can spare the time.'

'Oh, well, I suppose so. It's a busy day, is Friday, checking things, getting set up for the weekend.'

'I won't keep you long,' Pemberton assured him. 'I'm establishing the staff's movements on Wednesday, Mr Breckon, between seven and eight.'

'When the mistress goes out for her walk, you mean? Well, I don't start till half seven, you understand.'

'And what's your routine when you arrive?'

'Well, I come across the back yard, the way you came in now, and I come in through the kitchen door. I have a key for that. My first job it to open all the kitchen windows. The mistress liked fresh air when there's cooking so that was my first job. Then I'd open the front door, letting it stand wide open to show folks the mistress was in residence. We always kept the inner door closed and locked though. Then I did a quick check of the coal supplies, and coke and oil for the central heating, just in case we'd got through a lot, and after that I went round every room in the house, checking light bulbs to see if any had blown and then I'd replace them. And in winter and on cold days, I'd check the radiators, bleeding any with air locks. In summer, I'd open more ground-floor windows, in the morning room and lounge, for example. We'd keep them shut in the winter. And that took me to eight o'clock, winter and summer alike. The mistress would come back from her walk and go upstairs for a shower and change into her day clothes.'

'Regular with her time-keeping, was she?'

'Very regular, Mr Pemberton. You could set your clocks by her.'

'So you saw her leave at seven on Wednesday, for her walk. You told me that when we chatted before. But as a rule, you never saw her come back.'

284

'Not until she got into the house, Mr Pemberton, and sometimes not even then. You'd not see her coming unless you happened to be outside, on the back lane or in the yard. You can't see the lane from here, you see, or anywhere downstairs, because them buildings are in the way.'

'So until she was actually inside the Hall, you'd not be aware she'd returned?'

'No, though somebody might let me know – the mistress is back, they'd say – but I knew she'd be back anyway, she was always back at eight unless she had something to do at Mill House. Then she'd let us know.'

'And on Wednesday, you did not see her come back?'

'No, she didn't come back, did she? Well, if she had, I would have known.'

'Are you sure? Is it possible she might have returned unseen by anyone and gone out again, almost immediately, back to the bluebell field?'

'No, Mr Pemberton, I'd say not. If she'd come back and gone out again, we'd have known. Somebody on the staff would have known. I'd say it would be impossible for her to get back into the house without one of us knowing about it.'

'When she returned from her walk, Mr Breckon, what was her routine? I believe she had breakfast, for example.'

'Well, she would come in by the back

door, the entrance opposite my house, and take off her walking shoes or wet clothes if it was a bad morning, and hang them in the rear entrance. There's pegs there. She'd put her indoor shoes on, she'd left them there when she went out, and then go up to her room for a shower and get changed into her day clothes. Then she'd go into the dining-room for her breakfast.'

'What time did she sit down for breakfast?'

'Quarter past, twenty past eight.'

'She didn't eat in the kitchen?'

'No, never. She never thought it proper. Miss Farrow prepared her breakfast and took it to the dining-room. Usually, the post and papers had arrived so she would read her mail and the papers while having breakfast. That would take her to about quarter to nine, she had a light breakfast, Mr Pemberton, cereal and toast usually, nothing cooked, and then she'd go into the office to start work.'

'And where was Miss Farrow while the mistress was out walking?'

'Her duties started with breakfast. She always set the dining-room table the night before so it was ready for the mistress in the morning. I don't think the mistress expected Miss Farrow to be up at seven to see her off or anything, and so what usually happened was Miss Farrow was in the

286

kitchen by five to eight or thereabouts, preparing the toast, boiling the kettle, making the coffee, that sort of thing. It only took a few minutes, it wasn't needed until quarter past eightish. And it was her job to put the papers and post beside her place at the table.'

'And the mistress ate breakfast alone?'

'Yes, unless she had a house guest.'

'Did she have many guests?'

'No, not overnight stays. I think the last one was eight or nine years ago. Not like her parents. They were great ones for having friends in for the weekend. Nice friends, Mr Pemberton, gentry folk, like the Featleys from Harrogate way.'

'They knew Lady Featley, did they?'

'Oh, aye, long-standing friends, they were.'

'And Lady Consate? Did she ever come here?'

'I can't say I know that name, Mr Pemberton. But that doesn't mean to say she never came ... there was a lot of Ladyships whose names I never knew.'

'Thanks. Now to Miss Farrow, where did she have breakfast?'

'In the kitchen, Mr Pemberton. She was allowed to eat there instead of her own flat, and to use the house's food. Dinner as well as breakfast, and all ten o'clocks and tea-times. A perk for her, and the lads would come in for a coffee as well, before starting work. They brought pack-ups for their dinners though, and ate in the staff room, that's near the back door, a little room with chairs and a table in, and a pack of cards, dartboard and so on.'

'The former domestic staff room?'

'Yes. I didn't often use it or have coffee in the kitchen on a morning because I just live across the lane, but the others, who come from the village, would pop into the kitchen while Miss Farrow was making the coffee for the mistress, and have themselves a mug before starting work.'

'A nice start to the day!' smiled Pemberton.

'It was. They were supposed to start at eight, but nobody worried about ten minutes here or there so long as they got to the Hall on time to clock on. If they got here a bit early, they'd make their own coffees. The mistress knew about it, she didn't mind and said it got them off to a good start. If there was any extra work to be done, then they'd do it without grumbling, there was a lot of give and take. We liked it that way. I was usually doing my rounds by the time they came in for coffee. I start earlier than them, but I finish earlier.'

'So apart from you, all the others start work at eight o'clock? Even, I suppose, Miss Farrow.'

'Yes, they generally got here on time, they

didn't abuse the mistress's easy-going manner on timing.'

'Which way would they come to the Hall?'

'Up the main drive, by car, or bike.'

'Not across the old ironworks and along the lane over the railway viaduct?'

'Oh no, they never came that way. It's let off to Neil Potter these days, and he likes to keep the gate locked, to keep ramblers and wanderers out.'

'So they'd not be likely to come across their mistress returning from her walk?'

'No, Mr Pemberton, not them. They came up the front drive but they parked at the back of the Hall, so if they got here bang on eight they might have seen the mistress returning from her walk, crossing the back yard.'

'So there's only you working on the premises before eight?'

'Yes, just me. And Miss Farrow living in.'

'Did you see Miss Farrow on Wednesday morning? When you arrived in the kitchen? Or did you see her anywhere else when you started work?'

'No, but I never do, Mr Pemberton. She's not up as a rule. She wasn't up on Wednesday either, leastways if she was, I never saw her. She wasn't in the kitchen when I got there, nor in those parts of the house I see to first thing. She'd be in her flat, Mr Pemberton, getting ready for work, I expect.'

'So you'd be on your own for that first half-hour. Now, if the mistress wanted to talk to you about anything, Mr Breckon, either in person or as a group, when did she do that?'

'She'd call us into her office during the day, Mr Pemberton, unless it was something very personal in which case she would find us around the place, and arrange for a quiet chat somewhere.'

'How did she find you?'

'She would ask Miss Farrow to look out for us or go and find us. Miss Farrow always knew where we were, she kept tabs on us, she was like a second boss sometimes. Sometimes we said she'd have made a good sergeant major!' and he grinned ruefully. 'We all knew our place but sometimes Miss Farrow thought she was mistress of Milverdale!'

'And this Wednesday, Mr Breckon. Was there anything different about it? Staff not being where you'd expect them to be, being later than usual or earlier or doing something different?'

'No, there wasn't, Mr Pemberton... I hope you're not suggesting one of us...'

'No, nothing like that. But if somebody was watching the Hall and the staff, and watching for Miss Milverdale to leave for her walk, then the location of everyone here would be vital.'

'Somebody's been watching us, and planning all this while our backs were turned, you mean?'

'It's something I can't ignore, Mr Breckon. I'm trying to establish whether that might have happened, whether it could have happened, whether someone could have followed your mistress along her walk last Wednesday knowing you'd all be otherwise engaged on set tasks at particular times.'

'Oh, dear, that's awful, to think we might have been spied on.'

'You can see now why I need to know whether there was anything different about Wednesday morning. Anything not in its usual place, or someone not in their usual place...'

'Oh, I see. No, nothing was different, Mr Pemberton. She went off at seven like I said, and I expected her back at eight. Everything here was absolutely normal.'

'You didn't go over the viaduct, did you? For any reason?'

'Me? Good heavens, no, Mr Pemberton. Why would I want to do that? I haven't time for morning walks. No, I was here like I said, bang on half past seven, and I was about the house and grounds until dinner-time, that's twelve o'clock.'

'Was Miss Farrow in the kitchen making breakfast at her usual time, when the staff were having their coffees?'

'Yes, she was. I'd gone in as usual at half past seven, and was doing my rounds when I saw her in the kitchen, preparing breakfast as usual. No different from any other time.'

'What time would that be?'

'Just before eight, five to eight mebbe. It's hard to be exact. I'd gone in to fit a new bulb to the light over the sink, and then the lads got here and came for their coffees. Miss Farrow was making it, I knew because she asked if I fancied one and I did. Funnily enough, that morning I did have a coffee with her, Mr Pemberton, I'd done the mistress's room in good time, and then I went off to finish my rounds.'

'But the mistress did not return at eight that morning, as expected.'

'No, Miss Farrow asked if anyone had seen her come in because she was wondering whether to take her breakfast into the dining-room, but nobody had seen her.'

'Did anyone go and look for her?'

'No, not then, it was a bit too early. Miss Farrow took her breakfast into the dining-room so it would be ready for her when she came downstairs. But she never came, Mr Pemberton. Now we know why.'

'Yes, and I'm sorry. Now, did you see Miss Farrow leave to go and look for the mistress?'

'Yes, I saw her. I was in our kitchen washing my hands at dinner-time and saw her hurrying out. I had no idea where she was rushing off to, otherwise I'd have gone to help her, dinner or no dinner. If she'd asked, I'd have gone with her.'

'Mr Breckon, you've been most helpful. There's just one more thing. I understand you've come into some property?'

'Hall Cottage? Yes, it becomes mine, Mr Pemberton, but it won't make any difference to us, not at our stage of life. If the new folks will have us, we'll stay on.'

'And suppose they want to buy the house from you?'

'We'll have to think carefully about that, Mr Pemberton. Mebbe me and the wife will want to retire into the village, to be nearer the shop and post office for our pensions, but it's too early to talk about those kind of plans.'

'You knew the cottage would become yours, did you? On Alicia's death?'

'Aye, I did, Mr Pemberton, but I hope you don't think me or the missus bumped her off just to get our hands on that house. We'd not do that, would we? Not while we've got jobs. Not if it was going to be ours anyway ... that would be a daft thing to do.'

Pemberton smiled. 'Yes, it would, Mr Breckon. Thanks for helping me as you have. I can let you go now. Where will I find Miss Farrow?'

'I expect she'll be in her rooms, but there's a handbell in the main hall, you could ring that. She'll hear it and come to you.'

'Thanks,' and so Pemberton made his way into the main hall, found the bell and rang it. There were a few moments of deep silence in the empty house as he awaited some response and then he heard a door opening upstairs. Constance Farrow appeared on the landing.

'Superintendent Pemberton! You want to see me?'

12

Constance Farrow led Pemberton into the drawing-room and this time he refused a coffee, saying, 'No, thanks, I have a lot to do this morning. This is just a quick visit.'

'Has there been a development?' she asked as the tic appeared at the side of her mouth.

'No,' he said, with no intention of revealing to her that the sniping point had been discovered. 'It's just that I need to know where everyone was on Wednesday morning. I understand the men don't start work until eight, but they have a coffee in the kitchen first.'

'Yes, except Jim Breckon. He gets here at half past seven. He uses the back entrance. He lives right opposite, as I'm sure you know, so he comes straight in by the kitchen door, he has a key for it. The others come up the main drive, but enter the house by the kitchen door as well. It's open for them, of course.'

'Thank you. Now you, Miss Farrow. What are your hours?'

'I have no official starting time or finishing time, Mr Pemberton. My first job was to make sure Miss Milverdale's breakfast was on the table when she needed it – quarter or twenty past eight. She did not insist on rigid hours because I was in the house virtually all the time, from morning till night. My hours were very flexible, as I told you earlier.'

'So what was a normal morning for you?'

'I'm a methodical person, Mr Pemberton. I wake at seven, get up, have a shower, get dressed, then come down to start preparing breakfast.'

'You have your breakfast in the big house, not in your flat?'

'Yes, in the kitchen. On Wednesday, I ate before I made Alicia's breakfast as I always have. Afterwards, I washed my pots and started on her breakfast. Before then, though, I had my coffee with the men – I make it for them, you see. It provides an opportunity to relay any instructions to them, from the mistress, about anything that needs special attention during the day. Just after eight, they go to their posts. They did so on Wednesday and I made her breakfast, fresh and ready to put on the table when she came down from her shower.'

'So Wednesday was a perfectly ordinary day with no departure from the daily routine?'

'Except Miss Milverdale did not come back.'

'But the men came in at eight as usual,

you made coffee for them, then organised breakfast for the mistress?'

'Yes.'

'Were you up early on Wednesday?' he asked.

'Early?' The tic reappeared at the side of her mouth. 'I'm always up early, Mr Pemberton.'

'Earlier than usual, I mean,' he clarified the point.

'Well, yes, I suppose I was ... I never really thought about it. I do get up earlier sometimes.'

'It's just that you said you usually wake at seven but earlier you told me you saw the mistress leave at seven. You must have been up to have seen her. I recall from my visit to your flat that you can't see the rear entrance of the Hall from your bedroom or from anywhere in your flat.'

'I don't overlook that part of the Hall, Mr Pemberton.'

'So, on Wednesday morning, if you saw Miss Milverdale leave at seven, you must have been out of bed, Miss Farrow. So where were you when you saw her? Upstairs or downstairs? If you were downstairs, precisely where were you?'

He saw a look of uncertainty in her eyes, he saw the tic at the side of her mouth and he realised she was having to think furiously yet carefully before answering that question.

'It's difficult to be precise, Mr Pemberton. Such a lot has happened, memories aren't reliable after such a trauma. I am sure I was downstairs. I woke early, the noise of the birds singing wakes me up these mornings, the dawn chorus, you understand, and so I went downstairs. That's it. I was in the kitchen making myself an early cup of coffee when the mistress left the house.'

'At seven?'

'Yes, she was as punctual as ever.'

'Alone? Were you alone?'

'Yes, there is no one else on the premises.'

'Except for the mistress?'

'Yes, well, except for her.'

'Did she speak to you before she left for her walk? If you were in the kitchen, she might have seen you. She might have said goodbye or left instructions about the day's work.'

'No, she didn't see me. She wouldn't expect me to be there, would she?'

'So were the kitchen windows open or shut as you were making that early morning coffee?'

'Windows...' That tic appeared once again. 'Well,' and she stuttered now, just slightly. A sign of nervousness. 'Well, I have no idea... I never gave it a thought, it was very early.'

'Jim Breckon said the mistress liked the kitchen windows open.'

'Yes, but not all night. One of his duties

was to open them when he arrived at half past seven. That would be after I'd made that coffee. He opened them before breakfast was cooked, so they would be shut, wouldn't they?'

'How long do you think it took to make your early coffee?'

'I used hot water rather than hot milk, a few minutes. Quarter of an hour at the outside.'

'So you went back upstairs at ten or quarter past seven, or thereabouts?'

'Yes, I expect so. I wasn't keeping a detailed account of my movements, Mr Pemberton.'

'Of course not. So what did you do when you went back upstairs?'

'I returned to my flat, Mr Pemberton, I was in my nightdress. I took my drink with me and enjoyed it in bed...'

'Could anyone verify that?' was his unexpected question.

'Good God, no! I sleep alone, Mr Pemberton,' and there was a haughtiness in her voice. 'Then I got up and dressed before I came down for my day's duties. I'd be downstairs about twenty to eight or so. Quarter to perhaps.'

'And Mr Breckon, who starts work at half past seven, went into the kitchen just before eight, he said, about five to, and saw you there.'

'Yes, he did come in when I was there. That's after I had come down for the second time. He stayed for a coffee, rather unusually. Is all this relevant, Mr Pemberton? This preoccupation with trivia?'

'It is not trivia when I am trying to establish precisely where every member of the household was during those critical minutes between seven and eight on Wednesday morning.'

'You think someone was watching the house, you mean?'

'I think someone had made very careful plans to kill Alicia, and for those plans to be successful the killer would have had to make sure he was not seen by anyone. That's why I need to know exactly where everyone was. If I can work out where they were, I might be able to work out the killer's movements.'

'Well, I can't imagine how our very mundane comings and goings in the house matter when Alicia died such a long way from here, but of course I will help as best I can.'

'And then what did you do?'

'Well, after the men have had their coffee, I begin Alicia's breakfast.'

'And that is what you did on Wednesday?'

'Yes, when the men had gone, I prepared it as far as I could, but she did not return as expected. I waited, wondering why she hadn't told me she would be late, but one doesn't like to interfere or intrude, Mr Pemberton. There was no cause for concern at that stage, she had been delayed in the past without informing me. It was some time later that I became worried, so I began to ring Mill House... I never went out of the house though. Oh, except a trip to the shop. It's a regular weekly trip, I take a vehicle to the village and buy the necessary provisions.'

'And what time would that be?'

'In the middle of the morning, Mr Pemberton. Elevenish or so.'

'And was anyone around the grounds at that time? Unauthorised people, I mean?'

'No, I never saw anyone prowling around the grounds, either at that time or earlier, Mr Pemberton.'

'Well I think that's all for now, Miss Farrow. Thank you for being co-operative.'

'I just hope you find the person responsible, Mr Pemberton. Now, can I ask if there is any word about a funeral date?'

'No. The coroner will open the inquest shortly. He'll want us to make a few more enquiries before doing so, chiefly to establish whether her death was an accident or murder. I'll let you know just as soon as I can.'

'Thank you, Mr Pemberton.'

Before leaving Milverdale Hall, he succeeded in having talks with every member of the staff who'd been working on Wednesday morning, but none could provide any useful information. All arrived via the main drive, none had arrived before 7.50 a.m., consequently none had witnessed the departure of their mistress for her morning walk. All had gravitated towards the kitchen where they'd had a coffee around eight o'clock, with both Miss Farrow and Jim Breckon present.

Thanking them, Pemberton returned to the incident room.

During the morning, Gill Austin, mother of Adrian and one of the deputation who'd been to see Mrs Donaldson at the school, along with her friend, Anita Riley, mother of Henry, had been interviewed, but neither of their sons had ever been to Mill House. They had joined Neil Potter because he'd asked for some support, and because both mums had heard tales about Alicia in Mill House, they'd decided to support Neil. They could not help any further.

Miss Baines, the retired schoolteacher now living in Hexham, had also been interviewed by Northumbria police. When she was made aware of the rumours about Alicia Milverdale, she had terminated the children's unaccompanied trips to Mill House for either art lessons or pantomime rehearsals, but she had no personal knowledge of what actually occurred in the house. She did encourage Alicia to conduct her classes on school premises and this she had done, with great success. None of the children in Miss Baines's care had ever complained about Alicia's behaviour, and none of the children had ever expressed a wish not to attend Mill House.

A computer search of all local police records for the name of Lady Consate had drawn another blank. She had no criminal record, and her name did not appear for any other known reason. But Pemberton knew he'd come across her name ...

Detective Sergeant Rogers, who'd been in charge of the enquiries on board the 7 a.m. from Rainesbury to Long Barfield, had submitted his results. Every passenger had been subjected to very searching questions, but only one, a woman, had seen anything of interest. She had seen a fisherman. She'd been on the up train, sitting in the first coach midway along on the left and facing the engine. As the train had passed under the viaduct, she'd glanced to her left, towards Cam Beck and the bluebell field, and had seen a fisherman. Although she had not taken a lot of notice, she remembered it was a tall person dressed in dark waterproofs and carrying a bag of the kind that fishermen use to contain their fishing gear. He was walking quickly up the slope of the field towards the end of the viaduct, as if leaving the riverside.

Upon being shown a map of the area, she'd pointed close to the banks of Cam Beck and when Pemberton was shown the map, he saw it was almost directly opposite the island near Mill House.

'If he climbed to the top of that field,' he told Paul Larkin, 'he'd climb over the stile which brings him to the end of the viaduct. Turn left – and he goes towards Milverdale Hall. Turn right and it takes him along the disused track which crosses the old ironworks. It emerges on Bottom Road, over the wooden bridge.'

'If the fisherman walked across the iron-works and climbed the gate, he'd emerge on to Bottom Road, what, ten minutes, quarter of an hour later?' suggested Larkin.

'Yes, and in that case, he'd do so while Neil Potter was repairing his fence almost opposite! Potter was there for almost half an hour from seven thirty. He never saw any-one.'

'His fence was damaged by visitors,' Larkin reminded him. 'Our suspect fisher-man, perhaps?'

'I doubt it, Paul. The damage occurred on Tuesday, he was fixing it on Wednesday.

Unless it is someone boarding in the village. We'd better check bed-and-breakfast places, the pubs who take in guests and so on. Now, when's the fishing season?'

'It depends, sir. The trout season has started – with effect from 25th March. The close season for trout runs from 1st October until 24th March.'

'So our man could be a legitimate trout fisherman?'

'He could – provided he's got permission from Milverdale Estate for fishing in their waters, and the necessary licences. We're still in the close season for coarse fishing and there are no salmon in this beck. So it seems he was after trout.'

'If it was a man from the village, he might walk across Potter's field, climb his fence and go over the old ironworks for a spot of early morning fishing?'

'Quite possible, sir. I'll have the teams try and trace him. In the stuff you brought from the estate office, there was a list of people with permission to fish in Milverdale water. We'll go through them first, sir, they'll be on the computer now.'

'If we draw a blank, Paul, I'll organise a press appeal for the fisherman to come forward, but we'll keep it to ourselves for the moment. You'd think, though, if the fellow had walked over the ironworks just after half past seven, he'd have emerged on to Bottom Road before quarter to eight ... and he might have climbed Potter's fence, but Potter was there on Wednesday morning – that morning – and never saw anyone. The milkman who saw Potter fixing his fence never saw the fisherman either, did he?'

'No. He was quizzed pretty closely but never saw anyone else on Bottom Road, nor any car parked up or waiting.'

'So did the fisherman emerge on to that road, or did he vanish somewhere else?'

'There's nowhere else he could go without being seen, is there?' said Larkin. 'Except along the railway line.'

'There's Milverdale Hall,' Pemberton told him. 'If he'd turned left upon reaching the end of the viaduct, he could have gone into the Hall via the back entrance. Or he could have gone straight past the Hall, through the countryside, to emerge somewhere out of sight, on the moors above, say, where he might have had a car waiting. If he had no permission to be on that land he was trespassing, but if he was a professional killer that wouldn't worry him. But, apart from the lady on the train, no one else saw him, even though the Hall staff would be coming to work about that time. The Breckons never saw him either. He appears to have vanished into thin air, Paul, but we know that's impossible.'

'You're saying he could have gone into the

Hall, sir?' Larkin frowned at the implications of Pemberton's remarks.

'Suppose it was not a man in that gear, Paul, but a tall woman; suppose it was not fishing tackle in a case, but a rifle in a case. And suppose the person wore waders of the kind that left marks in the mud near the river edge...'

'Constance Farrow, you mean?'

'Why not?' asked Pemberton.

'But there's no motive, sir, she has no motive. She's lost her job and her home—'

'No, she hasn't,' Pemberton corrected him. 'Disposal of the estate is on hold for at least three years. According to the solicitor, she'll be asked to remain in the house to care for it during the interim period and that means she hasn't lost her home either. The estate will continue to pay her wages and the upkeep of the house, just as they will pay the wages of other members of staff. The trustees will run things, the estate will continue as it is now, and Constance still has a job and a home, at least for the foreseeable future.'

'Yes, but that doesn't give her a motive, sir. Killing an heiress generally implies some kind of strong motive, surely?'

'My sentiments exactly, Paul. So what kind of reason would there be to kill an heiress, even the last in the line?'

'Someone lurking in the background with

a grievance and a claim to the estate? To say nothing of the money it would generate. But there is no known heir is there? Unless we consider Beatrice Hammond, wherever she is.'

'We can't ignore her, Paul. We know that, somewhere out there, there *is* a child who carries Milverdale blood in her veins. There are three years for that child to show herself, three years to make a claim. We know Roderick was rather late in producing Alicia, the desired heir. I say desired because it seems he'd already fathered a child, one whose origins had to be hidden. It wouldn't surprise me if it was the result of rape but it was surely incest. Perhaps Audrey, in all her innocence, wanted her child to be the legitimate heir? We shall never know. It happened before Roderick junior's marriage, and I wonder if he got married because it was the right thing to do, rather than wanting to? Perhaps he thought his duty was to produce a legitimate heir? Which he did – Alicia. But she never married and now we know what he knew – that there was an older sister for Alicia who was the rightful heir, by blood. Were Roderick's words in that trust designed for this very reason, I wonder? We'll never know, but he never told his solicitors about Audrey's daughter and according to family records there is no heir. But we know different, Paul. We know there is. It's almost time for me to alert the solicitors to this development.'

'But the minute that heir makes a bid for the estate, she becomes a murder suspect – even if it is three years from now.'

'I know, Paul. I've been giving that a lot of thought. I've considered murder because of child abuse, I've considered accidental death from a flying bullet, I've considered tenants wanting rid of Alicia to get their hands on property. I've considered revenge or robbery and dozens of other scenarios. Not one of them stands up, Paul. Even the child abuse theory has not been proved and if we find the Robsons were telling the truth, that's the only case, and a very old one. The only person with the time and opportunity to kill Alicia is Constance Farrow and the only logical motive is one of inheritance, however obscured it might be.'

'How do you work that out?'

'Constance knows the precise movements of any member of staff at any time. They work to a pattern, Paul, as do so many domestics and manual staff in such a place. Even the mistress followed a pattern, a fairly rigid timetable. Constance knew that. Suppose she planned this crime in great detail, taking weeks, months or even years to bring it to a conclusion. She reasoned that she could get out of bed early on Wednesday morning, half past six or thereabouts, and go ahead of Alicia to the bluebell field. Nobody would see her. If there was anyone fishing or walking in that locality, she could avoid them – the woods are fairly dense and she's familiar with the terrain. She's been on that walk several times, she told us so, and the train driver's sightings support that. I think he saw Constance from time to time, not always Alicia. Might some of those trips have been a rehearsal or two? Having decided upon the right moment, she could simply lie in wait for Alicia, with the rifle resting on the rowan tree, a pre-selected site. I reckon Alicia appeared in the bluebell field around 7.25 a.m. and walked across it towards Mill House. That's when she was killed.'

'No one heard the shot, sir.'

'They wouldn't, Paul. The only people who might have heard it would be Farmer Midgley or his wife, but they were milking. And those milking machines make a lot of noise at close quarters, certainly enough to hide the sound of a rifle shot. Potter might have heard it, but he was fixing his fence at the actual time of her death, although I think he would have been too far away for the sound to reach him. I think Constance planned the shooting for the time the train came by – it would also drown the noise of the shot. The passing train and Midgley's milking were the only events that happened near the bluebell field, both were noisy and both were occurring at the same time. Around seven thirty. When Alicia was there. On the island, Constance would be hidden from the train. I think she waited for the train before shooting Alicia, having calculated she could pull the trigger as it was passing but without being seen. But that morning, the train was late – she had to make her move *before* the train came so she could hurry back to Milverdale Hall by eight o'clock, in time for coffee with the staff. That was her alibi. No one would know she'd been out of the house and no one would see her return, she'd make sure of that. Everything in the house would appear absolutely normal.'

'But there are loopholes in your hypothesis, sir. The fishing gear, her ability with the rifle, the rifle itself. Where did it come from? Where is it now?'

'Those are questions I have yet to answer, Paul. Proving my theories will not be easy – I need to think like Sherlock Holmes here – but I will try to elicit a confession from her. I shall use a little guile, subtle pressure of a kind, but I am convinced she has all the answers. She can handle a gun, I know that. I got her to hand me the weapons from the gun store at the Hall and she was very accustomed to handling them. So where was the rifle before she used it? It is surely a wartime relic – I thought it might be a Home Guard issue which was never returned? A souvenir retained by Mr Milverdale or one of his earlier staff? He was in charge of the local Home Guard, remember. And the fishing gear – there's fishing gear of every type in both Milverdale Hall and Mill House. But if I am to prove a case against Constance, I must find the rifle and that fishing gear I believe she used. I think she wore the fishing gear deliberately to make anyone spotting her think she was a fisherman – all part of her careful plan.'

'It would not be unusual to see a fisherman walking along the lanes, even through Milverdale land, would it? Some have permission to do that.'

'Exactly, Paul. But where is the gear now? In spite of a meticulous search, our teams did not find it or the rifle, did they?'

'They would never have regarded fishing gear, like waterproofs, rods or bags, as likely evidence in a murder case, sir, so that might mean another search'

'It won't be in the house now or any of its outbuildings, or anywhere near the bluebell field or in Mill House, Paul, not the stuff we need. It's all been hidden, it must have been by now. I'm sure it's been hidden with the rifle.'

'It can't be far away, though, can it? If

what you say is true, she had no time to take it far. Any ideas?'

'Yes. That passenger on the train saw the fisherman walking up the slope of the field where the path goes towards the end of the viaduct. Dressed in full gear. My train-driver witness, Mr Morgan, saw a woman hurrying across the viaduct towards the Hall. He thought it was Alicia – it was a woman, he was sure of that, marching along as if she was in a hurry, and she was not carrying anything. Alicia was not carrying anything either.'

'So?'

'It can't have been Alicia, Paul, she was dead.'

'Constance – or Mrs Breckon?'

'One or other of them – Constance, I'm sure. I think she had dumped the water-proofs and fishing gear by then – only minutes earlier though. They were probably hidden behind a wall or under a bush near the end of the viaduct before she hurried back to the Hall for eight. It's the only explanation.'

'We've not searched that part of the countryside, have we?'

'No, we haven't. There's never been a need to, until now.'

'The gear will have been moved now, surely, sir? Anyone could have found it.'

'Yes, I agree. Constance told us she went

313

into the village on Wednesday morning, to the shop, and she took the Landrover. We know that's true, she was seen there, and she made a point of telling me. Suppose she came out of the yard at the rear of the Hall – that's the way out for motor vehicles – but turned left not right. Right would take her around the Hall and down the main drive. A left turn out of the rear yard would take her along the lane and over the viaduct, using the rough track that leads towards the iron-works. That's no problem for a Landrover. She could retrieve the waterproofs and the rifle in its bag from their hiding place before anyone started to search for Alicia, drive into the old ironworks, dump the stuff down an old pit shaft or two, and either return the way she'd come or even continue across the old ironworks, unlock the gate and head into the village that way. She'd have access to the key of that gate, it's estate property even though it is let to Neil Potter.'

'So the rifle and waterproofs would be dumped down a pit shaft long before we arrived on the scene, and long before she raised the alarm?'

'Right, the evidence hidden long before we arrived, all part of her careful plan.'

'You've nothing to back up this theory, sir, have you?'

'Just the timing of her movements, Paul, along with the others. And her reaction to

314

some of my questions. I *know* she's guilty, Paul, but it's going to be very difficult proving it. If I ask her, she'll deny it, I know that.'

'So what's your next step?'

'A lot depends on what Lorraine finds out, Paul. I'll see what she turns up and I want to pop into York for words with the military authorities, and to visit a school, before I decide my next move.'

'The military?'

'Whoever used that .303 must have had military training, Paul. There are all kinds of available guns around here, but the killer chose a .303. I think that is most significant. It was probably because he or she had been expertly trained in the use of such a weapon.'

Lorraine returned from York just before Pemberton left and produced two shocks. He recognised the worry on her face and escorted her into his office at the incident room, sat her on his chair and said, 'What's wrong, Lorraine?'

'I got a letter,' she said. 'This morning, after you'd left. I've got to see a specialist. On Monday.'

'Well, I expected that. It will determine things, surely? And that must be good news.'

'I'm so worried, Mark, really I am. They've responded so quickly, it makes it look very urgent. I don't want to lose a breast... I couldn't bear the thought of that.'

'It might not come to that, it might not be cancer, darling... Look, you've got to go and you've got to submit to the tests, there's no alternative.'

'You'll come with me?' She looked pleadingly at him.

He almost said that his presence would depend on the progress of the enquiry, but he restrained himself in time. 'Yes,' he said. 'Yes, of course I'll come. I'll drive you there'

'But the enquiry?'

'There's no such thing as an indispensable person,' he smiled. 'Paul Larkin can run things in my absence – but that's on Monday. It's only Friday now. It might all be over by then,' and he informed her of the development at Hove. 'I think Constance Farrow might be that daughter, Lorraine. She might be heir to Milverdale Hall – which would explain a good deal about her behaviour. But I must be able to prove my theories. So how did things go in York?'

'Sorry, Mark. I'm going to knock your theory on the head,' she said with the faintest of smiles. 'Constance Farrow was not born in Hove, under the name of Beatrice Milverdale, alias Hammond. She was born in York, just as she told us. Constance Farrow is her real name. I've seen the entry for her birth – Constance

Farrow, born in York County Hospital on 6th September 1947, daughter of Sidney and Ethel Farrow who lived at Towsby, that's a suburb of York.'

'The same birthday as Audrey's child, then? I don't believe it!'

'It's true, Mark, and it's no great coincidence. Someone once told me that if you get a gathering of about twenty people in one room, there's a fair chance that two will share a birthday.'

'But these are the two women who feature most strongly in my enquiries – that *is* a coincidence!'

'But Audrey can't feature very strongly, surely? She's been dead for more than fifty years!'

'But she produced an heir to the Milverdale Estate, Lorraine. Has somebody discovered her rightful heritage? Is she setting about gaining what she sees as rightfully hers? After all, she is older than Alicia. Beatrice was the elder daughter of Roderick Milverdale, there's a certificate to prove it. She is Alicia's half-sister wherever she is, and she's full of Milverdale blood from both parents. She was cast aside as unwanted and I can imagine she's out for revenge. Hell hath no fury and all that...'

'You make it all sound very sinister and cruel.'

'Life is cruel, and planning a murder is

sinister for whatever reason.'

'But Constance, or Beatrice if that's who she is, wouldn't commit murder, Mark. Even if that was her motive, she'd fall under suspicion immediately, and she couldn't inherit the estate by committing murder. She has absolutely nothing to gain, Mark. No motive whatsoever.'

'Except revenge. I need to think more about this one. Anyway, did you discover anything else in York?'

'Yes. Like your Hove detective, I got around the houses. I went to Towsby. Even after the war it was a small village on the northern outskirts of York, but now it's all suburbia. But like all villages, some old folks still live there in what was the original village. I had words with a postman and he sent me to a cottage next to the shop. And I found an old lady called Lizzie Templeton who knew Sidney and Ethel Farrow, and their little girl, Constance.'

'I don't believe this,' muttered Pemberton. 'More proof that Constance was telling the truth...'

'Yes, and she recalls Constance going to the local primary school and then to a secondary school in York, leaving to get a job in a sweet shop. She followed it with several similar jobs, all within Lizzie Templeton's memory. She described Constance as a tall thin girl, not very pretty, with dark hair.'

'And in later life?'

'When Constance's parents died, Constance left home and got other work and Lizzie lost touch, but Constance did sometimes pop in to see her and Lizzie does recall her getting a job with Lady Consate. Constance came to tell her, saying how privileged she was to get such a good job in such a fine house and with such a nice lady. Then she lost touch altogether. She's never heard of Constance since that time and had no idea she was working at Milverdale Hall.'

'Lorraine, why does the name of Lady Consate keep niggling at me?' Pemberton asked. 'I know it from somewhere... I've come across it and I can't remember where.'

'In connection with work?' Lorraine asked.

'I think so, but I can't be absolutely sure.'

'Her home was at Holfield, just outside York. Holfield House. Were you ever stationed at York?'

'No.' He shook his head. 'No, I've never worked there... Oh, but hang on, I did a fortnight's undercover work there. We were keeping observations on some professional villains, burglars of good quality houses, and we needed police officers in disguise. We used those from outside the city whose faces wouldn't be known... Yes, so I did some police work there but only for a couple of weeks.'

'Would that be when you came across Lady Consate's name? Maybe the villains were going to raid her house or something? Did you stake it out?'

'No, we didn't do that...'

'When were you there?'

'Eight or nine years ago, so far as I remember. A lot has happened since then ... memories fade, Lorraine.'

'Have you still got your notebooks? I keep all mine.'

'They'll be somewhere about the house – in the attic, I reckon.'

'And if I know you, Mark Pemberton, they'll all be parcelled up in neat wrappings with the date on! Right, that's a job for you tonight after work – find your old notebooks and see if Lady Consate is mentioned for any reason. I can't see what she would have to do with this enquiry, but at least it will put your mind at rest!'

Having listened to Lorraine's account, Pemberton asked Larkin to join them, and he was acquainted with these details.

'So we're no further forward, are we, sir?' Larkin said. 'Constance Farrow is genuine, her account has been verified; she's not the missing heiress, and therefore she has no motive for bumping off Alicia. Where do we go from here?'

'The troops are still asking around the houses, are they? And doing all the ground work?'

'Yes, with no results ... nothing, sir.'

'It all makes me even more sure that the answer to our problems lies in Milverdale Hall, particularly with Constance Farrow. I need to exert pressure on her, Paul, so how about a very careful search of the old iron-works – disused pit shafts, buildings, river banks, undergrowth, tunnels ... a big job. Make it highly visible.'

'For the rifle, you mean?'

'Yes, and the fisherman's outfit. And tyre marks which I trust will match one of the estate vehicles. And footprints ... anything in fact.'

'Right, I'll get that under way, sir. But how will that put pressure on Constance?'

'She can see the old ironworks from the Hall,' smiled Pemberton. 'I want her to know we've decided to search that area.'

'Right, I'll fix that. Where will you be?'

'Before I go to York, I'm going home to dig out some of my old notebooks. I want to see if they contain a reference to Lady Consate,' and he explained why he felt there might be a note of some kind. 'If she is mentioned, I want to find out why. Why should this lady, who's now in the background to this enquiry, have featured in a previous police matter? That's what I hope to answer.'

'But she died, didn't she?' Larkin said. 'If I recall from Constance Farrow's antecedents, Lady Consate died in 1994. I can't see how she can be relevant to Alicia's death.'

'Nor can I until I check my old notebooks. Right, I'm off. More when I get back!'

Thanks to his efficiency and tidiness, Mark Pemberton quickly found his old notebooks and discovered that his period of special duty in York was during the summer of 1990. Two weeks from Sunday, 15th July until Saturday, 28th July inclusive. The entire fortnight was contained within one book and so he took it downstairs, made himself a cup of tea and sat at the kitchen table to examine the contents.

As he studied the entries relating to crimes and events in York, along with notes about the duties he undertook at that time, the memories returned and then he found what he wanted. The report of a woman missing from home. Or missing from her place of employment to be precise – and that place of employment was Holfield House at Holfield near York, the home of Lady Consate. And the name of the missing woman was Constance Farrow.

His pocket-book entry was necessarily brief, but it did say she'd left Holfield House to go for a walk on Tuesday, 17th July and had not returned. There followed a brief description – date of birth, 6th September 1947, making her forty-two at the time; five feet seven or eight inches tall, slim build, with dark brown hair worn bobbed, brown eyes, good teeth (all natural), local accent, wearing blue clip-on ear-rings, a cheap wrist-watch on her left wrist, a black skirt, red blouse, black jacket and black shoes. The report said she had not taken any personal belongings and thus there was slight concern for her safety, although she had not stolen anything from her employer nor was any local man known to be missing. The entry in his notebook had not been cancelled, indicating that she had not returned during his time at York.

Pemberton knew the system for recording people who were missing from home. If the person was an adult and there was no cause to be worried about their personal safety, or they were not suspected either of being a victim of crime or of having committed a crime, then no search was made. Their absence was noted in the 'Missing from Home' files but if they returned safe and sound, then no questions were asked. After all, an adult is perfectly entitled to leave home without reference to anyone. So had Constance returned after Pemberton's departure from York? He decided to check at Rainesbury police office.

Driving from home, he parked in his usual place at Rainesbury police station and entered the Control Room.

'Where do you keep old "Missing from Home" files?' he asked Inspector Thornton, the officer in charge.

'In the filing room, sir, bottom drawer. How far back do you want to go?'

'1990, a woman missing from York.'

'Yes, we've 1990 files intact. We have a clear-out every ten years.'

He found the printed 'Missing from Home' supplement, and located the entry for Constance Farrow. There was a small and rather indistinct black and white photograph taken when she was about thirty which made it difficult to compare with the same woman today but the entry had a cancellation line across it saying, 'Returned home, 14th March 1991.' And that was it. He knew there was no need to elaborate – she'd returned safe and sound and so she'd been crossed off the list.

He'd missed that amendment because her return was of no consequence to a busy detective working nearly fifty miles away. Now, though, he endorsed his own pocket-book accordingly – at least, he was up to date! She must have returned to Lady Consate's home because she was working there until her Ladyship died in 1994, after which she obtained employment with Lady

Featley. So where had she been, and why? Why disappear for nine months without a word to anyone. And was her disappearance, or her work with Lady Consate, of any significance to the current investigation?

And then he realised it was very significant.

Constance Farrow had brown eyes, according to her description as a missing person; the Constance Farrow at Milverdale Hall had grey eyes which, he remembered from his first meeting, matched her old grey cardigan.

13

Before leaving for York, Pemberton rang the Royal Corps of Military Police at their Provost Company Detachment offices and asked if Colonel McKay was available. He was, and Pemberton was connected.

'Ian,' he said. 'It's Mark Pemberton. I need a chat with you.'

'I'll be in my office for the rest of the day, Mark. Is it something I can be working on before you arrive?'

Pemberton explained about his investigation and said, 'I'm interested in a woman called Beatrice Hammond or Constance Farrow. She might have used the name Beatrice Milverdale. Date of birth – 6th September 1947. I think she might have been in the Army at some stage. Is there any way that can be checked?'

'No problem,' said McKay. 'What time do you expect to get here?'

'An hour or so from now.'

'See you then. I'll get my staff working on it,' and McKay replaced his telephone. The two men had often co-operated and such mutual assistance was a feature of their working relationship. Pemberton knew that

McKay would do his best to unearth anything of interest about the subject of his enquiry.

As he drove towards the ancient city of York, he realised he was working on little more than a hunch which was one reason he had kept the purpose of this mission to himself. If it went wrong, he would not be embarrassed. But, he told himself, Constance Farrow had revealed several military traits – the plain décor of her flat, the overall tidiness of the places within her area of responsibility, her meticulous timing, her capable handling of the guns, the knowledge that Alicia's death had been caused by a bullet rather than shotgun pellets, her knowledge that military personnel were allocated cutlery in their married quarters, the quick marching movements over the viaduct if indeed that had been Constance – and the fact that, if she was the killer, she had used a .303 rifle. That was a military weapon if ever there was one. If she had been in the Army during the 1960s – quite feasible given her age – she'd probably have been trained in the use of that weapon which might explain why she had not used any of the other weapons in the gun cupboard. A person highly trained and accustomed to using .303 rifles would not be so capable of handling a twelve-bore shotgun or even a light .22 rifle. It was these memories and her general behaviour which made Pemberton believe that Constance had served in some branch of HM Forces. The Army, with its specialised training, seemed likely.

Above all this speculation was the undoubted fact that the sheer skill of that single shot suggested it had been fired by someone with expertise in firearms, and a .303 rifle in particular. In addition, the killing did reveal some clever planning. Constance had been astute enough not to have claimed to have seen a stranger around the area – if she had seen one, then other members of the staff would have been likely to, and her lie might have been exposed. And so she remained silent, claiming to have seen nothing suspicious. The less she told the police, the less chance there was to reveal a lie. But her claimed sighting of Alicia at seven o'clock on Wednesday morning was a lie...

A clever woman, he mused. And Constance, he was sure, was not her name. Beatrice Hammond, born on the same day as Constance and of remarkably similar appearance, was probably the real name of the lady now at Milverdale Hall. So what had happened to the real Constance? According to Lorraine's research, details of Constance's life had matched the information provided by the housekeeper. The only question – in Pemberton's mind – was the real Constance's disappearance from her place of employment at Lady Consate's home at Holfield House near York. He hoped Lorraine might produce something more definitive about that.

He drove on, realising that his teams would now be starting their search of the old ironworks. He wanted Constance to see them at work. It might compel her into taking some kind of action although, to date, she had been remarkably cool and unemotional, with perhaps a few timely tears of sorrow at the loss of her mistress. In Pemberton's view she had, for reasons yet to be determined, coldly planned the murder in considerable detail and with undoubted skill.

In his mind, he ran over the probable sequence of events. Constance had risen earlier than usual on Wednesday morning, probably around six, and had hurried down to Mill House to establish herself in the firing position she'd earlier selected. With military precision, she'd rested the barrel in the fork of the tree and when Alicia had walked into her sights, she had pulled the trigger. Mr Morgan then saw her hurrying back to the Hall to be in the kitchen by eight o'clock, there to provide coffee to the incoming estate workers. Constance had not seen Alicia leave the Hall at seven on

Wednesday because she was not there to do so – she'd assumed she'd left at seven as was her practice, although Jim Breckon did confirm that.

And Constance had made a fuss at eight o'clock by asking the staff if anyone had seen Alicia return – something she would not normally do. Under normal circumstances, she would assume Alicia had returned and was preparing to come down for breakfast. But on Wednesday, she knew Alicia would not be there – and so she had asked the others if she'd returned, a show of concern, a means of showing the others she had no idea where Alicia was. A façade, in other words. She had shown restraint by not rushing off to 'seek' Alicia, but instead went about her daily routine, using the trip to the shops as a means of getting rid of the waterproofs, waders and rifle, hidden, albeit hastily and perhaps insecurely, until that moment, but disposed of prior to any search and before she informed the police. They'd be somewhere in the old ironworks, Pemberton was sure of that. There was nowhere else they could be. Then she'd gone to 'find' Alicia.

But where had the rifle been kept before being used to kill Alicia? The fishing clothes and equipment were no problem – a plentiful supply was kept both at the Hall and in Mill House. She could have helped herself to any of those. She must have entered Mill House to don the clothes; she could cross over to it from the island via the footbridge and let herself in with the available key. There'd be no footprints in the grounds of Mill House, the paths were made of flagstones. No one would see her wearing the gear, certainly no member of the staff. In Pemberton's mind, it was logical that the rifle had also been kept there, probably held illegally by the family although Constance might have smuggled it from the Army upon her demobilisation. That was unlikely; he favoured the idea that it had been kept at Mill House.

But even if she had committed the crime, even if she had had the time and the skill to do so, why had she killed Alicia?

Then his mobile phone bleeped. 'Pemberton,' he answered.

'DC Cashmore speaking, sir,' she said, using the formal address in case he was in the presence of another person. 'I have some information which I thought you ought to know immediately.'

'Go on, Lorraine,' he said, adding, 'I'm alone, by the way, in the car.'

'Thanks. Well, Constance did get work with Lady Consate and then she vanished in 1990. She was listed as a missing person. Lady Consate was still at home, not very mobile and not in full command of her mental faculties; she depended upon professional carers. After Constance vanished, another woman arrived. She said she'd been sent by the agency to care for Lady Consate while Constance was absent. The old lady was so muddled she accepted this, and the new woman started work. Others with responsibilities for Lady Consate thought she was genuine and it seems she did well. I've found a district nurse who remembers them both. But the point is the newcomer was called Hammond, sir. Beatrice Hammond.'

'Well, I'll be damned! And am I right in thinking Constance's personal papers would have been left in the house? She vanished without taking anything with her, not even her make-up, toiletries or clean underwear.'

'Yes, I've found the original report in York police station. She left everything behind – her birth certificate, work references, P45, income tax papers ... the lot. And her date of birth was the same as Beatrice Hammond's.'

'So are we suggesting that Beatrice Hammond assumed a new identity, that she became Constance Farrow?'

'That seems to have happened. When Lady Consate died, Lady Featley wanted a housekeeper and so Beatrice applied, and got the job. She had all the necessary references and papers to masquerade as

332

Constance Farrow. Someone – Beatrice more than likely – rang the police to say Constance had returned home. And so she was crossed off the missing lists, with no questions asked. That's how it works, as you know. And so Beatrice Hammond, alias Constance Farrow, worked for Lady Featley – who was known to the Milverdales – and when Featley went into a home due to her age and invalidity, "Constance" got the housekeeping job at Milverdale Hall. I think that is what she was aiming to do from the start – infiltrate the Milverdale household in some way. I think she'd researched the family records and decided she ought to have her rightful share of the estate...'

'I'm heading for the military police offices at York right now, Lorraine. I want to find out more about Beatrice Hammond, I think she has a military background. I want to check it out. Thanks for all that. I think we've got her... See you before too long. Love you as always...' and he blew a kiss down the phone.

Half an hour later, he was in Colonel McKay's office with a cup of tea and biscuits before him. They discussed their respective experiences since last meeting, with Pemberton outlining his current investigation, and then McKay passed him a file.

'It's all there, Mark. The military career of

your Beatrice Hammond. Have a look at it, and note what you want. I can authorise certified copies if you need them for evidence in criminal proceedings. Take it along the corridor to read, there's a quiet room there. Room 45.'

The file was comprehensive – and it included a head-and-shoulders photograph which was, beyond doubt, a younger version of the woman he knew as Constance Farrow. But this was Miss Beatrice Hammond, born on 6th September 1947 in Hove, and recruited from an address in York. After an unimpressive secondary education at York High School for Girls, she had joined the Women's Royal Army Corps as a single woman in October 1965 at the age of eighteen. At that time there was a limited range of careers for women, and she had initially opted for Catering although she had later transferred to Motor Transport. Her reason was that she preferred a career which took her outside the barracks and provided a greater stimulus. She rose through the non-commissioned ranks but was commissioned in 1970 and retired with the rank of Captain in 1987, after twenty-two years' service. She had not married during that time. That length of service entitled her to a pension, which was still being paid direct into a bank account in Rainesbury. He made a note of the account number – were withdrawals being made? There was nothing remarkable about her service, he felt; it followed the traditional pattern with a three-year spell in Germany, three years in Cyprus, three years in Northern Ireland and the rest at British bases. Among her achievements was captaincy of the national WRAC Rifle Shooting Team, membership of a joint services motor rally team and awards for the mechanical knowledge, both practical and theoretical, she had displayed on her initial training courses. But the thing that interested Pemberton more than any other was the name of her next-of-kin. This was given as Guy Hammond, her son. His address, the one at which he lived while she was serving, was in York, but there was no note of any maintenance payments being deducted from her salary. As the child bore her surname, he had not been adopted but appeared to have been otherwise cared for. By his father's family perhaps? The file did not say.

But if her maiden name was Hammond, then her son must have been illegitimate, and, reasoned Pemberton, he must have been born before she began her military career. To have become pregnant while serving would at that time have resulted in discharge from the WRAC.

The important thing was that 'Constance'

had a son! And due to his blood, he would be an heir to Milverdale Estate. Pemberton could see that if this man came forward to make his claim, his name would show no links with Constance Farrow, the housekeeper, but he could prove he was the son of Beatrice Hammond, the natural daughter of Audrey Milverdale. And so the Milverdale Estate would continue within the family. He thanked McKay for his assistance, took a photocopy of the entire file with a request that certified copies of all documents be made for the forthcoming murder trial, and left the premises. The question now was whether Pemberton should interview Guy Hammond immediately or wait until later. And then he wondered if Guy knew about his real ancestry – and if so, where had he been on Wednesday morning between the hours of seven and eight?

He'd surely have an alibi. An interview was imperative.

But first, Pemberton wanted to visit the High School for Girls before it closed. He drove across the city, parked in the staff area and found his way to the secretary's office complete with briefcase. Identifying himself, he asked for the head teacher; the secretary contacted her on the intercom and he was quickly escorted to her office. Mrs Foster welcomed him, bade him take a seat and smiled.

'Yes, superintendent, what can I do for you?'

She was a small dark-haired woman wearing thick horn-rimmed spectacles which produced an owlish impression but her face was wreathed in smiles. She would be in her late forties, he estimated.

'I'm engaged on a very delicate enquiry.' He had decided not to refer to the murder at this stage. 'I need to check the names of two of your former pupils, chiefly to establish whether or not they knew one another. I'm going back to the late fifties and early sixties, though, and wondered if your records went back to those days. Maybe a school photo might exist?'

'We can do better than that, superintendent. We have Mr Brown, Joseph Brown. He's been here longer than anyone and is due to retire next year. He came to the school in 1955 to teach English and has been with us ever since. Let me call him for you. He'll be in the library.'

She buzzed her intercom and said, 'Find Mr Brown will you, Julie, and ask him to come to my office immediately.'

Five minutes later, Joseph Brown arrived; he was a stooped and rather untidy man in a cheap grey suit, with a bald head surrounded by wisps of white hair and half-moon spectacles over which he peered at Mrs Foster and then at Pemberton.

'Joseph, this is Detective Superintendent Pemberton. He wants to test your memory!'

'It's not as sharp as it was, superintendent. At one point, you could have asked me anything about Milton and I could have answered with a quote from his works, but what can I do for you?'

'Two girls were at this school from around 1958 until 1964 or thereabouts,' he told them. 'Constance Farrow and Beatrice Hammond. I wondered if you remembered them?'

'I do indeed. The terrible twins, we called them. They were like two peas in a pod, superintendent, you'd have taken them for sisters. They shared the same birthday, you know, and went everywhere together. Amazing really, but there was no family connection. Beatrice's family moved here from the south, but Constance was a local girl.'

'That's just what I wanted,' beamed Pemberton. 'Do they keep in touch with the school?'

He shook his head. 'No. Constance wasn't very bright, she was no academic and left when she was sixteen, to work in a sweet shop of all things! Later, though, she branched out and became a housekeeper for the gentry, then she went missing. You would know that, of course?'

'Yes, she was working for Lady Consate at

the time. I was a policeman in York when we recorded her as missing, but she turned up eventually, according to our records.'

'Did she, by Jove? I never heard any more of her after that. I never saw her again. But the other girl, Beatrice, well, she was much brighter and could have done well, both academically and practically, in almost any profession she could have chosen, but she left school under a cloud – as I am sure you know.'

'Pregnant, you mean?' guessed Pemberton.

'Yes. She was only fifteen and so she left – her parents wanted nothing to do with the child or indeed with her, and so the parents of the father – one of our senior pupils – took the child in, a little boy, if I remember correctly. He grew up thinking his dad was his big brother. It was all something of a scandal at the time, but we managed to keep things as discreet as possible. She joined the WRAC eventually, Beatrice I mean, and I never heard any more of her.'

Pemberton eased the military file from his briefcase and revealed the photograph of Beatrice. 'So who is this?' he asked Mr Brown.

'Well, it could be either Beatrice or Constance,' he said. 'Really, I would not know, but after such a long time...'

'You've told me all I wish to know,' said

Pemberton. 'The two girls were close friends, sharing the same birthday and lots more experiences, I would imagine.'

'Yes indeed. Nice girls, but lively,' smiled Mr Brown.

'Thank you both for your help.' Pemberton took his leave and decided not to interview Guy Hammond at this stage. There was nothing to suggest that he was involved or that he knew anything about events within the Milverdale family. He turned towards the outer ring road and made for the incident room back at Campsthwaite. After explaining his theories to Paul Larkin with Lorraine adding her support, Pemberton asked, 'How's the search of the old ironworks going, Paul?'

'They've not found anything yet, sir, but they've been there since you ordered them.'

'Good. And now it's time to speak to Constance Farrow.'

14

'She's standing in the upstairs window,' said Pemberton as he drove up the drive to Milverdale Hall. 'See her? She's in Alicia's room.'

'She's expecting us?' suggested Lorraine.

'Perhaps. She's seen the activity at the old ironworks. She's wondering what's going on down there. It will have unsettled her – I hope! Made her uneasy.'

'She won't do anything silly, will she?' There was a note of anxiety in Lorraine's voice.

'I took the guns away,' he said.

'She could use something else...'

He eased to a halt outside the front door, parked to the left of the *porte-cochère*, collected his briefcase and went to ring the bell. There was a long delay, but eventually Constance opened the door. 'Superintendent.' She managed a weak smile. 'And Miss Cashmore. Do come in.'

She led them into the drawing-room, showed them to some seats and asked, 'Tea? Or sherry? Something else?'

'No, thank you, Miss Farrow,' and the tone of his voice, and perhaps the expression on his face, told her that this was no normal visit. 'Sit down, please.'

She obeyed, the tic on her face reacting to the changed circumstances in which she now found herself. He opened his briefcase, placing it on the occasional table before him, but did not reveal its contents. Not yet. But he did switch on the miniature tape recorder and he allowed her to note that he had done so.

'Miss Farrow. It is my belief that you killed Alicia Milverdale.' He decided on the direct shock approach. 'You shot her and, furthermore, I am now in a position to prove that allegation.'

'I see your officers are searching the old ironworks.' She spoke softly without answering his challenge, licking her dry lips as she studied him.

'We hope to find the rifle there, and some fishing gear, waterproofs and so on. There will be tyre marks too, from the estate vehicle you used. Footprints as well, I would hope, clear enough for us to match with your shoes. Lots of evidence, in other words. If the rifle – a .303, as I am sure you know – is hidden anywhere at the old ironworks, we shall find it, however long it takes, and when we do, I suspect that both it and the water-proofs will bear evidence that you handled them or wore them. There will be finger-print evidence, even if you tried to obliterate it, but more importantly there will be DNA residue, such a wonderful aid to modern crime detection. I have a sample from Alicia, by the way. And from you – from your hairbrush. I intend to make comparisons with those samples. Did you know we can prove paternity through DNA? Blood relationships?'

She looked at him steadily, her bright grey eyes showing a coolness and hardness he'd not previously encountered. She knew that her actions had been discovered, but in a show of defiance she held her head high and said, 'It was an accident ... a tragic, tragic accident, Mr Pemberton. I shall say it was an accident.'

'So you did shoot Alicia?'

'Yes, but it was an accident. I shall maintain it was an accident. A terrible accident.'

'You realise you are not obliged to say anything but what you do say may be given in evidence?' Having delivered the short version of the formal caution, he nodded to Lorraine whose notebook was already on her lap. She was noting the progress of this interview; the tape was recording their words.

'I understand, but I assure you it was an accident, superintendent. I was foolish, I tried to cover it up... It was wrong of me, I panicked, I just made things worse. I should have come to you immediately with the truth.'

'So what happened?' He spoke quietly and with apparent sympathy for her predicament.

'I went down to Mill House, very early, I was up and couldn't sleep and was angry, so angry...'

'Angry?'

'With Alicia, for letting down the Milverdale name. It had all boiled up inside me overnight, you must know what she was doing with those little boys. Well, I found out and I was so angry ... so I went down to Mill House. I knew the old rifle was there, it had been Mr Milverdale's, it was from his Home Guard days, he kept it away from the others, with the ammunition. Alicia showed me one day, sometimes she used it for her performances, without the ammunition of course, but she was going to surrender it next time you had a firearms amnesty. I wish she had. Anyway, on Wednesday I watched Alicia come down for her walk. She got to the bluebell field. I was waiting and I did point the gun at her. I shouted at her too, in anger. She knew I was there. I said I could kill her for what she was doing to the children and to the good name of the Milverdales and she shouted something back, I never heard what she said and then it went off ... the gun. Such a light trigger. I had no intention of shooting her, superintendent, no intention at all... I just wanted to frighten her into behaving like a true lady, to stop her damaging the good name of the Milverdales... I shall plead accident, Mr Pemberton. It was a dreadful accident.'

'The gun was loaded, Miss Farrow, you are lying and I can prove it,' said Pemberton, not elaborating. After a long wait without any response from Constance, he continued. 'You are a scheming woman, Miss Farrow. You wanted me to think Alicia had died because she was abusing children. You thought our enquiries would show that that was the motive behind her death, that she was killed by an angry parent. But her abuse of children has never been proven, Miss Farrow, I have no proof that she abused even one child. I am aware of the rumours, but have been unable to substantiate them. But you used those rumours as your shield and it almost worked.'

'But it was true!' she almost shouted. 'She was interfering with little boys ... such a dreadful thing ... suppose the press had found out? Think of the damage to the family name...'

'Your family name,' said Pemberton quietly.

'Mine?' She blinked at him now, the tic reappearing and disappearing in a moment.

He extracted the file from his briefcase.

'You are Beatrice Hammond, aren't you?

Born with the Milverdale name and with the Milverdale blood, but you were adopted to become Beatrice Hammond. You were cast aside by your own family for reasons I am sure you have discovered. You had a good career in the WRAC, you became a competent shot with a rifle, you retired with a pension. This is your military file. Then for some reason, in 1990, you went to Lady Consate's'

'You know it all,' she almost whispered. 'My God, you know it all... Yes, I did go to Lady Consate's, I went to see a friend, an old friend. But I found out she had left, she had vanished without a word.'

'That was the real Constance Farrow. She was registered as a missing person...'

'You must try to understand, super-intendent. During my Army career, I'd never tried to find my real parents, but when I came out I began to hunt them ... and when I did find out, I wanted to tell someone... I wanted to share the horror of being the result of incest ... me! Of all the people! The result of such a dirty, filthy act... I'd been friends with Constance all my life, we were like twins, like sisters, and I wanted to talk to her, she was the one person I could have told, but she'd gone, superintendent. Vanished without trace. The old lady thought I was her sister and that I'd come to take over her work ... so I stayed. It was so easy to take over. I had no job, and I found all Constance's papers and it was so easy to become her and to report her safe return. I did it to get closer to the Milverdales... I saw my opportunity, I wanted to regain what was really mine ... but if I did register a claim, it would mean revealing my shocking past. It put me in a dreadful dilemma.'

'But it was not done for you, Miss Farrow. You did not do this for yourself. You have a son, Guy. I know about him. You did it for him...'

'Oh my God.' Suddenly she was deflated. 'Look, Guy knows nothing of this. He has no idea of his family connections... I abandoned him when he was little, I have never seen him since, not officially, although I must admit I did watch him sometimes, going to school in his little cap and uniform, riding his bike, growing up... I knew him by sight, I've been watching him on and off all these years, I knew his father well, you see, and that family, his father's family, brought him up... They did well, superintendent, Guy is a lovely young man. So all this is his, now, isn't it? I cannot inherit, can I? If I am convicted of being a killer, I cannot inherit the estate, but he can, can't he?'

'So you think you have corrected the dreadful wrong you did to him? But whether he wants the estate will be up to

347

him. He will have to register a claim and subject himself to a blood test, or a DNA test, and I shall have to interview him.'

'You'll tell Mr Browning at the solicitors? Ask him to get Guy to make his claim? It means Milverdale Hall will stay in family hands, doesn't it? It means everything has come out right in the end, for the family.'

'Which is what you really wanted,' said Pemberton. 'And that is why I am arresting you for the murder of Alicia Milverdale.'

'Will all this come out at the trial?' she asked. 'It was an accident, you know, a real accident... You cannot prove otherwise, superintendent.'

'You'll have to discuss that with your defence counsel, he will liaise with the prosecution. But without trying to oppress you or force you to make a confession to murder, I should add that a plea of guilty might mean we don't have to provide all the prosecution evidence in open court; however, if you do persist in saying it was an accident, then I shall be obliged to reveal everything I know. To substantiate a motive, you see, and to prove guilt of the crime charged.'

'So by admitting murder, I go some way towards protecting the family name?'

'It is a matter to discuss with your defence counsel,' reiterated Pemberton.

'I will do all in my power to protect the

family name, superintendent. The Milverdale family has not had a very illustrious
past, has it? Incest, rape I wouldn't be
surprised, illegitimate children and now a
killer, all in recent times. God knows what
else there has been but happily little of those
scandals is known to the public. Now,
though, I hope it will have a renewed and
very fine future, through my son.'

The doorbell rang. Lorraine went to
answer it. It was Detective Inspector
Fowler. 'Just tell Mr Pemberton we've
found the rifle and the fishing gear,
Lorraine. And some footprints and tyre
marks around the pit shaft.'

'Thanks,' said Lorraine. 'I'll do that.'

She smiled; Mark would be available to
take her to the hospital on Monday and she
knew he would then reopen enquiries into
the disappearance of the real Constance
Farrow. And she wondered what would
happen to Mr and Mrs Breckon's house.

The publishers hope that this book has given you enjoyable reading. Large Print Books are especially designed to be as easy to see and hold as possible. If you wish a complete list of our books please ask at your local library or write directly to:

Magna Large Print Books
Magna House, Long Preston,
Skipton, North Yorkshire.
BD23 4ND

This Large Print Book for the partially sighted, who cannot read normal print, is published under the auspices of

THE ULVERSCROFT FOUNDATION